Henry Fitz Randolph

Fifty Years of English Song

Selections from the Poets of the Reign of Victoria

Henry Fitz Randolph

Fifty Years of English Song
Selections from the Poets of the Reign of Victoria

ISBN/EAN: 9783744767095

Printed in Europe, USA, Canada, Australia, Japan

Cover: Foto ©Andreas Hilbeck / pixelio.de

More available books at **www.hansebooks.com**

FIFTY YEARS

OF

ENGLISH SONG.

SELECTIONS FROM THE POETS

OF

THE REIGN OF VICTORIA.

EDITED AND ARRANGED BY

HENRY F. RANDOLPH.

* * * *

THE PRE-RAPHAELITE BROTHERHOOD.   THE BALLAD
AND SONG WRITERS.   THE RELIGIOUS POETS.

NEW YORK:
ANSON D. F. RANDOLPH & CO.
1888.

UNTO

J. H. F–R.

THIS VOLUME IS INSCRIBED.

CONTENTS.

———◆———

BIOGRAPHICAL

AND

BIBLIOGRAPHICAL NOTES.

BIOGRAPHICAL

AND

BIBLIOGRAPHICAL NOTES.

THE authorities for these notes, in addition to special biographies, and the biographical and bibliographical notes scattered through various anthologies and volumes of selections, are *Victorian Poets*, by Edmund Clarence Stedman, eleventh edition, 1886; *Celebrities of the Century*, edited by Lloyd C. Sanders, 1887; *The Men of the Reign*, 1885, and *The Men of the Time*, twelfth edition, 1887, both edited by Thomas Humphry Ward. The authors marked with an asterisk (*) are still living.

ALFORD, THE VERY REV. HENRY, D.D. (1810–1871). Born in London, and educated at Trinity College, Cambridge, where he took the Bell scholarship, and afterwards a fellowship. Shortly after his ordination he became curate of Ampton, and in 1835 he was presented with the living of Wymeswold. In 1841 he became Hulsean Lecturer at Cambridge, and was from 1853 to 1857 officiating minister of Quebec Street Chapel. In the latter year he succeeded Dean Lyall to the deanery of Canterbury, which he held till his death. He was the first editior of *The Contemporary Review*, and is best known by his edition of the Greek Testament, which appeared in five volumes between 1841 and 1861. His poetical works are *Poems and Poetical Fragments*, 1831; *The School of the Heart, and other Poems*, 1835.

* ALLINGHAM, WILLIAM (1828). Born at Ballyshannon in the northwest of Ireland, and descended from an old Anglo-Irish family. In his youth he was influenced strongly by the 'Pre-Raphaelite Brotherhood,' and was for many years editor of

Fraser. In 1874 he married Miss Helen Paterson, the artist. He has published *Poems*, 1850; *The Music Master, and Day and Night Songs*, 1854; *Lawrence Bloomfield in Ireland: a Modern Poem, in Twelve Chapters*, 1864; *Songs, Poems, and Ballads*, 1877; *Evil May-Day*, 1883; *Ashley Manor* (Drama), 1883; *Blackberries picked off Many Bushes*, 1884.

* BARING-GOULD, THE REV. SABINE (1834). Born at Exeter, and educated at Clare College, Cambridge, where he took his degree of A. M., in 1856. He was appointed incumbent of Dalton Thirsk in 1869, and rector of East Mersea, Colchester, in 1871. From 1871 to 1873, he was editor of *The Sacristy*, a quarterly review of ecclesiastical art and literature. He has been a voluminous writer on subjects connected with religious thought and modern criticism, and is the author of several remarkable novels. He has published one volume of verse, *The Silver Store*, 1868.

BARNES, THE REV. WILLIAM, D.D. (1820–1886). Born in the Vale of Blackmore, Dorset, and for a time kept a school at Dorchester, but was appointed curate of Whitcombe in 1847, and rector of Winterbourne Came in 1862. He devoted his life to the study of the Dorsetshire dialect, and was the author of several volumes on philology and early English history. He published *Poems of Rural Life in the Dorset Dialect*, three successive series, subsequently collected in one volume in 1879; *Rural Poems.*

* BENNETT, WILLIAM COX, LL.D. (1820). Born at Greenwich, and has devoted himself to the cause of education for the people. He was instrumental in establishing a popular literary institution at Greenwich, acted as auditor for the Associates for the Repeal of the Taxes on Knowledge, and was the secretary to the Greenwich branch of the National Education League. He has also taken an active interest in politics, and, in 1868, he proposed the election of Mr. Gladstone for Greenwich, and organized the committee which secured his return. He was attached to the staff of *The Weekly Dispatch* during the years 1869–70, and in 1869 he received the degree of LL.D. from the University of Tusculum. From 1883 to 1884 he was the editor of a monthly periodical, entitled *The Lark; Songs, Ballads and Recitations for the People.* He has published *Poems,* 1850; *War Songs,* 1855; *Queen Eleanor's Vengeance, and other Poems,* 1857; *Songs by a Song-Writer,* 1859; *Baby May, and other Poems on Infants,* 1861; *The Worn Wedding Ring,* 1861; *Songs for Sailors,* 1872; *Prometheus the Fire-giver,* 1877; *Sea Songs,* 1878; *Songs for Soldiers,* 1879.

* BICKERSTETH, THE RIGHT REV. EDWARD HENRY, D.D. (1825). Born at Islington, and educated at Trinity College, Cambridge, which he entered in 1843, and where he won the Chancellor's medal in 1844, 1845, and 1846. He took his degree A.B. in 1847. He was ordained deacon in 1848, and shortly afterwards became curate of Benningham, Norfolk. In 1851 he accepted a curacy at Tunbridge Wells, and a few months later became rector of Hinton Martell, Dorset. He was successively vicar of Christ Church, Hampstead, in 1855, chaplain to the Bishop of Ripon in 1861, and rural dean of Highgate in 1878. In 1870 he made a brief visit to the United States, and succeeded Dr. Temple as Bishop of Exeter in 1885. He has published *Poems and Hymns,* 1849; *Nineveh, a Poem,* 1851; *Yesterday, To-Day, and For Ever: a Poem in Twelve Books,* 1867; *The Two Brothers, and Other Poems,* 1871. He is also the author of several prose works on the subject of practical religion, and the editor of a popular collection of hymns known as *The Hymnal Companion to the Book of Common Prayer,* 1870.

* BONAR, HORATIUS, D.D. (1808). Born at Edinburgh, and educated at the High-School and University of his native city. For several years he acted as a missionary at Leith, and in 1837 he was ordained the pastor of the Presbyterian church of Kelso, where he shortly afterwards commenced the publication of the *Kelso Tracts.* At the disruption of the Church of Scotland in 1843, he joined the Free Church, and since 1866 has been the pastor of the Chalmers Memorial Free Church in Edinburgh. He was for a long period the editor of *The Journal of Prophecy,* and subsequently of *The Christian Treasury.* In addition to several prose works on religious subjects, he has published

Songs for the Wilderness, two series, 1843-44; *The Bible Hymn Book*, 1845; *Hymns Original and Selected*, 1850; *Hymns of Faith and Hope*, first series, 1857, second series, 1861, third series, 1866.

* DIXON, THE REV. RICHARD WATSON (1833). Born in London, and educated at King Edward's School and at Pembroke College, Oxford, where he started, in conjunction with Mr. Burne-Jones and Mr. William Morris, *The Oxford and Cambridge Magazine*, advocating Pre-Raphaelite principles. He became curate of St. Mary-the-Less, Lambeth, in 1858, and was made hon. canon of Carlisle in 1874. He was vicar of Hayton from 1875 to 1883, when he became vicar of Warkworth. He has published *Christ's Company, and other Poems*, 1861; *Historical Odes*, 1863; *Mano*, 1883; *Odes and Eclogues*, privately printed, 1884. He is also the author of a voluminous history of the Church of England.

* DOYLE, SIR FRANCIS HASTINGS CHARLES, Bart. (1810). Born at Nunappleton, near Tadcaster, Yorkshire, and educated at Eton and Christ Church, Oxford. He was called to the bar in 1831, and after holding an office in the Customs, was in 1867 elected Professor of Poetry at Oxford, which chair he occupied for two terms of five years each. He has published one volume of verse, *The Return of the Guards, and other Poems*, 1866.

FABER, FREDERICK WILLIAM, D. D. (1814-1863). Born at Calverley, Yorkshire, and educated at Harrow. In 1832 he entered Balliol College, Oxford, and three years later, University College, having obtained one of its scholarships, and in 1836 gained the Newdigate prize by his poem, *The Knights of St. John*. He graduated A. B. in 1836, and the following year obtained a Fellowship and the Johnson Divinity Scholarship. While at Oxford he had come under the influence of the Tractarian movement, and was a diligent attendant at the Church of St. Mary's, Oxford, of which Dr. (afterwards Cardinal) Newman was the incumbent; and after graduation translated the seven books of Optatus for the *Library of the Fathers*. He was ordained deacon in 1837, and priest two years later, and in 1843 was presented to the living of Elton, Huntingdonshire. After a visit to Rome, and an interview with Pope Gregory XVI., he was, in 1845, received into the Church of Rome. Three years later he was received into the Oratory of St. Philip Neri, and in October of the following year was appointed Superior of the Oratory in London. He published *Hymns*, 1848; *Jesus and Mary*, 1849; *Jesus and Mary*, new and enlarged edition, 1852; *The Oratory Hymn Book*, 1854; *Hymns*, 1861.

FERGUSON, SIR SAMUEL, Q.C., LL.D. (1810–1886). Born at Belfast, and educated at Trinity College, Dublin. He was called to the bar 1838, and to the Inner Bar 1859. He acted as First Deputy Keeper of the Records for Ireland from 1867, and served for a time as President of the Royal Irish Academy. As a reward for his services as Deputy Keeper, he was knighted in 1878. He achieved considerable reputation by his translations from the Irish, and devoted considerable time and skill to the study of the relics of early Irish art. He published *Lays of the Western Gael*, 1865; *Congal, a Poem in Five Books*, 1872; *Poems*, 1880.

* HOWITT, MRS. MARY BOTHAM (1805). Born at Uttoxeter, and the wife of Mr. William Howitt. Most of her literary work was done in conjunction with her husband, and she was for three years the editor of the *Drawing-Room Scrap-Book*. In addition to numerous prose works she has published in verse *The Seven Temptations*, 1830; *Ballads and Other Poems*, 1847; in conjunction with her husband, *The Forest Minstrel*, 1823, and *The Desolation of Eyan*, 1827.

KEBLE, THE REV. JOHN, M.A. (1792–1866). Born at Fairford, entered Corpus Christi, Oxford, in 1806, having obtained a scholarship, and was elected a Fellow of Oriel College in 1811. He was ordained in 1815, became a college tutor in 1818, and in 1825 accepted a curacy at Fairford. In 1831 he was elected Professor of Poetry in Oxford, and occupied that chair for ten years. During the term of his professorship he took a prominent part in the organization of the Tractarian movement,

to which he was inclined by both his High Church views and
personal interest in many of the leaders of that movement,
especially in Hurrell Froude, who had been his favorite pupil at
Fairford. In 1835 he was appointed to the vicarage of Hursley,
which he held to the time of his death. In 1845 he had attempted to secure the foundation in Oxford of a ' Poor Man's
College,' designed for the education of priests for the English
Church; but the scheme was at the time wholly unsuccessful,
except that a plot of land was purchased on the top of Head-
ington Hill as a site. After his death, however, the project was
revived, and pushed forward with great rapidity, and in 1870,
Keble College, Oxford, was opened as a memorial of him. In
addition to numerous works in prose, he published *The Christian Year*, 1827 ; *Lyra Innocentium*, 1845 ; *Poems* (posthumously).
He was also one of the contributors to the *Lyra Apostolica*,
1836.

LYTE, THE REV. HENRY FRANCIS (1793–1847). Born at
Ednam, near Kelso, Scotland, and in 1812 entered Trinity
College, Dublin, where he thrice won the prize for English
poetry. Originally intending to become a physician, he abandoned that purpose for the church, and took orders in the Irish
Establishment in 1815. His first curacy was at Wexford, but
he was obliged to quit Ireland on account of ill health, and after
several changes, was, in 1826, appointed to the perpetual curacy
of the district chapel of Lower Brixham in Devonshire, which
he held for twenty years. He published in verse, *Poems, chiefly
Religious*, 1833 ; *Spirit of the Psalms*, 1834. An edition of his
selected poems was published in Edinburgh in 1868.

MACAULAY, THOMAS BABINGTON (1800–1859). Born at Rothley Temple, and after being educated privately, entered Trinity
College, Cambridge, where he won the Craven Scholarship, and
of which he was elected a Fellow in 1824. In 1826 he was called
to the bar, and though attached to the northern Circuit for a
time, never seriously practised his profession. In 1830 he was
returned to Parliament from the borough of Calne, where he sup-
ported the Reform Bill, and on the passage of the Reform Act,
became one of the commissioners of the Board of Control, and

in 1833 became member for Leeds. In 1834 he accepted the post
of member of the Supreme Indian Council, and remained in India
four years, during which time he drafted what has subsequently
become the Indian penal code. On his return to England in 1838
he was returned member for Edinburgh, and the following year
became Secretary of War, with a seat in the Cabinet of Lord
Melbourne's ministry. The ministry lasted only two years, and
after its fall he devoted himself to his historical studies; but
with the return of the Whigs to power in 1846, he accepted the
office of Paymaster-General in Lord John Russell's administra-
tion. In 1847 he was defeated at the Edinburgh election, chiefly
on account of his lack of sympathy with the Free Church. In
1848 the first two volumes of his *History of England* were published, and had an unprecedented success. In 1852 Edinburgh
returned him unsolicited to Parliament, and in 1857, after the
publication of four volumes of his history, he was, on account of
his literary eminence, raised to the peerage, under the title of
Baron Macaulay of Rothley. He published *Lays of Ancient
Rome*, 1843.

MacCarthy, Denis Florence (1817–1882). Born at Dublin,
and a member of the Irish bar, but never practised. His first
literary work was contributed to the Irish *Nation*, and he was
especially noted for his linguistic attainments ; his poems includ-
ing, in addition to original verse, translations from nearly all of
the modern European languages. In 1881 he received from the
Royal Academy of Spain a medal for his translations of the
works of Calderon. He published *Ballads, Poems and Lyrics*,
1850; *The Bell Founder*, 1857 ; *Underglimpses, and Other Poems*,
1857. His translations of Calderon were published 1853-1873.

Mahony, Francis (1804–1866). Born at Cork and educated
in his native city, and afterwards at a college of the Jesuits abroad,
where he acquired the intimate knowledge of Latin which was
such a prominent characteristic of his scholarship. He entered
the Roman Catholic priesthood, but practised his profession for
only about two years, officiating during that time at the Chapel
of the Bavarian Legation, London. In 1834 he commenced to
contribute to *Fraser's Magazine* the *Prout Papers*, which were

modelled on the *Noctes Ambrosianæ* of *Blackwood*, and had for
their *nom de plume* the name of a Roman Catholic priest, who
had lived for many years at Watergrass Hill in the County of
Cork.   In 1846 he visited Rome as the special correspondent of
the London *Daily News*, and during the last years of his life was
the foreign correspondent of the London *Globe* at Paris.

* MASSEY, GERALD (1828).   Born at Tring, in Hertfordshire,
and educated at the British and National schools.   At eight years
of age he was put to work in a silk manufactory, and at fifteen
found employment in London as an errand boy.   In 1849 he became editor of *The Spirit of Freedom*, a cheap journal to which
the contributors were exclusively workingmen, and the following
year was one of the secretaries of the 'Christian Socialists,' — an
organization with which the Revs. Charles Kingsley and F. D.
Maurice were associated.   He was for ten years on the staff of
The Athenæum.   As early as 1852 he had commenced to devote
considerable attention to mesmerism, spiritualism, and other
kindred subjects, and has lectured a number of times on such
matters both in the United States and the British Colonies.   Of
late years he has devoted himself almost exclusively to the for-
mation of societies for the promotion of spiritualism and social-
ism.   He has published *Voices of Freedom and Lyrics of Love*,
1850; *The Ballad of Babe Christabel, and other Poems*, 1854; *War
Wails*, 1855; *Craigcrook Castle*, 1856; *A Tale of Eternity, and
other Poems*, 1869.

* MORRIS, WILLIAM (1834).   Born at Walthamstow, and educated at Marlborough and Exeter College, Oxford, and was associated with Canon Dixon and Mr. Burne-Jones in starting *The
Oxford and Cambridge Magazine*, for the advocacy of pre-Raphaelite principles, defraying the cost of this periodical through
the twelve months of its existence.   In 1856 he took his degree
and was articled to an architect, but failed to serve the full
time of articles.   In 1863 he started, under the name of Morris,
Marshall, Faulkner & Co., the establishment, which is now carried on under his name alone, for the manufacture of various
,articles, especially wall-paper, stained glass, tiles, and household
decorations.   He has since 1877 lectured much on art, and has

recently become a leading spirit of the Socialist League and a contributor to *The Commonweal*, the official organ of the League. He has published *The Defence of Guenevere, and Other Poems*, 1858; *The Life and Death of Jason*, 1867; *The Earthly Paradise*, 1868-1870; *Love is Enough, or the Freeing of Pharamond. A Morality*, 1873; *The Æneid of Virgil done into English Verse*, 1876; *The Story of Sigurd the Volsung, and the Fall of the Niblungs*, 1878. He has also, in collaboration with Mr. Eirikr Magnusson, published several prose translations from the Icelandic Sagas.

* MYERS, FREDERICK W. H. (1843). He has published *St. Paul; The Renewal of Youth and other Poems*, 1882. He is also the author of the monograph on Wordsworth, in the *English Men of Letters* series.

* NEWMAN, HIS EMINENCE JOHN HENRY, Cardinal Deacon of the Holy Roman Church (1801). Born in London, and while still a boy developed a strong passion for theology. From an early age he entertained the idea of entering the church, and at fifteen made a voluntary vow of celibacy, believing that his 'calling in life would require such a sacrifice as celibacy involved,' having at that time been strongly drawn for some years to missionary work among the heathen. In 1816 he entered Trinity College, Oxford, graduated in classical honors in 1820, and two years later was elected a Fellow of Oriel College. In 1824 he took orders, and the following year was appointed Vice-Principal of St. Albans Hall, of which Dr. [afterwards Archbishop) Whately was Principal. Under the influence of Dr. Whately he gradually abandoned the Calvinistic tendency towards which he had leaned from boyhood, and drifted towards the liberal movement in the Church of England, of which Dr. Whately was a prominent exponent. 'The truth is,' he says in his *Apologia*, 'I was beginning to prefer intellectual excellence to moral; I was drifting in the direction of liberalism. I was rudely awakened from my dream at the end of 1827, by two great blows, — illness and bereavement.' The occasion of the formal break with Dr. Whately was the attempted re-election of Sir Robert Peel to Parliament from Oxford, although Newman's

opposition rested ' on a simple academical, not at all an ecclesiastical or political ground,' insisting that 'a great University
ought not to be bullied, even by a great Duke of Wellington.'
Moreover, it was at this time that he came under the influence
of Richard Hurrell Froude and John Keble. From 1826 to
1831 he was a tutor at Oriel, and in 1828 became incumbent of
St. Mary's, Oxford, which he held until 1843, together with the
chaplaincy of Littlemore. In 1833 the Oxford movement, in which
Newman played such a conspicuous part, was definitely started
by Keble's Assize Sermon on 'National Apostasy,' preached in
July of that year, and which gained a certain amount of tempo-
rary strength by the *Hampden Controversy*, which brought the
conflict between the Tractarians and the Broad Church party to
a crisis. The problem whose solution was attempted by the
movement was, how to ' keep the Church from being liberalized.'
An association was formed, of which Newman, Keble, Froude,
and Pusey were the most conspicuous members, and the publication of the famous *Tracts for the Times* commenced, which
culminated in *Tract XC.*, written by Newman, wherein the author advanced the opinion that the Thirty-Nine Articles were
directed, not against the doctrines of the Church of Rome as
interpreted by the Council of Trent, but against earlier heresies
disavowed by that Council. The Tract was severely condemned
by the University authorities and the Episcopal bench, and in
1842 Newman resigned the living of St. Mary's, and retired
to Littlemore, where he and a small band of religious-minded
associates formed themselves into a community, conducted on
an ascetic model. In 1845 he was formally received into the
Church of Rome, and shortly after his ordination as priest, was
appointed head of the Oratory of St. Philip Neri at Birmingham.
In 1850 he founded the Brompton Oratory, but removed in 1852
to the new Oratory at Edgbaston, near Birmingham, where he has
remained, with the exception of the years 1854–58, when he was
Rector of the Roman Catholic University at Dublin. The intemperate attack upon him by the Rev. Charles Kingsley in *Macmil-
lan's Magazine* for January, 1864, and a pamphlet entitled *What
then does Dr. Newman mean ?* led to the publication, in 1865, of
the famous *Apologia pro Vita Sua*. In 1877 he was elected an
honorary Fellow of Trinity College, Oxford, and was created a

Cardinal Deacon by Pope Leo XIII, in 1879. In addition to various theological and historical works, he has published *Verses on Religious Subjects*, 1855; *Verses on Various Occasions*, 1867. He was also one of the contributors to the *Lyra Apostolica*, 1836.

NORTON, HON. MRS. CAROLINE ELIZABETH, subsequently LADY STIRLING–MAXWELL (1808–1877). The second daughter of Mr. Thomas Sheridan, sister of Lady Dufferin, and said to be the loveliest of the 'Three Graces,' as the Sheridan sisters were called in their youthful days. In 1827 she married the Hon. George Norton; but the marriage was an unfortunate one, and after three years a judicial separation was effected between the parties. Her husband seems to have regarded his wife as simply a tool for obtaining position and money, and his persecutions finally culminated in an action for divorce, in which Lord Melbourne was made the co-respondent. The trial resulted, however, in the complete vindication of Mrs. Norton; but for forty years afterwards the husband spared no means to annoy his wife, and was not above appropriating to his own use the copyright of her books. She edited *The Ladies' Magazine* for several years, and *The Keepsake* and *Fraser's Drawing-Room Scrap-Book* for a short time. In 1877, a little less than two years after her husband's death, and only three months before her own, she was married to Sir William Stirling-Maxwell. Mrs. Norton is said to be the original of Diana Antonio Merion, in Mr. George Meredith's novel *Diana of the Crossways*. She has published *The Dandies' Rout*, 1825; *The Sorrows of Rosalie*, 1829; *The Undying One*, 1831; *The Dream, and Other Poems*, 1841; *The Child of the Islands*, 1846; *Aunt Carry's Ballads for Children*, 1847; *The Lady of La Garaye*, 1863. Mrs. Norton was also the author of three novels.

PROCTER, ADELAIDE ANNE (1825–1864). Born in London, and daughter of Bryan Waller Procter (Barry Cornwall). Her earliest literary work consisted of poetical contributions published under the pseudonym of Miss Mary Berwick, in *Household Words*, conducted by Charles Dickens. Dickens himself had no suspicion of the real authorship of the poems until the warm approval expressed by him to Mr. and Mrs. Procter, of a poem by Miss Berwick, published in the Christmas number of *Household Words*, 1854, led Miss Procter to disclose her identity. Some years before her death, Miss Procter became a Roman Catholic, and took a great interest in charitable work in London. It was for the benefit of a lodging house for homeless women in London that her *Chaplet of Verses* was written. She published *Legends and Lyrics*, 1858, and an enlarged edition, 1861 ; *A Chaplet of Verses*, 1862.

PROCTER, BRYAN WALLER (1787–1874). Born in London, and educated at Harrow, where Byron was one of his schoolfellows. He was articled to a solicitor in Wiltshire, and subsequently entered a conveyancer's office in London. In 1821 his tragedy of *Mirandola* was produced with complete success at Covent Garden, Macready acting the part of Mirandola, Charles Kemble that of Guido, and Miss Foote playing Isidora. In 1824 he married a daughter of Mrs. Basil Montagu, and he was called to the bar in 1831. Shortly afterwards he was appointed a Commissioner of Lunacy, an office which he held till 1861. He published *Dramatic Scenes, and other Poems*, 1819; *Marcian Colonna* (Drama), 1820; *Mirandola* (Drama), 1821 ; *A Sicilian Story*, 1821 ; *Flood of Thessaly*, 1823; *English Songs*, first edition, 1832, and new edition, with additional poems, 1851.

ROSSETTI, GABRIEL CHARLES DANTE (1828–1882). Born in London, and early in his professional career modified his name into Dante Gabriel Rossetti. He was the brother of Christina Georgina Rossetti, and son of Gabriele Rossetti, an Italian poet-patriot, who escaped to England as a political exile after the failure of the Neapolitan insurrection in 1821. In 1835 Dante Gabriel entered King's College School, where he remained for eight years, when he studied first at an Art academy, and afterwards at the Royal Academy Antique School. He left the academy in 1848, and the following year exhibited his first picture, *The Girlhood of Mary Virgin*. In 1848 he associated with Holman Hunt and Thomas Woolner in founding the Pre-Raphaelite Brotherhood, and two years later contributed *The Blessèd Damozel* to *The Germ*, which had been started as the official organ of that movement. In 1856 he became one of the contributors to *The Oxford and Cambridge Magazine,* which also advocated Pre-Raphaelite principles. In 1860 he married Elizabeth Eleanor Siddal, his model and pupil, who died two years later, under tragic circumstances, being found dead in her bed from the effects of an overdose of laudanum. Under stress of deep grief, he impulsively buried in his wife's coffin the manuscript copies of both his published and unpublished poems, which he eight years later permitted to be exhumed at the earnest solicitation of his friends. The poems thus recovered were revised for publication, and appeared in 1870. It was this volume which inspired Mr. Robert Buchanan's article, *The Fleshly School of Poetry,* in *The Contemporary Review.* The strictures of this critic, followed by others equally harsh, served to make Rossetti, always retiring in his habits, almost a recluse. Shortly before the publication of Mr. Buchanan's criticism, he had resorted to chloral as a remedy for insomnia, and his disturbed condition of mind caused by the hostile reception given to his poems led him into such excessive use of the drug, as to ultimately cause his death. He published *The Early Italian Poets* (translation), 1861 ; *Poems,* 1870, and a new edition 1881 ; *Dante and his Circle* (translations), 1874; *Ballads and Sonnets,* 1881. A collected edition of his poems and translations, edited by his brother, Mr. William Michael Rossetti, was published in 1887.

STANLEY, THE VERY REV. ARTHUR PENRHYN, D.D. (1815–1881). Born at Alderley in Cheshire, educated at a private school, and in 1824 went to Rugby, where he formed a passionate attachment for Dr. Arnold, whose biographer he subsequently became. In 1834 he entered Balliol College, Oxford, having gained a scholarship, and his career at the University was marked by a series of triumphs, gaining, among others, the Newdigate prize for English poetry by his poem, *The Gipsies.* He took orders in 1839, and was elected a Fellow of University College in 1840, where he remained twelve years as a tutor. In 1851 he was presented to a canonry at Canterbury, which he resigned in 1858 for that of Christ Church, having been appointed to the chair of Ecclesiastical History at Oxford in 1853. In 1862 he accompanied the Prince of Wales to the East, and in the following year was appointed to the Deanery of Westminster. In 1863 he was married to Lady Augusta Bruce, and in 1874 visited St. Petersburg to solemnize the marriage of the Duke and Duchess of Edinburgh according to the English Ritual.   Dean Stanley was a conspicuous member of the Broad Church party, and not infrequently found himself in conflict with many of the clergy, notably on the occasion of his appointment to the deanery at Westminster, when the appointment was violently opposed by Dr. Wordsworth, afterwards Bishop of Lincoln, on the ground of Canon Stanley's alleged heterodoxy. No collected edition of his poems has been published.

THORNBURY, GEORGE WALTER (1828–1876).   The son of a London solicitor, and for a short time studied painting, but eventually took up literature as a profession.   In 1845 he became a contributor of topographical and antiquarian papers to *The Bristol Journal,* and contributed to *The Athenæum* in 1857 a series of papers on the Courts of the Crystal Palace.   He was noted for the extreme versatility of his productions, which comprised poetry, fiction, biography, and critical and antiquarian works. He published *Lays and Legends of the New World,* 1851 ; *Songs of the Cavaliers and Roundheads,* 1857 ; *Historical and Legendary Ballads and Songs,* 1873.

TOWNSHEND, REV. CHAUNCEY HARE (1800–1868).   Born in Surrey and educated at Trinity Hall, Cambridge, where he graduated B. A. in 1821, and obtained his Master's degree in 1824.   He obtained the University prize for English verse by his poem *Jerusalem,* in 1828.   He published *Sermons in Sonnets, with other Poems,* 1851 ; *The Three Gates,* 1859.

TRENCH, THE MOST REV. RICHARD CHENEVIX, D. D. (1807–1886).   Born in Dublin, and educated at Harrow and Trinity College, Cambridge, where he graduated in 1829, and the same year was ordained deacon.   He became incumbent of Curdridge in 1833, but resigned that living in 1841, to become curate of Archdeacon Wilberforce at Alverstoke.   In 1845 he was appointed rector of Itchin Stoke, and a year later became Professor of Theology in King's College, London.   In 1856 he was appointed Dean of Westminster, and in 1864, Archbishop of

Dublin, which latter office he held for twenty years. In addition to numerous and valuable prose works, he published in verse *Justin Martyr, and other Poems,* 1835; *Honor Neale,* 1838; *Genoveva,* 1842; *Sacred Poems,* 1846; *Alma, and other Poems,* 1855.

* WOOLNER, THOMAS, R. A. (1825). Born at Hadleigh in Suffolk, educated in a school at Ipswich, and at the age of thirteen was placed in the studio of Mr. William Behnes, the sculptor. In 1843 he exhibited at the Royal Academy his first model, *Eleanor Sucking the Poison from Prince Edward's Wound,* since which time he has executed many celebrated works in bronze and marble, as well as several busts and statues of distinguished contemporaries. In 1858 he joined the ' Pre-Raphaelite Brotherhood,' and took a leading part in establishing *The Germ,* to which he contributed a series of poems, subsequently published under the title of *My Beautiful Lady.* He was elected an Associate of the Royal Academy in 1871, and was nominated a Royal Academician five years later. From 1877 to 1879 he was Professor of Sculpture in the Royal Academy. He has published *My Beautiful Lady,* 1863; *Pygmalion,* 1881; *Silenus,* 1884; *Tiresias,* 1886.

THE

PRE-RAPHAELITE BROTHERHOOD.

I

PRE-RAPHAELITE BROTHERHOOD.

GABRIEL CHARLES DANTE ROSSETTI.

THE KING'S TRAGEDY.[1]

JAMES I. OF SCOTS — 20TH FEBRUARY, 1437.

I CATHERINE am a Douglas born,
  A name to all Scots dear;
And Kate Barlass they 've called me now
  Through many a waning year.

This old arm 's withered now.   'T was once
  Most deft 'mong maidens all
To rein the steed, to wing the shaft,
  To smite the palm-play ball.

In hall adown the close-linked dance
  It has shone most white and fair;
It has been the rest for a true lord's head,
And many a sweet babe's nursing-bed,
  And the bar to a King's chambère.

Aye, lasses, draw round Kate Barlass,
  And hark with bated breath
How good King James, King Robert's son,
  Was foully done to death.

Against the coming of Christmastide
    That year the King bade call
I' the Black Friars' Charterhouse of Perth
    A solemn festival.

And we of his household rode with him
    In a close-ranked company;
But not till the sun had sunk from his throne
    Did we reach the Scotish Sea.

That eve was clenched for a boding storm,
    'Neath a toilsome moon half seen;
The cloud stooped low and the surf rose high;
And where there was a line of the sky,
    Wild wings loomed dark between.

And on a rock of the black beach-side,
    By the veiled moon dimly lit,
There was something seemed to heave with life
    As the King drew nigh to it.

And was it only the tossing furze
    Or brake of the waste sea-wold?
Or was it an eagle bent to the blast?
When near we came, we knew it at last
    For a woman tattered and old.

But it seemed as though by a fire within
    Her writhen limbs were wrung;
And as soon as the King was close to her,
    She stood up gaunt and strong.

'T was then the moon sailed clear of the rack
    On high in her hollow dome;
And still as aloft with hoary crest
    Each clamorous wave rang home,
Like fire in snow the moonlight blazed
    Amid the champing foam.

And the woman held his eyes with her eyes : —
  'O King, thou art come at last ;
But thy wraith has haunted the Scotish Sea
  To my sight for four years past.

'Four years it is since first I met,
  'Twixt the Duchray and the Dhu,
A shape whose feet clung close in a shroud,
  And that shape for thine I knew.

'A year again, and on Inchkeith Isle
  I saw thee pass in the breeze,
With the cerecloth risen above thy feet
  And wound about thy knees.

'And yet a year, in the Links of Forth,
  As a wanderer without rest,
Thou cam'st with both thine arms i' the shroud
  That clung high up thy breast.

'And in this hour I find thee here,
  And well mine eyes may note
That the winding-sheet hath passed thy breast
  And risen around thy throat.

'And when I meet thee again, O King,
  That of death hast such sore drouth, —
Except thou turn again on this shore, —
The winding-sheet shall have moved once more
  And covered thine eyes and mouth.

'O King, whom poor men bless for their King,
  Of thy fate be not so fain ;
But these my words for God's message take,
And turn thy steed, O King, for her sake
  Who rides beside thy rein !'

While the woman spoke, the King's horse reared
  As if it would breast the sea,
And the Queen turned pale as she heard on the gale
  The voice die dolorously.

When the woman ceased, the steed was still,
  But the King gazed on her yet,
And in silence save for the wail of the sea
  His eyes and her eyes met.

At last he said : — ' God's ways are His own ;
  Man is but shadow and dust.
Last night I prayed by His altar-stone ;
To-night I wend to the Feast of His Son ;
  And in Him I set my trust.

' I have held my people in sacred charge,
  And have not feared the sting
Of proud men's hate, — to His will resigned
Who has but one same death for a hind
  And one same death for a King.

' And if God in His wisdom have brought close
  The day when I must die,
That day by water or fire or air
My feet shall fall in the destined snare
  Wherever my road may lie.

' What man can say but the Fiend hath set
  Thy sorcery on my path,
My heart with the fear of death to fill,
And turn me against God's very will
  To sink in His burning wrath ? '

The woman stood as the train rode past,
  And moved nor limb nor eye ;
And when we were shipped, we saw her there
  Still standing against the sky.

As the ship made way, the moon once more
   Sank slow in her rising pall ;
And I thought of the shrouded wraith of the King,
   And I said, ' The Heavens know all.'

And now, ye lasses, must ye hear
   How my name is Kate Barlass : —
But a little thing, when all the tale
   Is told of the weary mass
Of crime and woe which in Scotland's realm
   God's will let come to pass.

'T was in the Charterhouse of Perth
   That the King and all his Court
Were met, the Christmas Feast being done,
   For solace and disport.

'T was a wind-wild eve in February,
   And against the casement-pane
The branches smote like summoning hands
   And muttered the driving rain.

And when the wind swooped over the lift
   And made the whole heaven frown,
It seemed a grip was laid on the walls
   To tug the housetop down.

And the Queen was there, more stately fair
   Than a lily in garden set;
And the King was loth to stir from her side;
For as on the day when she was his bride,
   Even so he loved her yet.

And the Earl of Athole, the King's false friend,
   Sat with him at the board ;
And Robert Stuart the chamberlain
   Who had sold his sovereign Lord.

Yet the traitor Christopher Chaumber there
  Would fain have told him all,
And vainly four times that night he strove
  To reach the King through the hall.

But the wine is bright at the goblet's brim
  Though the poison lurk beneath ;
And the apples still are red on the tree
Within whose shade may the adder be
  That shall turn thy life to death.

There was a knight of the King's fast friends
  Whom he called the King of Love;
And to such bright cheer and courtesy
  That name might best behove.

And the King and Queen both loved him well
  For his gentle knightliness ;
And with him the King, as that eve wore on,
  Was playing at the chess.

And the King said, (for he thought to jest
  And soothe the Queen thereby ;) —
' In a book 't is writ that this same year
  A King shall in Scotland die.

' And I have pondered the matter o'er,
  And this have I found, Sir Hugh, —
'There are but two Kings on Scotish ground,
  And those Kings are I and you.

' And I have a wife and a new-born heir,
  And you are yourself alone ;
So stand you stark at my side with me
  To guard our double throne.

' For here sit I and my wife and child,
  As well your heart shall approve,

In full surrender and soothfastness,
  Beneath your Kingdom of Love.'

And the Knight laughed, and the Queen too smiled;
  But I knew her heavy thought,
And I strove to find in the good King's jest
  What cheer might thence be wrought.

And I said, 'My Liege, for the Queen's dear love
  Now sing the song that of old
You made, when a captive Prince you lay,
And the nightingale sang sweet on the spray,
  In Windsor's castle-hold.'

Then he smiled the smile I knew so well
  When he thought to please the Queen;
The smile which under all bitter frowns
  Of hate that rose between,
For ever dwelt at the poet's heart
  Like the bird of love unseen.

And he kissed her hand and took his harp,
  And the music sweetly rang;
And when the song burst forth, it seemed
  'T was the nightingale that sang.

.   .   .   .

And oft have I heard again in dreams
  The voice of dire appeal
In which the King then sang of the pit
  That is under Fortune's wheel.

'*And under the wheel beheld I there*
  An ugly Pit as deep as hell,
That to behold I quaked for fear:
  And this I heard, that who therein fell
  Came no more up, tidings to tell:

Whereat, astound of the fearful sight,
I wist not what to do for fright.'

And oft has my thought called up again
   These words of the changeful song : —
' *Wist thou thy pain and thy travàil*
To come, well might'st thou weep and wail !'
   And our wail, O God ! is long.

But the song's end was all of his love ;
   And well his heart was graced
With her smiling lips and her tear-bright eyes
   As his arm went round her waist.

And on the swell of her long fair throat
   Close clung the necklet-chain
As he bent her pearl-tired head aside,
And in the warmth of his love and pride
   He kissed her lips full fain.

And her true face was a rosy red,
   The very red of the rose
That, couched on the happy garden-bed,
   In the summer sunlight glows.

And all the wondrous things of love
   That sang so sweet through the song
Were in the look that met in their eyes,
   And the look was deep and long.

'T was then a knock came at the outer gate,
   And the usher sought the King.
' The woman you met by the Scotish Sea,
   My Liege, would tell you a thing ;
And she says that her present need for speech
   Will bear no gainsaying.'

And the King said: 'The hour is late;
  To-morrow will serve, I ween.'
Then he charged the usher strictly, and said:
  'No word of this to the Queen.'

But the usher came again to the King.
  'Shall I call her back?' quoth he:
'For as she went on her way, she cried,
  "Woe! Woe! then the thing must be!"'

And the King paused, but he did not speak.
  Then he called for the Voidee-cup:
And as we heard the twelfth hour strike,
There by true lips and false lips alike
  Was the draught of trust drained up.

So with reverence meet to King and Queen,
  To bed went all from the board;
And the last to leave of the courtly train
Was Robert Stuart the chamberlain
  Who had sold his sovereign lord.

And all the locks of the chamber-door
  Had the traitor riven and brast;
And that Fate might win sure way from afar,
He had drawn out every bolt and bar
  That made the entrance fast.

And now at midnight he stole his way
  To the moat of the outer wall,
And laid strong hurdles closely across
  Where the traitors' tread should fall.

But we that were the Queen's bower-maids
  Alone were left behind;
And with heed we drew the curtains close
  Against the winter wind.

    .   .   .   .

And now beneath the window arose
  A wild voice suddenly:
And the King reared straight, but the Queen fell back
  As for bitter dule to dree;
And all of us knew the woman's voice
  Who spoke by the Scotish Sea.

'O King,' she cried, 'in an evil hour
  They drove me from thy gate;
And yet my voice must rise to thine ears;
  But alas! it comes too late!

'Last night at mid-watch, by Aberdour,
  When the moon was dead in the skies,
O King, in a death-light of thine own
  I saw thy shape arise.

'And in full season, as erst I said,
  The doom had gained its growth;
And the shroud had risen above thy neck
  And covered thine eyes and mouth.

'And no moon woke, but the pale dawn broke,
  And still thy soul stood there;
And I thought its silence cried to my soul
  As the first rays crowned its hair.

'Since then have I journeyed fast and fain
  In very despite of Fate,
Lest Hope might still be found in God's will:
  But they drove me from thy gate.

'For every man on God's ground, O King,
  His death grows up from his birth
In a shadow-plant perpetually;
And thine towers high, a black yew-tree,
  O'er the Charterhouse of Perth!'

That room was built far out from the house;
   And none but we in the room
Might hear the voice that rose beneath,
   Nor the tread of the coming doom.

For now there came a torchlight-glare,
   And a clang of arms there came;
And not a soul in that space but thought
   Of the foe Sir Robert Græme.

Yea, from the country of the Wild Scots,
   O'er mountain, valley, and glen,
He had brought with him in murderous league
   Three hundred armèd men.

The King knew all in an instant's flash,
   And like a King did he stand;
But there was no armor in all the room,
   Nor weapon lay to his hand.

And all we women flew to the door
   And thought to have made it fast;
But the bolts were gone and the bars were gone
   And the locks were riven and brast.

And he caught the pale, pale Queen in his arms
   As the iron footsteps fell, —
Then loosed her, standing alone, and said,
   'Our bliss was our farewell!'

And 'twixt his lips he murmured a prayer,
   And he crossed his brow and breast;
And proudly in royal hardihood
Even so with folded arms he stood, —
   The prize of the bloody quest.

Then on me leaped the Queen like a deer: —
   'O Catherine, help!' she cried.

And low at his feet we clasped his knees
  Together side by side.
'Oh! even a King, for his people's sake,
  From treasonous death must hide!'

'For *her* sake most!' I cried, and I marked
  The pang that my words could wring.
And the iron tongs from the chimney-nook
  I snatched and held to the King:—
'Wrench up the plank! and the vault beneath
  Shall yield safe harboring.'

With brows low-bent, from my eager hand
  The heavy heft did he take;
And the plank at his feet he wrenched and tore;
And as he frowned through the open floor,
  Again I said, 'For her sake!'

Then he cried to the Queen, 'God's will be done!'
  For her hands were clasped in prayer.
And down he sprang to the inner crypt;
And straight we closed the plank he had ripped
  And toiled to smooth it fair.

(Alas! in that vault a gap once was
  Wherethro' the King might have fled:
But three days since close-walled had it been
By his will; for the ball would roll therein
  When without at the palm he played.)

Then the Queen cried, 'Catherine, keep the door,
  And I to this will suffice!'
At her word I rose all dazed to my feet,
  And my heart was fire and ice.

And louder ever the voices grew,
  And the tramp of men in mail;
Until to my brain it seemed to be

As though I tossed on a ship at sea
   In the teeth of a crashing gale.

Then back I flew to the rest; and hard
   We strove with sinews knit
To force the table against the door
   But we might not compass it.

Then my wild gaze sped far down the hall
   To the place of the hearthstone-sill;
And the Queen bent ever above the floor,
   For the plank was rising still.

And now the rush was heard on the stair,
   And ' God, what help ? ' was our cry.
And was I frenzied or was I bold ?
I looked at each empty stanchion-hold,
   And no bar but my arm had I !

Like iron felt my arm, as through
   The staple I made it pass : —
Alack ! it was flesh and bone — no more !
'T was Catherine Douglas sprang to the door,
   But I fell back Kate Barlass.

With that they all thronged into the hall,
   Half dim to my failing ken ;
And the space that was but a void before
   Was a crowd of wrathful men.

Behind the door I had fall'n and lay,
   Yet my sense was wildly aware,
And for all the pain of my shattered arm
   I never fainted there.

Even as I fell, my eyes were cast
   Where the King leaped down to the pit;
And lo ! the plank was smooth in its place,
   And the Queen stood far from it.

And under the litters and through the bed
  And within the presses all
The traitors sought for the King, and pierced
  The arras around the wall.

And through the chamber they ramped and stormed
  Like lions loose in the lair,
And scarce could trust to their very eyes, —
  For behold! no King was there.

Then one of them seized the Queen, and cried, —
  ' Now tell us, where is thy lord ? '
And he held the sharp point over her heart :
She drooped not her eyes nor did she start,
  But she answered never a word.

Then the sword half pierced the true true breast :
  But it was the Græme's own son
Cried, ' This is a woman, — we seek a man ! '
  And away from her girdle-zone
He struck the point of the murderous steel ;
  And that foul deed was not done.

And forth flowed all the throng like a sea,
  And 't was empty space once more ;
And my eyes sought out the wounded Queen
  As I lay behind the door.

And I said : ' Dear Lady, leave me here,
  For I cannot help you now ;
But fly while you may, and none shall reck
  Of my place here lying low.'

And she said, ' My Catherine, God help thee ! '
  Then she looked to the distant floor,
And clasping her hands, ' O God help *him*,'
  She sobbed, ' for we can no more ! '

But God He knows what help may mean,
  If it mean to live or to die ;
And what sore sorrow and mighty moan
On earth it may cost ere yet a throne
  Be filled in His house on high.

.   .   .   .

And what I say next I partly saw
  And partly I heard in sooth,
And partly since from the murderers' lips
  The torture wrung the truth.

For now again came the armèd tread,
  And fast through the hall it fell ;
But the throng was less : and ere I saw,
  By the voice without I could tell
That Robert Stuart had come with them
  Who knew that chamber well.

And over the space the Græme strode dark
  With his mantle round him flung ;
And in his eye was a flaming light
  But not a word on his tongue.

And Stuart held a torch to the floor,
  And he found the thing he sought ;
And they slashed the plank away with their swords ;
  And O God ! I fainted not !

And the traitor held his torch in the gap,
  All smoking and smouldering ;
And through the vapor and fire, beneath
  In the dark crypt's narrow ring,
With a shout that pealed to the room's high roof
  They saw their naked King.

Half naked he stood, but stood as one
  Who yet could do and dare :

With the crown, the King was stript away, —
The Knight was reft of his battle-array, —
　　But still the Man was there.

From the rout then stepped a villain forth, —
　　Sir John Hall was his name;
With a knife unsheathed he leapt to the vault
　　Beneath the torchlight-flame.

Of his person and stature was the King
　　A man right manly strong,
And mightily by the shoulder-blades
　　His foe to his feet he flung.

Then the traitor's brother, Sir Thomas Hall,
　　Sprang down to work his worst;
And the King caught the second man by the neck
　　And flung him above the first.

And he smote and trampled them under him;
　　And a long month thence they bare
All black their throats with the grip of his hands
　　When the hangman's hand came there.

And sore he strove to have had their knives,
　　But the sharp blades gashed his hands.
Oh James! so armed, thou hadst battled there
　　Till help had come of thy bands;
And oh! once more thou hadst held our throne
　　And ruled thy Scotish lands!

But while the King o'er his foes still raged
　　With a heart that nought could tame,
Another man sprang down to the crypt;
And with his sword in his hand hard-gripped,
　　There stood Sir Robert Græme.

(Now shame on the recreant traitor's heart
　　Who durst not face his King　　　　.

Till the body unarmed was wearied out
   With two-fold combating !

Ah ! well might the people sing and say.
   As oft ye have heard aright : —
'*O Robert Græme, O Robert Græme,*
Who slew our King, God give thee shame !'
   For he slew him not as a knight.)

And the naked King turned round at bay,
   But his strength had passed the goal,
And he could but gasp : — ' Mine hour is come ;
But oh ! to succor thine own soul's doom,
   Let a priest now shrive my soul ! '

And the traitor looked on the King's spent strength
   And said : — ' Have I kept my word ? —
Yea, King, the mortal pledge that I gave?
No black friar's shrift thy soul shall have,
   But the shrift of this red sword ! '

With that he smote his King through the breast ;
   And all they three in that pen
Fell on him and stabbed and stabbed him there
   Like merciless murderous men.

Yet seemed it now that Sir Robert Græme,
   Ere the King's last breath was o'er,
Turned sick at heart with the deadly sight
   And would have done no more.

But a cry came from the troop above : —
   ' If him thou do not slay,
The price of his life that thou dost spare
   Thy forfeit life shall pay ! '

O God ! what more did I hear or see,
   Or how should I tell the rest?

But there at length our King lay slain
  With sixteen wounds in his breast.

O God! and now did a bell boom forth,
  And the murderers turned and fled; —
Too late, too late, O God, did it sound! —
And I heard the true men mustering round,
  And the cries and the coming tread.

But ere they came, to the black death-gap
  Somewise did I creep and steal;
And lo! or ever I swooned away,
Through the dusk I saw where the white face lay
  In the Pit of Fortune's Wheel.

And now, ye Scotish maids who have heard
  Dread things of the days grown old, —
Even at the last, of true Queen Jane
  May somewhat yet be told,
And how she dealt for her dear lord's sake
  Dire vengeance manifold.

'T was in the Charterhouse of Perth,
  In the fair-lit Death-chapelle,
That the slain King's corpse on bier was laid
  With chaunt and requiem-knell.

And all with royal wealth of balm
  Was the body purified;
And none could trace on the brow and lips
  The death that he had died.

In his robes of state he lay asleep
  With orb and sceptre in hand;
And by the crown he wore on his throne
  Was his kingly forehead spanned.

And the Queen sat by him night and day,
   And oft she knelt in prayer,
All wan and pale in the widow's veil
   That shrouded her shining hair.

And I had got good help of my hurt;
   And only to me some sign
She made; and save the priests that were there
   No face would she see but mine.

And the month of March wore on apace;
   And now fresh couriers fared
Still from the country of the Wild Scots
   With news of the traitors snared.

And still as I told her day by day,
   Her pallor changed to sight,
And the frost grew to a furnace-flame
   That burnt her visage white.

And evermore as I brought her word,
   She bent to her dead King James,
And in the cold ear with fire-drawn breath
   She spoke the traitors' names.

But when the name of Sir Robert Græme
   Was the one she had to give,
I ran to hold her up from the floor;
For the froth was on her lips, and sore
   I feared that she could not live.

And the month of March wore nigh to its end,
   And still was the death-pall spread;
For she would not bury her slaughtered lord
   Till his slayers all were dead.

And now of their dooms dread tidings came,
   And of torments fierce and dire;

And nought she spake, — she had ceased to speak, —
  But her eyes were a soul on fire.

But when I told her the bitter end
  Of the stern and just award,
She leaned o'er the bier, and thrice three times
  She kissed the lips of her lord.

And then she said, — 'My King, they are dead!'
  And she knelt on the chapel-floor,
And whispered low with a strange proud smile, —
  'James, James, they suffered more!'

Last she stood up to her queenly height,
  But she shook like an autumn leaf,
As though the fire wherein she burned
Then left her body, and all were turned
  To winter of life-long grief.

And 'O James!' she said, — 'My James!' she said, —
  'Alas for the woful thing,
That a poet true and a friend of man,
In desperate days of bale and ban,
  Should needs be born a King!'

THE BLESSÈD DAMOZEL.

THE blessèd damozel leaned out
  From the gold bar of heaven;
Her eyes were deeper than the depth
  Of waters stilled at even;
She had three lilies in her hand,
  And the stars in her hair were seven.

Her robe, ungirt from clasp to hem,
  No wrought flowers did adorn,

But a white rose of Mary's gift,
   For service meetly worn;
Her hair that lay along her back
   Was yellow like ripe corn.

Herseemed she scarce had been a day
   One of God's choristers;
The wonder was not yet quite gone
   From that still look of hers;
Albeit, to them she left, her day
   Had counted as ten years.

(To one, it is ten years of years,
   .   .   . Yet now, and in this place,
Surely she leaned o'er me — her hair
   Fell all about my face.   .   .   .
Nothing: the autumn fall of leaves.
   The whole year sets apace.)

It was the rampart of God's house
   That she was standing on;
By God built over the sheer depth
   The which is Space begun;
So high, that looking downward thence
   She scarce could see the sun.

It lies in Heaven, across the flood
   Of ether, as a bridge.
Beneath, the tides of day and night
   With flame and darkness ridge
The void, as low as where this earth
   Spins like a fretful midge.

Around her, lovers, newly met
   'Mid deathless love's acclaims,
Spoke evermore among themselves
   Their heart-remembered names;

And the souls mounting up to God
   Went by her like thin flames.

And still she bowed herself and stooped
   Out of the circling charm;
Until her bosom must have made
   The bar she leaned on warm,
And the lilies lay as if asleep
   Along her bended arm.

From the fixed place of Heaven she saw
   Time like a pulse shake fierce
Through all the worlds.   Her gaze still strove
   Within the gulf to pierce
Its path; and now she spoke as when
   The stars sang in their spheres.

The sun was gone now; the curled moon
   Was like a little feather
Fluttering far down the gulf; and now
   She spoke through the still weather.
Her voice was like the voice the stars
   Had when they sang together.

(Ah sweet! Even now, in that bird's song,
   Strove not her accents there,
Fain to be hearkened?   When those bells
   Possessed the mid-day air,
Strove not her steps to reach my side
   Down all the echoing stair?)

'I wish that he were come to me,
   For he will come,' she said.
'Have I not prayed in Heaven? — on earth,
   Lord, Lord, has he not prayed?
Are not two prayers a perfect strength?
   And shall I feel afraid?

‘When round his head the aureole clings,
 And he is clothed in white,
I ’ll take his hand and go with him
 To the deep wells of light;
As unto a stream we will step down,
 And bathe there in God’s sight.

‘We two will stand beside that shrine,
 Occult, withheld, untrod,
Whose lamps are stirred continually
 With prayer sent up to God;
And see our old prayers, granted, melt
 Each like a little cloud.

‘We too will lie i’ the shadow of
 That living mystic tree
Within whose secret growth the Dove
 Is sometimes felt to be,
While every leaf that His plumes touch
 Saith His Name audibly.

‘And I myself will teach to him,
 I myself, lying so,
The songs I sing here; which his voice
 Shall pause in, hushed and slow,
And find some knowledge at each pause,
 Or some new thing to know.’

(Alas! We two, we two, thou say’st!
 Yea, one wast thou with me
That once of old. But shall God lift
 To endless unity
The soul whose likeness with thy soul
 Was but its love for thee?)

‘We two,’ she said, ‘will seek the groves
 Where the lady Mary is,

With her five handmaidens, whose names
  Are five sweet symphonies,
Cecily, Gertrude, Magdalen,
  Margaret and Rosalys.

  Circlewise sit they, with bound locks
    And foreheads garlanded ;
  Into the fine cloth white like flame
    Weaving the golden thread,
  To fashion the birth-robes for them
    Who are just born, being dead.

  ' He shall fear, haply, and be dumb :
    Then will I lay my cheek
  To his, and tell about our love,
    Not once abashed or weak :
  And the dear Mother will approve
    My pride, and let me speak.

  ' Herself shall bring us, hand in hand,
    To Him round whom all souls
  Kneel, the clear-ranged unnumbered heads
    Bowed with their aureoles :
  And angels meeting us shall sing
    To their citherns and citoles.

  ' There will I ask of Christ the Lord
    Thus much for him and me : —
  Only to live as once on earth
    With Love, only to be,
  As then awhile, for ever now
    Together, I and he.'

  She gazed and listened and then said,
    Less sad of speech than mild, —

'All this is when he comes.'   She ceased.
   The light thrilled towards her, filled
With angels in strong level flight.
   Her eyes prayed, and she smiled.

(I saw her smile.)   But soon their path
   Was vague in distant spheres :
And then she cast her arms along
   The golden barriers,
And laid her face between her hands,
   And wept.   (I heard her tears.)

FROM 'THE HOUSE OF LIFE : A SONNET SEQUENCE.'[2]

A SONNET is a moment's monument, —
   Memorial from the Soul's eternity
   To one dead deathless hour.   Look that it be,
Whether for lustral rite or dire portent,
Of its own arduous fulness reverent :
   Carve it in ivory or in ebony,
   As Day or Night may rule ; and let Time see
Its flowering crest impearled and orient.

A Sonnet is a coin : its face reveals
   The soul, — its converse, to what Power 't is due : —
Whether for tribute to the august appeals
   Of Life, or dower in Love's high retinue,
It serve ; or, 'mid the dark wharf's cavernous breath,
In Charon's palm it pay the toll to Death.

FROM 'PART I., YOUTH AND CHANGE.'

SONNET XIX.

SILENT NOON.

YOUR hands lie open in the long fresh grass, —
   The finger-points look through like rosy blooms :
   Your eyes smile peace. The pasture gleams and glooms
'Neath billowing skies that scatter and amass.
All round our nest, far as the eye can pass,
   Are golden kingcup-fields with silver edge
   Where the cow-parsley skirts the hawthorn-hedge.
'T is visible silence, still as the hour-glass.

Deep in the sun-searched growths the dragon-fly
Hangs like a blue thread loosened from the sky : —
   So this winged hour is dropt to us from above.
Oh ! clasp we to our hearts, for deathless dower,
This close-companioned inarticulate hour
   When twofold silence was the song of love.

SONNET XXIV.

PRIDE OF YOUTH.

EVEN as a child, of sorrow that we give
   The dead, but little in his heart can find,
   Since without need of thought to his clear mind
Their turn it is to die and his to live : —
Even so the winged New Love smiles to receive
   Along his eddying plumes the auroral wind,
   Nor, forward glorying, casts one look behind
Where night-rack shrouds the Old Love fugitive.

There is a change in every hour's recall,
  And the last cowslip in the fields we see
  On the same day with the first corn-poppy.
Alas for hourly change! Alas for all
The loves that from his hand proud Youth lets fall,
  Even as the beads of a told rosary!

SONNET XXXI.

HER GIFTS.

HIGH grace, the dower of queens; and therewithal
  Some wood-born wonder's sweet simplicity;
  A glance like water brimming with the sky
Or hyacinth-light where forest-shadows fall;
Such thrilling pallor of cheek as doth enthral
  The heart; a mouth whose passionate forms imply
  All music and all silence held thereby;
Deep golden locks, her sovereign coronal;
A round reared neck, meet column of Love's shrine
  To cling to when the heart takes sanctuary;
  Hands which for ever at Love's bidding be,
And soft-stirred feet still answering to his sign:—
  These are her gifts, as tongue may tell them o'er.
  Breathe low her name, my soul; for that means more.

SONNET XLIII.

LOVE AND HOPE.

BLESS love and hope. Full many a withered year
  Whirled past us, eddying to its chill doomsday;
  And clasped together where the blown leaves lay,
We long have knelt and wept full many a tear.
Yet lo! one hour at last, the Spring's compeer,

Flutes softly to us from some green byway :
Those years, those tears are dead, but only they : —
Bless love and hope, true soul; for we are here.

Cling heart to heart ; nor of this hour demand
    Whether in very truth, when we are dead,
    Our hearts shall wake to know Love's golden head
Sole sunshine of the imperishable land ;
    Or but discern, through night's unfeatured scope,
    Scorn-fired at length the illusive eyes of Hope.

SONNET XLVII.

BROKEN MUSIC.

THE mother will not turn, who thinks she hears
    Her nursling's speech first grow articulate ;
    But breathless with averted eyes elate
She sits, with open lips and open ears,
That it may call her twice.   'Mid doubts and fears
    Thus oft my soul has hearkened; till the song,
    A central moan for days, at length found tongue,
And the sweet music welled and the sweet tears.

But now, whatever while the soul is fain
    To list that wonted murmur, as it were
The speech-bound sea-shell's low importunate strain, —
    No breath of song, thy voice alone is there,
O bitterly beloved ! and all her gain
    Is but the pang of unpermitted prayer.

SONNET LIII.

WITHOUT HER.

WHAT of her glass without her ?   The blank gray
    There where the pool is blind of the moon's face.
    Her dress without her ?   The tossed empty space

Of cloud-rack whence the moon has passed away.
Her paths without her? Day's appointed sway
  Usurped by desolate night.   Her pillowed place
  Without her? Tears, ah me! for love's good grace,
And cold forgetfulness of night or day.

What of the heart without her? Nay, poor heart,
  Of thee what word remains ere speech be still?
  A wayfarer by barren ways and chill,
Steep ways and weary, without her thou art,
Where the long cloud, the long wood's counterpart,
  Sheds doubled darkness up the laboring hill.

FROM 'PART II., CHANGE AND FATE.'

SONNET LXII.

THE SOUL'S SPHERE.

SOME prisoned moon in steep cloud-fastnesses, —
  Throned queen and thralled; some dying sun whose pyre
  Blazed with momentous memorable fire; —
Who hath not yearned and fed his heart with these?
Who, sleepless, hath not anguished to appease
  Tragical shadow's realm of sound and sight
  Conjectured in the lamentable night? . . . .
Lo! the soul's sphere of infinite images!

What sense shall count them? Whether it forecast
  The rose-winged hours that flutter in the van
  Of Love's unquestioning unrevealèd span, —
Visions of golden futures: or that last
Wild pageant of the accumulated past
  That clangs and flashes for a drowning man.

SONNET LXVI.

THE HEART OF THE NIGHT.

FROM child to youth; from youth to arduous man;
　　From lethargy to fever of the heart;
　　From faithful life to dream-dowered days apart;
From trust to doubt; from doubt to brink of ban; —
Thus much of change in one swift cycle ran
　　Till now.　Alas, the soul! — how soon must she
　　Accept her primal immortality, —
The flesh resume its dust whence it began?

O Lord of work and peace!　O Lord of life!
　　O Lord, the awful Lord of will! though late,
　　Even yet renew this soul with duteous breath:
That when the peace is garnered in from strife,
　　The work retrieved, the will regenerate,
　　This soul may see thy face, O Lord of death!

SONNET LXIX.

AUTUMN IDLENESS.

THIS sunlight shames November where he grieves
　　In dead red leaves, and will not let him shun
　　The day, though bough with bough be over-run.
But with a blessing every glade receives
High salutation; while from hillock-eaves
　　The deer gaze calling, dappled white and dun,
　　As if, being foresters of old, the sun
Had marked them with the shade of forest-leaves.

Here dawn to-day unveiled her magic glass;
　　Here noon now gives the thirst and takes the dew;
Till eve bring rest when other good things pass.
　　And here the lost hours the lost hours renew
While I still lead my shadow o'er the grass,
　　Nor know, for longing, that which I should do.

SONNET LXXVIII.

BODY'S BEAUTY.

Of Adam's first wife, Lilith, it is told
   (The witch he loved before the gift of Eve,)
    That, ere the snake's, her sweet tongue could deceive,
And her enchanted hair was the first gold.
And still she sits, young while the earth is old,
    And, subtly of herself contemplative,
    Draws men to watch the bright web she can weave,
Till heart and body and life are in its hold.

The rose and poppy are her flowers; for where
    Is he not found, O Lilith, whom shed scent
And soft-shed kisses and soft sleep shall snare?
    Lo! as that youth's eyes burned at thine, so went
    Thy spell through him, and left his straight neck bent
And round his heart one strangling golden hair.

SONNET LXXXVI.

LOST DAYS.

The lost days of my life until to-day,
    What were they, could I see them on the street
    Lie as they fell?   Would they be ears of wheat
Sown once for food but trodden into clay?
Or golden coins squandered and still to pay?
    Or drops of blood dabbling the guilty feet?
    Or such spilt water as in dreams must cheat
The undying throats of Hell, athirst alway?

I do not see them here; but after death
    God knows I know the faces I shall see,
Each one a murdered self, with low last breath.
    'I am thyself, — what hast thou done to me?'
'And I — and I — thyself,' (lo! each one saith,)
 . 'And thou thyself to all eternity!'

3

SONNET XCVII.

A SUPERSCRIPTION.

Look in my face ; my name is Might-have-been ;
  I am also called No-more, Too-late, Farewell ;
  Unto thine ear I hold the dead-sea shell
Cast up thy Life's foam-fretted feet between ;
Unto thine eyes the glass where that is seen
  Which had Life's form and Love's, but by my spell
  Is now a shaken shadow intolerable,
Of ultimate things unuttered the frail screen.

Mark me, how still I am !   But should there dart
  One moment through thy soul the soft surprise
  Of that winged Peace which lulls the breath of sighs,—
Then shalt thou see me smile, and turn apart
Thy visage to mine ambush at thy heart
  Sleepless with cold commemorative eyes.

AVE.

Mother of the Fair Delight,
Thou handmaid perfect in God's sight,
Now sitting fourth beside the Three,
Thyself a woman-Trinity, —
Being a daughter borne to God,
Mother of Christ from stall to rood,
And wife unto the Holy Ghost : —
Oh when our need is uttermost,
Think that to such as death may strike
Thou once wert sister sisterlike !
Thou headstone of humanity,
Groundstone of the great Mystery,
Fashioned like us, yet more than we !

Mind'st thou not (when June's heavy breath
Warmed the long days in Nazareth,)

That eve thou didst go forth to give
Thy flowers some drink that they might live
One faint night more amid the sands?
Far off the trees were as pale wands
Against the fervid sky: the sea
Sighed further off eternally
As human sorrow sighs in sleep.
Then suddenly the awe grew deep,
As of a day to which all days
Were footsteps in God's secret ways:
Until a folding sense, like prayer,
Which is, as God is, everywhere,
Gathered about thee; and a voice
Spake to thee without any noise,
Being of the silence: — 'Hail,' it said,
'Thou that art highly favorèd;
The Lord is with thee here and now;
Blessèd among all women thou.'

Ah! knew'st thou of the end, when first
That Babe was on thy bosom nursed? —
Or when He tottered round thy knee
Did thy great sorrow dawn on thee? —
And through His boyhood, year by year
Eating with Him the Passover,
Didst thou discern confusedly
That holier sacrament, when He,
The bitter cup about to quaff,
Should break the bread and eat thereof? —
Or came not yet the knowledge, even
Till on some day forecast in Heaven
His feet passed through thy door to press
Upon His Father's business? —
Or still was God's high secret kept?

Nay, but I think the whisper crept
Like growth through childhood.   Work and play,

Things common to the course of day,
Awed thee with meanings unfulfilled;
And all through girlhood, something stilled
Thy senses like the birth of light,
When thou hast trimmed thy lamp at night
Or washed thy garments in the stream;
To whose white bed had come the dream
That He was thine and thou wast His
Who feeds among the field-lilies.
O solemn shadow of the end
In that wise spirit long contained!
O awful end! and those unsaid
Long years when It was Finishèd!

Mind'st thou not (when the twilight gone
Left darkness in the house of John,)
Between the naked window-bars
That spacious vigil of the stars? —
For thou, a watcher even as they,
Wouldst rise from where throughout the day
Thou wroughtest raiment for His poor;
And, finding the fixed terms endure
Of day and night which never brought
Sounds of His coming chariot,
Wouldst lift through cloud-waste unexplored
Those eyes which said, 'How long, O Lord?'
Then that disciple whom He loved,
Well heeding, haply would be moved
To ask thy blessing in His name;
And that one thought in both, the same
Though silent, then would clasp ye round
To weep together, — tears long bound,
Sick tears of patience, dumb and slow.
Yet, 'Surely I come quickly,' — so
He said, from life and death gone home.
Amen: even so, Lord Jesus, come!

But oh! what human tongue can speak
That day when Michael came to break
From the tired spirit, like a veil,
Its covenant with Gabriel
Endured at length unto the end?
What human thought can apprehend
That mystery of motherhood
When thy Beloved at length renewed
The sweet communion severèd, —
His left hand underneath thine head
And His right hand embracing thee? —
Lo! He was thine, and this is He!

Soul, is it Faith, or Love, or Hope,
That lets me see her standing up
Where the light of the Throne is bright?
Unto the left, unto the right,
The cherubim, arrayed, conjoint,
Float inward to a golden point,
And from between the seraphim
The glory issues for a hymn.
O Mary Mother, be not loth
To listen, — thou whom the stars clothe,
Who seëst and mayst not be seen!
Hear us at last, O Mary Queen!
Into our shadow bend thy face,
Bowing thee from the secret place,
O Mary Virgin, full of grace!

William Morris.

Her slender fingers scarce could hold
The wet reins; yea, and scarcely, too,
She felt the foot within her shoe
Against the stirrup; all for this,
To part at last without a kiss
Beside the haystack in the floods.

For when they neared that old soaked hay,
They saw across the only way
That Judas, Godmar, and the three
Red running lions dismally
Grinned from his pennon, under which,
In one straight line along the ditch,
They counted thirty heads.

        So then,
While Robert turned round to his men,
She saw at once the wretched end,
And, stooping down, tried hard to rend
Her coif the wrong way from her head,
And hid her eyes; while Robert said:
' Nay, love, 't is scarcely two to one,
At Poictiers where we made them run
So fast — why, sweet my love, good cheer,
The Gascon frontier is so near,
Nought after this.'

        But, ' O,' she said,
' My God! My God! I have to tread
The long way back without you; then
The court at Paris; those six men;
The gratings of the Chatelet;
The swift Seine on some rainy day
Like this, and people standing by,
And laughing, while my weak hands try
To recollect how strong men swim.

All this, or else a life with him,
For which I should be damned at last,
Would God that this next hour were past!'

He answered not, but cried his cry,
'St. George for Marny!' cheerily;
And laid his hand upon her rein.
Alas! no man of all his train
Gave back that cheery cry again;
And, while for rage his thumb beat fast
Upon his sword-hilts, some one cast
About his neck a kerchief long,
And bound him.

           Then they went along
To Godmar; who said: 'Now, Jehane,
Your lover's life is on the wane
So fast, that, if this very hour
You yield not as my paramour,
He will not see the rain leave off —
Nay, keep your tongue from gibe and scoff,
Sir Robert, or I slay you now.'

She laid her hand upon her brow,
Then gazed upon the palm, as though
She thought her forehead bled, and — 'No.'
She said, and turned her head away,
As there were nothing else to say,
And everything were settled: red
Grew Godmar's face from chin to head:
'Jehane, on yonder hill there stands
My castle, guarding well my lands:
What hinders me from taking you,
And doing that I list to do
To your fair wilful body, while
Your knight lies dead?'

              A wicked smile
Wrinkled her face, her lips grew thin,
A long way out she thrust her chin:
'You know that I should strangle you
While you were sleeping; or bite through
Your throat, by God's help — ah!' she said,
'Lord Jesus, pity your poor maid!
For in such wise they hem me in,
I cannot choose but sin and sin,
Whatever happens: yet I think
They could not make me eat or drink,
And so should I just reach my rest.'
'Nay, if you do not my behest,
O Jehane! though I love you well,'
Said Godmar, 'would I fail to tell
All that I know.'   'Foul lies,' she said.
'Eh? lies my Jehane?   By God's head,
At Paris folks would deem them true!
Do you know, Jehane, they cry for you,
"Jehane the brown! Jehane the brown!
Give us Jehane to burn or drown!" —
Eh — gag me, Robert! — sweet my friend,
This were indeed a piteous end
For those long fingers, and long feet,
And long neck, and smooth shoulders sweet;
An end that few men would forget
That saw it — So, an hour yet:
Consider, Jehane, which to take
Of life or death!'

              So, scarce awake,
Dismounting, did she leave that place,
And totter some yards: with her face
Turned upward to the sky she lay,
Her head on a wet heap of hay,
And fell asleep; and while she slept,

And did not dream, the minutes crept
Round to the twelve again; but she,
Being waked at last, sighed quietly,
And strangely childlike came, and said:
'I will not.'   Straightway Godmar's head,
As though it hung on strong wires, turned
Most sharply round, and his face burned.

For Robert — both his eyes were dry,
He could not weep, but gloomily
He seemed to watch the rain; yea, too,
His lips were firm; he tried once more
To touch her lips; she reached out, sore
And vain desire so tortured them,
The poor gray lips, and now the hem
Of his sleeve brushed them.

                        With a start
Up Godmar rose, thrust them apart;
From Robert's throat he loosed the bands
Of silk and mail; with empty hands
Held out, she stood and gazed, and saw
The long bright blade without a flaw
Glide out from Godmar's sheath, his hand
In Robert's hair; she saw him bend
Back Robert's head; she saw him send
The thin steel down; the blow told well,
Right backward the knight Robert fell,
And moaned as dogs do, being half dead,
Unwitting, as I deem: so then
Godmar turned grinning to his men,
Who ran, some five or six, and beat
His head to pieces at their feet.

Then Godmar turned again and said:
'So, Jehane, the first fitte is read!

Take note, my lady, that your way
Lies backward to the Chatelet!'
She shook her head and gazed awhile
At her cold hands with a rueful smile,
As though this thing had made her mad.

This was the parting that they had
Beside the haystack in the floods.

FROM 'THE EARTHLY PARADISE.'[8]

AN APOLOGY.

Of Heaven or Hell I have no power to sing,
I cannot ease the burden of your fears,
Or make quick-coming death a little thing,
Or bring again the pleasure of past years,
Nor for my words shall ye forget your tears,
Or hope again for aught that I can say,
The idle singer of an empty day.

But rather, when aweary of your mirth,
From full hearts still unsatisfied ye sigh,
And, feeling kindly unto all the earth,
Grudge every minute as it passes by,
Made the more mindful that the sweet days die, —
— Remember me a little then, I pray,
The idle singer of an empty day.

The heavy trouble, the bewildering care
That weighs us down who live and earn our bread,
These idle verses have no power to bear;
So let me sing of names remembered,
Because they, living not, can ne'er be dead,
Or long time take their memory quite away
From us poor singers of an empty day.

Dreamer of dreams, born out of my due time,
Why should I strive to set the crooked straight?
Let it suffice me that my murmuring rhyme
Beats with light wing against the ivory gate,
Telling a tale not too importunate
To those who in the sleepy region stay,
Lulled by the singer of an empty day.

Folk say, a wizard to a northern king
At Christmas-tide such wondrous things did show,
That through one window men beheld the spring,
And through another saw the summer glow,
And through a third the fruited vines arow,
While still, unheard, but in its wonted way,
Piped the drear wind of that December day.

So with this Earthly Paradise it is,
If ye will read aright, and pardon me,
Who strive to build a shadowy isle of bliss
Midmost the beating of the steely sea,
Where tossed about all hearts of men must be ;
Whose ravening monsters mighty men shall slay,
Not the poor singer of an empty day.

FROM 'PROLOGUE — THE WANDERERS.'

Two gates unto the road of life there are,
And to the happy youth both seem afar, —
Both seem afar, so far the past one seems,
The gate of birth, made dim with many dreams,
Bright with remembered hopes, beset with flowers ;
So far it seems he cannot count the hours
That to this midway path have led him on
Where every joy of life now seemeth won,
So far, he thinks not of the other gate,
Within whose shade the ghosts of dead hopes wait

To call upon him as he draws anear,
Despoiled, alone, and dull with many a fear,
'Where is thy work? how little thou hast done,
Where are thy friends, why art thou so alone?'
How shall he weigh his life? slow goes the time
The while the fresh dew-sprinkled hill we climb,
Thinking of what shall be the other side,
Slow pass perchance the minutes we abide
On the gained summit, blinking at the sun;
But when the downward journey is begun
No more our feet may loiter, past our ears
Shrieks the harsh wind scarce noted midst our fears,
And battling with the hostile things we meet,
Till, ere we know it, our weak, shrinking feet
Have brought us to the end and all is done.

'*THE MAN BORN TO BE KING.*'

FROM '**MARCH.**'

.   .   .   .

So wandering, to a fountain's side
He came, and o'er the basin hung,
Watching the fishes, as he sung
Some song remembered from of old,
Ere yet the miller won that gold.
But soon made drowsy with his ride,
And the warm, hazy autumn-tide,
And many a musical sweet sound,
He cast him down upon the ground,
And watched the glittering water leap,
Still singing low, nor thought to sleep.
But scarce three minutes had gone by
Before, as if in mockery,
The starling chattered o'er his head,

And nothing he remembered,
Nor dreamed of aught that he had seen.

Meanwhile unto that garden green
Had come the Princess, and with her
A maiden that she held right dear,
Who knew the inmost of her mind.
Now those twain, as the scented wind
Played with their raiment or their hair,
Had late been running here and there,
Chasing each other merrily,
As maids do, thinking no one by ;
But now, well wearied therewithal,
Had let their gathered garments fall
About their feet, and slowly went :
And through the leaves a murmur sent,
As of two happy doves that sing
The soft returning of the spring.
Now of these twain the Princess spoke
The less, but into laughter broke
Not seldom, and would redden oft,
As on her lips her fingers soft
She laid, as still the other maid,
Half grave, half smiling, follies said.
So in their walk they drew anigh
That fountain in the 'midst, whereby
Lay Michael sleeping, dreaming naught
Of such fair things so nigh him brought ;
They, when the fountain shaft was passed,
Beheld him on the ground downcast,
And stopped at first, until the maid
Stepped lightly forward to the shade,
And when she had gazed there awhile
Came running back again, a smile
Parting her lips, and her bright eyes
Afire with many fantasies ;

And ere the Lady Cecily
Could speak a word, ' Hush ! hush ! ' said she ;
' Did I not say that he would come
To woo thee in thy peaceful home
Before thy father brought him here ?
Come, and behold him, have no fear !
The great bell would not wake him now,
Right in his ears.'

     ' Nay, what dost thou ?'
The Princess said ; 'let us go hence ;
Thou know'st I give obedience
To what my father bids ; but I
A maid full fain would live and die,
Since I am born to be a queen.'

 ' Yea, yea, for such as thou hast seen,
That may be well,' the other said.
' But come now, come ; for by my head
This one must be from Paradise ;
Come swiftly then, if thou art wise
Ere aught can snatch him back again.'

 She caught her hand, and not in vain
She prayed ; for now some kindly thought
To Cecily's brow fair color brought,
And quickly 'gan her heart to beat
As Love drew near those eyes to greet,
Who knew him not till that sweet hour.

 So over the fair, pink-edged flower,
Softly she stepped ; but when she came
Anigh the sleeper, lovely shame
Cast a soft mist before her eyes
Full filled of many fantasies.
But when she saw him lying there
She smiled to see her mate so fair ;
And in her heart did Love begin
To tell his tale, nor thought she sin

To gaze on him that was her own,
Not doubting he was come alone
To woo her, whom midst arms and gold
She deemed she should at first behold:
And with that thought love grew again
Until departing was a pain,
Though fear grew with that growing love,
And with her lingering footsteps strove
As from the place she turned to go,
Sighing and murmuring words full low.
But as her raiment's hem she raised,
And for her merry fellow gazed
Shamefaced and changed, she met her eyes
Turned grave and sad with ill surprise;
Who while the princess mazed did stand
Had drawn from Michael's loosened band
The King's scroll, which she held out now
To Cecily, and whispered low,
' Read, and do quickly what thou wilt, —
Sad, sad! such fair life to be spilt:
Come further first.'
                    With that they stepped
A space or two from where he slept,
And then she read,
                    ' Lord Seneschal,
On thee and thine may all good fall;
Greeting hereby the King sendeth,
And biddeth thee to put to death
His enemy who beareth this;
And as thou lovest life and bliss,
And all thy goods thou holdest dear,
Set thou his head upon a spear
A good half-furlong from the gate,
Our coming hitherward to wait, —
So perish the King's enemies!'
    She read, and scarcely had her eyes

Seen clear her father's name and seal,
Ere all love's power her heart did feel,
That drew her back in spite of shame,
To him who was not e'en a name
Unto her a short hour agone.
Panting she said, 'Wait thou alone
Beside him, watch him carefully
And let him sleep if none draw nigh ;
If of himself he waketh, then
Hide him until I come again,
When thou hast told him of the snare, —
If thou betrayest me, beware !
For death shall be the least of all
The ills that on thine head shall fall, —
What say I ? — thou art dear to me,
And doubly dear now shalt thou be,
Thou shalt have power and majesty,
And be more queen in all than I. —
Few words are best, be wise, be wise !'

Withal she turned about her eyes
Once more, and swiftly as a man
Betwixt the garden trees she ran,
Until, her own bower reached at last,
She made good haste, and quickly passed
Unto her secret treasury.
There, hurrying since the time was nigh
For folk to come from meat, she took
From 'twixt the leaves of a great book
A royal scroll, signed, sealed, but blank,
Then, with a hand that never shrank
Or trembled, she the scroll did fill
With these words, writ with clerkly skill, —
'Unto the Seneschal Sir Rafe,
Who holdeth our fair castle safe,
Greeting and health ! O well-beloved,

4

Know that at this time we are moved
To wed our daughter, so we send
Him who bears this, our perfect friend,
To be her bridegroom; so do thou
Ask nought of him, since well we know
His race and great nobility,
And how he is most fit to be
Our son; therefore make no delay,
But wed the twain upon the day
Thou readest this : and see that all
Take oath to him, whate'er shall fall,
To do his bidding as our heir ;
So doing still be lief and dear
As I have held thee yet to be.'
   She cast the pen down hastily
At that last letter, for she heard
How even now the people stirred
Within the hall : nor dared she think
What bitter portion she must drink
If now she failed, so falsely bold
That life or death did she infold
Within its cover, making shift
To seal it with her father's gift,
A signet of carnelian.

   Then swiftly down the stairs she ran
And reached the garden ; but her fears
Brought shouts and thunder to her ears,
That were but lazy words of men
Full-fed, far off; nay, even when
Her limbs caught up her flying gown
The noise seemed loud enough to drown
The twitter of the autumn birds,
And her own muttered breathless words
That to her heart seemed loud indeed.
   Yet therewithal she made good speed

And reached the fountain seen of none,
Where yet abode her friend alone,
Watching the sleeper, who just now
Turned in his sleep and muttered low.
Therewith fair Agnes saying naught
From out her hand the letter caught;
And while she leaned against the stone
Stole up to Michael's side alone,
And with a cool, unshrinking hand
Thrust the new scroll deep in his band,
And turned about unto her friend;
Who, having come unto the end
Of all her courage, trembled there
With face upturned for fresher air,
And parted lips grown gray and pale,
And limbs that now began to fail,
And hands wherefrom all strength had gone,
Scarce fresher than the blue-veined stone
That quivering still she strove to clutch.

But when she felt her lady's touch,
Feebly she said, 'Go! let me die
And end this sudden misery
That in such wise has wrapped my life,
I am too weak for such a strife,
So sick I am with shame and fear;
Would thou hadst never brought me here!'

But Agnes took her hand and said,
'Nay, Queen, and must we three be dead
Because thou fearest? All is safe
If boldly thou wilt face Sir Rafe.'

So saying, did she draw her hence,
Past tree and bower, and high pleached fence
Unto the garden's further end,
And left her there, and back did wend,
And from the house made haste to get
A gilded maund, wherein she set

A flask of ancient island wine,
Ripe fruits and wheaten manchets fine,
And many such a delicate
As goddesses in old time ate,
Ere Helen was a Trojan queen;
So passing through the garden green
She cast her eager eyes again
Upon the spot where he had lain,
But found it empty, so sped on
Till she at last the place had won
Where Cecily lay weak and white
Within that fair bower of delight.

Her straight she made to eat and drink,
And said, ' See now thou dost not shrink
From this thy deed; let love slay fear
Now, when thy life shall grow so dear,
Each minute should seem loss to thee
If thou for thy felicity
Couldst stay to count them; for I say,
This day shall be thy happy day.'

Therewith she smiled to see the wine
Embracèd by her fingers fine;
And her sweet face grow bright again
With sudden pleasure after pain.

Again she spoke, ' What is this word
That, dreaming, I perchance have heard,
But certainly remember well;
That some old soothsayer did tell
Strange things unto my lord, the King,
That on thy hand the spousal ring
No Kaiser's son, no King should set,
But one a peasant did beget, —
What say'st thou? '

                     But the Queen flushed red;
' Such fables I have heard,' she said;
' And thou — is it such scath to me,

The bride of such a man to be ?'
  ' Nay,' said she, ' God will have him King;
How shall we do a better thing
With this or that one than He can ?
God's friend must be a goodly man.'
  But with that word she heard the sound
Of folk who through the mazes wound
Bearing the message; then she said,
' Be strong, pluck up thine hardihead,
Speak little, so shall all be well,
For now our own tale will they tell.'

  And even as she spoke they came,
And all the green place was aflame
With golden raiment of the lords ;
While Cecily, noting not their words,
Rose up to go ; and for her part
By this had fate so steeled her heart,
Scarce otherwise she seemed, than when
She passed before the eyes of men
At tourney or high festival.
But when they now had reached the hall,
And up its very steps they went,
Her head a little down she bent ;
Nor raised it till the daïs was gained
For fear that love some monster feigned
To be a god, and she should be
Smit by her own bolt wretchedly.
But at the rustling, crowded daïs
She gathered heart her eyes to raise,
And there beheld her love, indeed,
Clad in her father's serving weed,
But proud, and flushed, and calm withal.
Fearless of aught that might befall,
Nor too astonied, for he thought, —
' From point to point my life is brought

Through wonders till it comes to this;
And trouble cometh after bliss,
And I will bear all as I may,
And ever, as day passeth day,
My life will hammer from the twain,
Forging a long-enduring chain.'
   But midst these thoughts their young eyes met,
And every word did he forget
Wherewith men name unhappiness,
As read again those words did bless
With double blessings his glad ears.
And if she trembled with her fears,
And if with doubt, and love, and shame,
The rosy color went and came
In her sweet cheeks and smooth bright brow,
Little did folk think of it now,
But as of maiden modesty,
Shamefaced to see the bridegroom nigh.
   And now when Rafe the Seneschal
Had read the message down the Hall,
And turned to her, quite calm again
Her face had grown, and with no pain
She raised her serious eyes to his,
Grown soft and pensive with his bliss,
And said:
                  'Prince, thou art welcome here,
Where all my father loves is dear,
And full trust do I put in thee,
For that so great nobility
He knoweth in thee; be as kind
As I would be to thee, and find
A happy life from day to day,
Till all our days are passed away.'
   What more than found the bystanders
He found within this speech of hers,
I know not; some faint quivering

In the last words ; some little thing
That checked the cold words' even flow,
But yet they set his heart aglow,
And he in turn said eagerly : —
  'Surely I count it naught to die
For him who brought me unto this ;
For thee, who givest me this bliss ;
Yea, even dost me such a grace
To look with kind eyes in my face,
And send sweet music to my ears.'
  But at his words she, mazed with tears,
Seemed faint, and failing quickly, when
Above the low hum of the men
Uprose the sweet bells' sudden clang,
As men unto the chapel rang ;
While just outside the singing folk
Into most heavenly carols broke.
And going softly up the hall
Boys bore aloft the verges tall
Before the bishop's gold-clad head.
  Then forth his bride young Michael led,
And naught to him seemed good or bad
Except the lovely hand he had ;
But she the while was murmuring low,
'If he could know, if he could know,
What love, what love, his love should be ! '

  But while mid mirth and minstrelsy
The ancient Castle of the Rose
Such pageant to the autumn shows
The King sits ill at ease at home,
For in these days the news is come
That he who in his line should wed
Lies in his own town stark and dead,
Slain in a tumult in the street.

Brooding on this he deemed it meet,
Since nigh the day was come when she
Her bridegroom's visage looked to see,
To hold the settled day with her,
And bid her at the least to wear
Dull mourning guise for gold and white.
So on another morning bright,
When the whole promised month was past,
He drew anigh the place at last
Where Michael's dead head, looking down
Upon the highway with a frown,
He doubted not at last to see.
So 'twixt the fruitful greenery
He rode, scarce touched by care the while,
Humming a roundel with a smile.

Withal, ere yet he drew anigh,
He heard their watch-horn sound from high,
Nor wondered, for their wont was so,
And well his banner they might know
Amidst the stubble-lands afar:
But now a distant point of war
He seemed to hear, and bade draw rein,
But listening cried, ' Push on again !
They do but send forth minstrelsy
Because my daughter thinks to see
The man who lieth on his bier,'
So on they passed, till sharp and clear
They heard the pipe and shrill fife sound ;
And restlessly the King glanced round
To see that he had striven for,
The crushing of that sage's lore,
The last confusion of that fate.

But drawn still higher to the gate
They turned a sharp bend of the road,
And saw the pageant that abode
The solemn coming of the King.

For first on each side, maids did sing,
Dressed in gold raiment; then there came
The minstrels in their coats of flame;
And then the many-colored lords,
The knights' spears, and the swordmen's swords,
Backed by the glittering wood of bills.

So now, presaging many ills,
The King drew rein, yet none the less
He shrank not from his hardiness,
But thought, ' Well, at the worst I die,
And yet perchance long life may lie
Before me — I will hold my peace;
The dumb man's borders still increase.'

But as he strengthened thus his heart
He saw the crowd before him part,
And down the long melodious lane,
Hand locked in hand there passed the twain,
As fair as any earth has found,
Clad as kings' children are, and crowned.
Behind them went the chiefest lords,
And two old knights with sheathèd swords
The banners of the kingdom bore.

But now the King had pondered sore,
By when they reached him, though, indeed,
The time was short unto his need,
Betwixt his heart's first startled pang
And those old banner-bearers' clang
Anigh his saddle-bow; but he
Across their heads scowled heavily,
Not saying aught awhile; at last,
Ere any glance at them he cast,
He said, ' Whence come ye? what are ye?
What play is this ye play to me?'

None answered — Cecily, faint and white,
The rather Michael's hand clutched tight,
And seemed to speak, but not one word

The nearest to her could have heard.
Then the King spoke again, — ' Sir Rafe,
Meseems this youngling came here safe
A week agone ? '
                         ' Yea, sir,' he said ;
' Therefore the twain I straight did wed,
E'en as thy letters bound me to.'
' And thus thou diddest well to do,'
The King said.   ' Tell me on what day
Her old life she did put away.'
' Sire, the eleventh day this is
Since that they gained their earthly bliss,'
Quoth old Sir Rafe.   The King said naught,
But with his head bowed down in thought,
Stood a long while ; but at the last
Upward a smiling face he cast,
And cried aloud above the folk :
' Shout for the joining of the yoke
Betwixt these twain ! and thou, fair lord,
Who dost so well my every word,
Nor makest doubt of anything,
Wear thou the collar of thy king ;
And a duke's banner, cut foursquare,
Henceforth shall men before thee bear
In tourney and in stricken field.
    ' But this mine heir shall bear my shield,
Carry my banner, wear my crown,
Ride equal with me through my town,
Sit on the same step of the throne ;
In nothing will I reign alone ;
Nor be ye with him miscontent,
For that with little ornament
Of gold and folk to you he came ;
For he is of an ancient name
That needeth not the clink of gold —
The ancientest the world doth hold ;

For in the fertile Asian land,
Where great Damascus now doth stand,
Ages agone his line was born,
Ere yet men knew the gift of corn ;
And there, anigh to Paradise,
His ancestors grew stout and wise ;
And certes he from Asia bore
No little of their piercing lore.
　‘ Look then to have great happiness,
For every wrong shall he redress.’

　　　.　　.　　.　　　.　　.　　.

So mid sweet song and taboring,
And shouts amid the apple-grove,
And soft caressing of his love,
Began the new King Michael’s reign.
Nor will the poor folk see again
A king like him on any throne,
Or such good deeds to all men done :
For then, as saith the chronicle,
It was the time, as all men tell,
When scarce a man would stop to gaze
At gold crowns hung above the ways.

FROM ‘LOVE IS ENOUGH.’[4]

MUSIC (with singing).

DAWN talks to-day
Over dew-gleaming flowers,
　Night flies away
Till the resting of hours :
　Fresh are thy feet
And with dreams thine eyes glistening,
　Thy still lips are sweet
Though the world is a-listening.

O Love, set a word in my mouth for our meeting,
Cast thine arms round about me to stay my heart's beating!
O fresh day, O fair day, O long day made ours!

    Morn shall meet noon
  While the flower-stems yet move,
    Though the wind dieth soon
  And the clouds fade above.
    Loved lips are thine
  As I tremble and hearken;
    Bright thine eyes shine,
  Though the leaves thy brow darken.
O Love, kiss me into silence, lest no word avail me,
Stay my head with thy bosom lest breath and life fail me!
O sweet day, O rich day, made long for our love!

    Late day shall greet eve,
  And the full blossoms shake,
    For the wind will not leave
  The tall trees while they wake.
    Eyes soft with bliss,
  Come nigher and nigher!
    Sweet mouth I kiss,
  Tell me all thy desire!
Let us speak, Love, together some words of our story,
That our lips as they part may remember the glory!
O soft day, O calm day, made clear for our sake!

    Eve shall kiss night,
  And the leaves stir like rain
  · As the wind stealeth light
  O'er the grass of the plain.
    Unseen are thine eyes
  Mid the dreamy nights' sleeping,
    And on my mouth there lies
  The dear rain of thy weeping.

Hold silence, Love, speak not of the sweet day departed,
Cling close to me, Love, lest I waken sad-hearted !
O kind day, O dear day, short day, come again !

THE MUSIC.

LOVE is enough : ho ye who seek saving,
    Go no further ; come hither ; there have been who have
        found it,
And these know the House of Fulfilment of Craving;
    These know the Cup with the roses around it ;
    These know the World's Wound and the balm that
        hath bound it :
Cry out, the World heedeth not, ' Love, lead us home ! '

He leadeth, He hearkeneth, He cometh to you-ward ;
    Set your faces as steel to the fears that assemble
Round his goad for the faint, and his scourge for the
        froward :
    Lo his lips, how with tales of last kisses they tremble !
    Lo his eyes of all sorrow that may not dissemble !
Cry out, for he heedeth, ' O Love, lead us home ! '

O hearken the words of his voice of compassion :
    ' Come cling round about me, ye faithful who sicken
Of the weary unrest and the world's passing fashion !
    As the rain in mid-morning your troubles shall thicken,
    But surely within you some Godhead doth quicken,
As ye cry to me heeding, and leading you home.

'Come — pain ye shall have, and be blind to the ending !
    Come — fear ye shall have, mid the sky's overcasting !
Come — change ye shall have, for far are ye wending !
    Come — no crown ye shall have for your thirst and
        your fasting,
    But the kissed lips of Love and fair life everlasting !
Cry out, for one heedeth, who leadeth you home ! '

Is he gone ? was he with us ? — ho ye who seek saving,
  Go no further; come hither; for have we not found it?
Here is the House of Fulfilment of Craving;
  Here is the Cup with the roses around it;
  The World's Wound well healed, and the balm that hath
      bound it :
Cry out ! for he heedeth, fair Love that led home.

RICHARD WATSON DIXON.

FROM 'MANO.'[5]

WHAT MOVED FERGANT TO WRITE.

BOOK I., CANTO I.

I, FERGANT, living now my latest days,
Gerbert's disciple once, but long a monk
Of Sant Evreult, for that in many ways
   I have beheld God's strokes upon the trunk
Of rotten trees: and seen the cedars tall
Fall on the hills, because the earth has shrunk
   From nourishing, herself washed down by fall
Of pelting rains, and crumbled by the sun,
So that no state may be perpetual:
   And knowing how things dwindle one by one
To him who clings to this world's misery
Some longer while, ere to the grave he run:
   I, looking soon for that; and since that I
Have seen some things that shall not happen twice,
And days return not that be once gone by:
   And for the cause that many calumnies
Concerning my great Master now be spread,
Gerbert the Pope, that doctor high and wise;
   And of the fate which took him from our head,
And of his arts, his magic spells and songs,
Because that many things be lewdly said:
   And likewise of Sir Mano and his wrongs,
(Who was the friend of Gerbert at the first)
Because that many move their evil tongues;

For this, — well knowing how they long conversed
In love, till anger rose betwixt them twain,
And by what angry cause their love was cursed:
    I, Fergant, now begin this work of pain,
To vindicate their glory from all foes,
And set the truth in order clear and plain.
        Nor less in duteous memory of those
Who loved my famous master or his friend
Tell I that history, which I marked so close.
    All things shall be recounted, if God send
Strength to this heart, and still with life upstay
The hand that writes, until it reach the end.
        And partly I my master's mind obey,
Who charged me still to hold his memory dear:
Which I refuse not, though, the truth to say,
    Some acts in him of doubtful praise appear;
Nor could my dark mind apprehend the fate
Which cast him suddenly from throne to bier. —
        I, then, if God give aid, shall celebrate
The prodigies, the portents, and events
Of fifty years agone, beginning late:
    Yea, great are my concernments and intents
Touching that time, when bursting seemed the earth
With dissolution's sighs and throes and rents
    About the millenary of the Lord's birth:
For we believed that at the thousandth year
The thing would cease in blood and pest and dearth:
    And, as the fatal hour prefixed drew near,
We saw creation cracking, and the signs
Of Antichrist multiplied in our fear.
    For from above depended still the lines
Of God, which heavily the nations beat,
And underneath were laid His secret mines.
    But Gerbert, bold when Nature's shaking seat
The pride of man began to check and quell,
On honor's ladder placed his venturous feet.

He to the topmost round mounted full well,
And with him to have carried did intend
Sir Mano, who clomb high, but deeply fell.

For Gerbert, though he counted him his friend,
So soon as once he marked in him defect,
Or thought it, of their friendship made an end :

He was a man who could a man reject,
And oft required beyond what man could owe :
They who climb honor's hill the sky suspect.

They who suspect the sky, look not below :
And Gerbert, gazing his high purpose, stood,
Nor pity upon failure would bestow :

While Mano, who had fierceness in his blood,
At the first question drew himself away ;
Woe, for the quarrels of the brave and good !

This was that Mano who was Thurold's stay,
And in the Italian field the man of note,
Where Thurold had the Normans in his sway.

Mightily played he in those realms remote,
And was in all men's sight uplifted high,
Until dark destiny his voyage smote,

And rent his sail sinful calamity.
But I believe, whatever Gerbert did
Concerning him, when they brake amity,

Was done with pain, albeit the pain was hid.

HOW MANO CAST HIS LOVE AT BLANCHE: AND HER SISTER AT HIM.

BOOK I., CANTO VII.

Now in the chapel, ye shall understand,
When sat those knights and ladies, gazing all
On one another, ranged on either hand,

Ere that the chants began, it did befall
That Mano cast his eyes on Blanche the Fair ;

5

And of a bitter love became the thrall;
  Oh, bitterly love's thrall, Oh, then and there.
So that, although erewhile to Italy
He had been purposed swiftly to repair,
  His mind was changed, and he gan secretly
Devise to tarry longer in that place:
Which was his first fall from integrity.
          Nor less Joanna to her fate did race,
Who that same hour went into love as deep
With him, as he with Blanche.   O cruel case!
  I, to whom mortal love is sin, can weep
At the most fatal stroke of love, which still
Of ordered joys makes but a tangled heap:
  When I consider all the bitter ill
Which came thereof: how Mano his life's peace
Lost in the mournful frenzy of his will:
  And how Joanna, till her soul's release,
Never knew joy, but hungrily did watch
The love which all so nigh her did increase:
  But, though so nigh, no glimmer could she catch,
Nor any ray of warmth: ah fate unkind,
That love's designs and deeds so ill should match!
  I say that I, though with a zealous mind
Devoted to the Benedictine rule,
Which blessed Odo on his monks did bind,
  And all my life instructed so to school
My senses to exclude love's very thought,
And turn from him who is love's slave and fool;
  Yet in my secret'st heart I never sought
To shut out pity for such misery;
So blessed Maiolus and Aylmer taught:
  They pitied too that human woe: and I
Who learned of them in youth, and still observed
Of those great men the grave austerity,
  Deem that in age I shall not thence have swerved,
If with full heart I write of what befell

Through love's great force: nay, thereto am I nerved,
  And in the thought of them think I do well:
Their reverend zeal and aspect so benign,
And their old age of toil within me dwell.

  When I and other youths, compeers of mine,
To evil thoughts gave way, and restless grew
Under the burden of our vows divine,
  Then Maiolus and Aylmer ever threw
Themselves between us and the gates of sin
With lifted hands and eyes of lovely hue:

  And their sweet counsel probed so deeply in
Our stormy hearts with loving words and wise,
That we with penitence would soon begin;
  Yea, break in tears, and strong tempestuous sighs,
And soon our feeble zeal was re-illumed
From their bright torch, with clearer flame to rise.

  For they victorious emblems had assumed
Over the flesh, while we were fighting still:
They fly not fast whose souls for heaven be plumed:
  But by God's law on earth they tarry till
Others grow strong who feebler pennons wave:
Nor did they this command austerely fill.

  Oft in their dehortation mild they gave
Strange knowledge how in youth themselves were tried
By wiles from which themselves they could not save:
  But if they stood, through grace it did betide:
And many a wondrous miracle they told
In which heaven's grace in them was magnified:

  And many a penance undergone of old,
Through which their evil nature was subdued:
That we against the flesh might wax more bold.
      Then we ourselves in labors stern and rude,
Fasts, vigils, chantings, stripes, by slow degrees
Arose above each passion wild and lewd;

  And as life passed, grew more and more at ease.
 But life was well-nigh passed ere that, as now,

My mind her thoughts was able to appease,
  And live by memory in times gone through,
And so collected as to gaze upon
The joys of others without present woe,
  Their griefs without malignity thereon:
And even now at times I feel the wrong
Of having lived my woful life alone.
  Why should I serve this toil? though I belong
Through this, I trust, to heaven's elected bands?
So feels the priest, when comes the nuptial throng,
  Which day by day approaches where he stands
White-robed, awaiting, that they may partake
The holy marriage blessing from his hands.
  No joy is stored for him, although he make
The joys of others holy, last of all
To be remembered, let him smile or ache.
  Yet in this sadness it is usual
To find great peace: and only pity grows
In me beholding how men's woes befall.
  But I will say, if ever aught arose
In me akin to thoughts which women move,
Joanna sweetest, sacred through her woes
To me — but what has that to do with love?

HOW MANO PARTED FROM FERGANT.

BOOK IV., CANTO VI.

OH, mind of man, whose thoughts with travel sore
Cannot arrive the ground where simple sense
In the beginning stood: thou, who the more
  Thou strivest in the sum of things immense,
The less achieving, seest that centre firm,
Where thou wouldst plant thy footing, to move thence
  Crumbling resolve itself from term to term,

And leave unsure the measure that remains:
Thou, taking thought, canst not thyself confirm.
   Thou canst not from the incorporeal plains
Of the old atomic chaos separate
Thyself: not that contained from that contains.
   Nothing canst thou by thought discriminate;
For all is one and one is all by thought,
And motion cannot be in nature's state.
      But by the senses winged, thou sett'st at nought
The halting intellect: and at a bound
Reachest thy ends, which else were never raught.
   Thy deeds and being thought would fain confound,
And call not possible: but thou dost live,
Nor knowest thyself by mockeries wrapped and wound.
   So great a might to thee the senses give.
But when, cut off from sense, in sleep sopite,
The soul, not sensible, but sensitive,
   Takes her own instruments, of finer might
Than eye or ear, though fashioned to the same
Of purpose, then she sees further than sight,
   Hears more than sound: then doth her skill acclaim
O'er moveless thought her wider victories:
Then, if she sport, she maketh better game,
   And boldly spreads the shows she doth devise:
Or if to heaviness her mood be bent,
Being perplexed or troubled anywise,
   More swiftly then by her the cloud is rent
Which bears the thundrous store of threatening fate:
For past and last future to her present.
      So to the coming evil gave the date
That dream predictive, which the noble knight
Told to my ears, and did the same debate.
   The heads of things to come in wavering light
Moved up and down therein, as on the wall
Beyond my bed the arras shook in sight;
   And its inwoven heads did rise and fall

Above the wood-fire's smoke invisible,
Which made them quiver and grow dim withal.
  Sad grew my heart to hear what he did tell,
But sadder, when he said, ' I must be gone:
Therefore, dear fellow, bid I thee farewell:
  ' But have no fear, I shall return anon ;
For, as it seems to me, I soon shall find
Diantha, whom our quest is set upon.
  ' But this may be to hurt: for to my mind
The thing that I have met seems verily
To show success to us, with harm behind.'
          Then bade I him to go, sith what must be
None may prevent: and from my chamber door
He passed: and soon was armed: and forth went he,
Whom living on this earth I saw no more.

THE END.

BOOK IV., CANTO XVII.

I, FERGANT, living now my latest days
Have brought to term this heavy history,
Showing how all things pass, and nothing stays:
  How Fate may mar, and evil destiny.
And my last hand in age and sickness weak
Setting hereto, to God great thanks give I.
  For God hath granted me so far to speak ;
Yea He who showed the purpose to be sought,
Made straight the way, and gave the strength to seek
  That I by serving might be served of thought,
In living might the life of others try,
And at the cost of pain to truth be brought :
  That I might trace the maze of misery,
And make again dead Virtue, noble toil
Rise from the bed of low indignity :

That I from envy's weeds the wasted soil,
Which holds the memory of friends, might clear,
And Falsehood of her vaunting crown despoil :
    That I that dreadful age might make appear,
As 't was in this world's sickness, death, and birth,
Before, and in and forth the thousandth year.
    Much have I overpassed in my poor dearth
Of words and memory and method true ;
But let me not have failed to heaven and earth
    In setting forth with order not undue
The mighty workers of this world's affairs,
Fatality, infinity, these two,
The one the only yoke the other wears.

THOMAS WOOLNER.

FROM 'PYGMALION.'[6]

CYTHEREA.

FROM BOOK II.

UPRISEN from the sea when Cytherea,
Shining in primal beauty, paled the day,
The wondering waters hushed.   They yearned in sighs
That shook the world : tumultuously heaved
To a great throne of azure laced with light
And canopied in foam to grace their Queen.
Shrieking for joy came Oceanides,
And swift Nereides rushed from afar
Or clove the waters by.   Came eager-eyed
Even shy Naiades from inland streams,
With wild cries headlong darting thro' the waves ;
And Dryads from the shore stretched their lorn arms.
While hoarsely sounding heard was Triton's shell ;
Shoutings uncouth ; sudden, bewildered sounds ;
And the innumerable splashing feet
Of monsters gambolling around their God,
Forth shining on a sea-horse, fierce, and finned.
Some bestrode fishes glinting dusky gold,
Or angry crimson, or chill silver bright ;
Others jerked fast on their own scaly tails ;
And seabirds, screaming upwards either side,
Wove a vast arch above the Queen of Love,
Who, gazing on this multitudinous
Homaging to her beauty, laughed :

                                She laughed
The soft delicious laughter that makes mad ;
Low warblings in the throat that clench man's life
Tighter than prison bars.
                          Then swayed a breath
Of odorous rose and scented myrtle mixed,
That toyed the golden radiance round her brows
To wavy flames. When lo ! sweet murmurings
Spread sudden silence on that gathered host !
And, as sped arrows to their mark ; as bees
Drop promptly on the honeyed flower, as one
Shone the three daughters of Eurynome,
Aglaia, and Thalia ; each an arm
In reverence taking fondled tenderly ;
Then pressed their blushing cheeks against her breasts :
And loved Euphrosyne, scarcely less fair
Than Cytherea's self, lay her white length
Kissing the sacred feet.
                        Such honor paid
The powers of nature to the power of Love,
Creation's longed-for Wonder sprung to life !

Now as a man lifts up a little child,
 Placing it down where he would have it walk,
The wave of night's azure forward driven
By magic impulse sheer in downward slope
Fell, then drawn backward sank, and was no more ;
Leaving the Goddess on her Cyprian coast.
And when her feet first touched the trembling sand,
She fired awakened Earth's remotest veins
To strange ethereal ecstasies ; as birds
Brighten to clamor by the fires of morn.
Thus to Pygmalion beamed the wondrous Birth ;
And this in pure immortal marble he
Labored to show ; bound by those rules of Art
The wise had found inexorably fixed.

THE RESPONSE OF APHRODITE TO PYGMALION'S PRAYER.

FROM BOOK IV.

KNOW you that I
Breathe in the lilies' perfume : daffodils
Awake surprise, taking their light from me.
I teach the tender nightingales my thought,
Rejoicingly they warble in the moon.
I start the thistle down's adventurous quest
For increase in some happy spot.   I nerve
Doves to such boldness hawks would they attack :
And lions soothe to gentleness so fond,
Harmless they sport as playful butterflies.
To spin like maids bent I strong Heracles,
And Zeus I tempted to become a swan !
I draw his clouds together ; make them fight ;
Embrace in flame, and breed live thunderbolts
For Him.   I put the edge on war, to peace
I add the honey.
             You have felt my power:
And shown due reverence by sacrifice,
Fitting obeisance, and observances
The negligent and savage disregard,
The burden borne attests the mortals' faith ;
And hissing flesh on altars rich men give
Often but vaulted unfelt offerings
Costing the giver not one cup of joy !
   The prayers and sacrifices loved of Gods
Are man's delight in giving up delights,
And checked impulses of the yielding will.
Your blameless life has been devotedness
To worship of my beauty through your love.
You, wandering darkly, on a starless waste,

Tho' worn and sore from stumbling, have not paused
In faithfulness, and true to early bent
Have sought my succor in perplexity.
   This my reward, your Hebe shall have life
And immortality.   Far times to come
Shall sing your story.   Not the sweetest dream,
As stretched you lay on shadowed forest bank,
Has ever promised such a paradise
As mine awaiting you.
                  But hark! Before
These high Olympian gifts are yours to hold,
Braced must you be to battle for your own.
Dire hate will strew your path with scorpions,
And dog you for your life.   Foul calumny
Will taint your name with poisonous lies, truth-tinged,
Whereat familiar friends fall back appalled,
While other loved ones fledge the barbèd lies.
   For Gods do not their rarest gifts bestow
Without sure test and payment.   Men cannot,
In earthly state handle pure truth and fire,
The means of Gods, and still remain unscorched.
But you are strong; the prize shines bright in view,
Cost what it may a pathway must be cleared.
And if you forward press unfalteringly,
Pallas Athena may beside you march.

THE

BALLAD AND SONG WRITERS.

BALLAD AND SONG WRITERS.

BRYAN WALLER PROCTER.

A REPOSE.

SHE sleeps amongst her pillows soft
  (A dove, now wearied with her flight),
And all around, and all aloft,
  Hang flutes and folds of virgin white :
Her hair out-darkens the dark night,
  Her glance out-shines the starry sky;
But now her locks are hidden quite,
  And closèd is her fringèd eye !

She sleepeth : wherefore doth she start?
  She sigheth; doth she feel no pain?
None, none ! the Dream is near her heart;
  The Spirit of sleep is in her brain.
He cometh down like golden rain,
  Without a wish, without a sound;
He cheers the sleeper (ne'er in vain),
  Like May, when earth is winter-bound.

All day within some cave he lies,
  Dethroned from his nightly sway, —
Far fading when the dawning skies
  Our souls with wakening thoughts array.

Two Spirits of might doth man obey;
  By each he 's wrought, from each he learns :
The one is Lord of life by day ;
  The other when starry Night returns.

SONG OF WOOD-NYMPHS.

COME here, come here, and dwell
In forest deep !
Come here, come here, and tell
Why thou dost weep !
Is it for love (sweet pain !)
That thus thou dar'st complain
Unto our pleasant shades, our summer leaves,
Where naught else grieves ?

Come here, come here, and lie
By whispering stream !
Here no one dares to die
For love's sweet dream ;
But health all seek, and joy,
And shun perverse annoy,
And race along green paths till close of day,
And laugh — alway !

Or else, through half the year,
On rushy floor,
We lie by waters clear,
While skylarks pour
Their songs into the sun !
And when bright day is done,
We hide 'neath bells of flowers or nodding corn,
And dream — till morn !

THE SEA.

THE Sea! the Sea! the open Sea!
The blue, the fresh, the ever free!
Without a mark, without a bound,
It runneth the earth's wide regions 'round;
It plays with the clouds; it mocks the skies;
Or like a cradled creature lies.

I'm on the Sea! I'm on the Sea!
I am where I would ever be;
With the blue above, and the blue below,
And silence wheresoe'er I go;
If a storm should come and awake the deep,
What matter? *I* shall ride and sleep.

I love (oh! *how* I love) to ride
On the fierce foaming bursting tide,
When every mad wave drowns the moon,
Or whistles aloft his tempest tune,
And tells how goeth the world below,
And why the south-west blasts do blow.

I never was on the dull, tame shore,
But I loved the great Sea more and more,
And backward flew to her billowy breast,
Like a bird that seeketh her mother's nest;
And a mother she *was*, and *is* to me;
For I was born on the open Sea!

The waves were white, and red the morn,
In the noisy hour when I was born;
The whale it whistled, the porpoise rolled,
And the dolphins bared their backs of gold;
And never was heard such an outcry wild
As welcomed to life the Ocean-child.

6

I have lived since then, in calm and strife,
Full fifty summers a sailor's life,
With wealth to spend and a power to range,
But never have sought, nor sighed for change;
And Death, whenever he come to me,
Shall come on the wide unbounded Sea!

SIT DOWN, SAD SOUL.

SIT down, sad soul, and count
    The moments flying;
Come, tell the sweet amount
    That 's lost by sighing!
How many smiles? — a score?
Then laugh, and count no more;
        For day is dying!

Lie down, sad soul, and sleep,
    And no more measure
The flight of time, nor weep
    The loss of leisure;
But here, by this lone stream,
Lie down with us, and dream
        Of starry treasure!

We dream; do thou the same;
    We love, — forever;
We laugh, yet few we shame, —
    The gentle never.
Stay, then, till sorrow dies;
Then — hope and happy skies
        Are thine forever!

INSCRIPTION FOR A FOUNTAIN.

REST ! This little Fountain runs
　　Thus for aye : — It never stays
For the look of summer suns,
　　Nor the cold of winter days.
Whosoe'er shall wander near,
　　When the Syrian heat is worst,
Let him hither come, nor fear
　　Lest he may not slake his thirst :
He will find this little river
　　Running still, as bright as ever.
Let him drink, and onwards hie,
　　Bearing but in thought, that I,
EROTAS, bade the Naiad fall,
　　And thank the great god Pan for all !

A PETITION TO TIME.

TOUCH us gently, Time !
　　Let us glide adown thy stream
Gently — as we sometimes glide
　　Through a quiet dream !
Humble voyagers are We,
Husband, wife, and children three —
(One is lost — an angel, fled
To the azure overhead !)

Touch us gently, Time !
　　We 've not proud nor soaring wings :
Our ambition, *our* content,
　　Lies in simple things.
Humble voyagers are We,
O'er Life's dim, unsounded sea,
Seeking only some calm clime : —
Touch us *gently*, gentle Time !

SOFTLY WOO AWAY HER BREATH.

SOFTLY woo away her breath,
    Gentle death !
Let her leave thee with no strife,
    Tender, mournful, murmuring life !
She hath seen her happy day, —
    She hath had her bud and blossom ;
Now she pales and shrinks away,
    Earth, into thy gentle bosom !

She hath done her bidding here,
    Angels dear !
Bear her perfect soul above,
    Seraph of the skies, — sweet love !
Good she was, and fair in youth ;
    And her mind was seen to soar,
And her heart was wed to truth :
    Take her, then, forevermore, —
    Forever — evermore !

FOR MUSIC.

Now whilst he dreams, O Muses, wind him round !
  Send down thy silver words, O murmuring Rain !
Haunt him, sweet Music !   Fall, with gentlest sound, —
  Like dew, like night, upon his weary brain !
Come, Odors of the rose and violet, — bear
Into his charmèd sleep all visions fair !
So may the lost be found,
So may his thoughts by tender Love be crowned,
And Hope come shining like a vernal morn,
And with its beams adorn
The Future, till he breathes diviner air,
In some soft Heaven of joy, beyond the range of Care !

HISTORY OF A LIFE.

DAY dawned; within a curtained room,
Filled to faintness with perfume,
A lady lay at point of doom.
Day closed; a child had seen the light:
But, for the lady fair and bright,
She rested in undreaming night.
Spring rose; the lady's grave was green;
And near it, oftentimes, was seen
A gentle boy with thoughtful mien.
Years fled; he wore a manly face,
And struggled in the world's rough race,
And won at last a lofty place.
And then he died! behold before ye
Humanity's poor sum and story;
Life — Death — and all that is of Glory.

LORD MACAULAY.

IVRY:

A SONG OF THE HUGUENOTS.

Now glory to the Lord of Hosts, from whom all glories
    are !
And glory to our Sovereign Liege, King Henry of Na-
    varre !
Now let there be the merry sound of music and of dance,
Through thy corn-fields green, and sunny vines, oh pleasant
    land of France !
And thou, Rochelle, our own Rochelle, proud city of the
    waters,
Again let rapture light the eyes of all thy mourning daugh-
    ters.
As thou wert constant in our ills, be joyous in our joy,
For cold, and stiff, and still are they who wrought thy walls
    annoy.
Hurrah ! Hurrah ! a single field hath turned the chance of
    war,
Hurrah ! Hurrah ! for Ivry, and Henry of Navarre.

Oh ! how our hearts were beating, when, at the dawn of day,
We saw the army of the League drawn out in long array ;
With all its priest-led citizens, and all its rebel peers,
And Appenzel's stout infantry, and Egmont's Flemish
    spears.
There rode the brood of false Lorraine, the curses of our
    land ;

And dark Mayenne was in the midst, a truncheon in his
    hand :
And, as we looked on them, we thought of Seine's empur-
    pled flood,
And good Coligni's hoary hair all dabbled with his blood ;
And we cried unto the living God, who rules the fate of
    war,
To fight for His own holy name, and Henry of Navarre.

The King is come to marshal us, in all his armor drest,
And he has bound a snow-white plume upon his gallant
    crest.
He looked upon his people, and a tear was in his eye ;
He looked upon the traitors, and his glance was stern and
    high.
Right graciously he smiled on us, as rolled from wing to
    wing,   •
Down all our line, a deafening shout, ' God save our Lord
    the King ! '
' And if my standard-bearer fall, as fall full well he may,
For never saw I promise yet of such a bloody fray,
Press where ye see my white plume shine, amidst the ranks
    of war.
And be your oriflamme to-day the helmet of Navarre.'

Hurrah ! the foes are moving. Hark to the mingled din
Of fife, and steed, and trump, and drum, and roaring cul-
    verin.
The fiery Duke is pricking fast across Saint Andre's plain,
With all the hireling chivalry of Guelders and Almayne.
Now by the lips of those ye love, fair gentlemen of France,
Charge for the golden lilies, — upon them with the lance !
A thousand spurs are striking deep, a thousand spears in
    rest,
A thousand knights are pressing close behind the snow-
    white crest ;

And in they burst, and on they rushed, while, like a guiding star,
Amidst the thickest carnage blazed the helmet of Navarre.

Now, God be praised, the day is ours. Mayenne hath
turned his rein.
D'Aumale hath cried for quarter. The Flemish count is
slain.
Their ranks are breaking like thin clouds before a Biscay
gale ;
The field is heaped with bleeding steeds, and flags, and
cloven mail.
And then we thought on vengeance, and, all along our van,
' Remember St. Bartholomew,' was passed from man to
man.
But out spake gentle Henry, ' No Frenchman is my foe :
Down, down with every foreigner, but let your brethren go.'
Oh ! was there ever such a knight, in friendship or in war,
As our Sovereign Lord, King Henry, the soldier of Navarre ?

Right well fought all the Frenchmen who fought for France
to-day,
And many a lordly banner God gave them for a prey.
But we of the religion have borne us best in fight ;
And the good Lord of Rosny has ta'en the cornet white.
Our own true Maximilian the cornet white hath ta'en,
The cornet white with black, the flag of false Lorraine.
Up with it high ; unfurl it wide ; that all the host may know
How God hath humbled the proud house which wrought
His church such woe.
Then on the ground, while trumpets sound their loudest
point of war,
Fling the red shreds, a footcloth meet for Henry of Navarre.

Ho ! maidens of Vienna ; Ho ! matrons of Lucerne ;
Weep, weep, and rend your hair for those who never shall
return.

Ho! Philip, send, for charity, the Mexican pistoles,
That Antwerp monks may sing a mass for thy poor spear-
men's souls.
Ho! gallant nobles of the League, look that your arms be
bright;
Ho! burghers of Saint Genevieve, keep watch and ward
to-night.
For our God hath crushed the tyrant, our God hath raised
the slave,
And mocked the counsel of the wise, and the valor of the
brave.
Then glory to His holy name, from whom all glories are;
And glory to our Sovereign Lord, King Henry of Navarre.

THE BATTLE OF NASEBY.

(By Obadiah Bind-their-kings-in-chains-and-their-nobles-with-
links-of-iron, Sergeant in Ireton's Regiment.)

OH! wherefore come ye forth, in triumph from the North,
  With your hands, and your feet, and your raiment all red?
And wherefore doth your rout send forth a joyous shout?
  And whence be the grapes of the wine-press which ye
    tread?

Oh evil was the root, and bitter was the fruit,
  And crimson was the juice of the vintage that we trod;
For we trampled on the throng of the haughty and the strong,
  Who sate in the high places, and slew the saints of God.

It was about the noon of a glorious day of June,
  That we saw their banners dance, and their cuirasses
    shine,
And the Man of Blood was there, with his long essenced hair,
  And Astley, and Sir Marmaduke, and Rupert of the Rhine.

Like a servant of the Lord, with his Bible and his sword,
  The General rode along us to form us to the fight,
When a murmuring sound broke out, and swelled into a shout
  Among the godless horsemen upon the tyrant's right.

And hark ! like the roar of the billows on the shore,
  The cry of battle rises along their charging line !
For God ! for the Cause ! for the Church ! for the Laws !
  For Charles King of England, and Rupert of the Rhine !

The furious German comes, with his clarions and his drums,
  His bravoes of Alsatia, and pages of Whitehall ;
They are bursting on our flanks.   Grasp your pikes, close
      your ranks ;
  For Rupert never comes but to conquer or to fall.

They are here !   They rush on !   We are broken !   We are
      gone !
  Our left is borne before them like stubble on the blast.
O Lord, put forth thy might !   O Lord, defend the right !
  Stand back to back, in God's name, and fight it to the last.

Stout Skippon hath a wound ; the centre hath given ground :
  Hark ! hark ! — What means the trampling of horsemen
      on our rear ?
Whose banner do I see, boys ?   'T is he, thank God, 't is
      he, boys.
  Bear up another minute : brave Oliver is here.

Their heads all stooping low, their points all in a row,
  Like a whirlwind on the trees, like a deluge on the dykes,
Our cuirassiers have burst on the ranks of the Accurst,
  And at a shock have scattered the forest of his pikes.

Fast, fast, the gallants ride, in some safe nook to hide
  Their coward heads, predestined to rot on Temple Bar :
And he — he turns, he flies : — shame on those cruel eyes
  That bore to look on torture, and dare not look on war !

Ho! comrades, scour the plain; and, ere ye strip the slain,
  First give another stab to make your search secure,
Then shake from sleeves and pockets their broad-pieces
      and lockets,
  The tokens of the wanton, the plunder of the poor.

Fools! your doublets shone with gold, and your hearts
      were gay and bold,
  When you kissed your lily hands to your lemans to-day;
And to-morrow shall the fox, from her chambers in the rocks,
  Lead forth her tawny cubs to howl above the prey.

Where be your tongues that late mocked at heaven and hell
      and fate,
  And the fingers that once were so busy with your blades,
Your perfumed satin clothes, your catches and your oaths,
  Your stage-plays and your sonnets, your diamonds and
      your spades?

Down, down, for ever down with the mitre and the crown,
  With the Belial of the Court, and the Mammon of the Pope.
There is woe in Oxford Halls: there is wail in Durham's
      Stalls:
  The Jesuit smites his bosom: the Bishop rends his cope.

And She of the seven hills shall mourn her children's ills,
  And tremble when she thinks on the edge of England's
      sword;
And the Kings of earth in fear shall shudder when they hear
  What the hand of God hath wrought for the Houses and
      the Word.

EPITAPH ON A JACOBITE.

To my true king I offered free from stain
Courage and faith; vain faith, and courage vain.
For him, I threw lands, honors, wealth, away,
And one dear hope, that was more prized than they.

For him I languished in a foreign clime,
Gray-haired with sorrow in my manhood's prime;
Heard on Lavernia Scargill's whispering trees,
And pined by Arno for my lovelier Tees;
Beheld each night my home in fevered sleep,
Each morning started from the dream to weep;
Till God, who saw me tried too sorely, gave
The resting place I asked, an early grave.
Oh thou, whom chance leads to this nameless stone,
From that proud country which was once mine own,
By those white cliffs I never more must see,
By that dear language which I spake like thee,
Forget all feuds, and shed one English tear
O'er English dust.   A broken heart lies here.

WILLIAM BARNES.

NAÏGHBOUR PLAŸMEÄTES.

O JAŸ betide the dear wold mill,
　My naïghbour plaÿmeätes' happy hwome,
Wi' rollèn wheel, an' leäpèn foam,
　Below the overhangèn hill,
　　Where, wide an' slow,
　　The stream did flow,
An' flags did grow, an' lightly vlee
Below the grey-leav'd withy tree,
While clack, clack, clack, vrom hour to hour,
Wi' whirlèn stwone, an' streamèn flour,
Did goo the mill by cloty Stour.

An' there in geämes by evenèn skies,
　When Meäry zot her down to rest,
The broach upon her pankèn breast,
　Did quickly vall an' lightly rise,
　　While swans did zwim
　　In steätely trim.
An' swifts did skim the water, bright
Wi' whirlèn froth, in western light;
An' clack, clack, clack, that happy hour,
Wi' whirlèn stwone, an' streamèn flour,
Did goo the mill by cloty Stour.

Now mortery jeints, in streaks o' white,
　Along the geärdèn wall do show

In Maÿ, an' cherry boughs do blow,
  Wi' bloomèn tutties, snowy white,
    Where rollèn round,
    Wi' rumblèn sound,
The wheel woonce drown'd the vaice so dear
To me.   I faïn would goo to hear
The clack, clack, clack, vor woone short hour,
Wi' whirlèn stwone, an' streamèn flour,
Bezide the mill on cloty Stour.

But should I vind a-heavèn now
  Her breast wi' aïr o' thik dear pleäce ?
Or zee dark locks by such a brow,
  Or het o' plaÿ on such a feäce ?
    No !   She 's now staïd,
    An' where she plaÿ'd,
There 's noo such maïd that now ha' took
The pleäce that she ha' long vorsook,
Though clack, clack, clack, vrom hour to hour,
Wi' whirlèn stwone an' streamèn flour,
Do goo the mill by cloty Stour.

An' still the pulley rwope do heist
  The wheat vrom red-wheeled waggon beds,
An' ho'ses there wi' lwoads of grist,
  Do stand an' toss their heavy heads ;
    But on the vloor,
    Or at the door,
Do show noo mwore the kindly feäce
Her father show'd about the pleäce,
As clack, clack, clack, vrom hour to hour,
Wi' whirlèn stwone, an' streamèn flour,
Did goo his mill by cloty Stour.

THE LOVE CHILD.

WHERE the bridge out at Woodley did stride,
  Wi' his wide arches' cool sheäded bow,
Up above the clear brook that did slide
  By the popples, befoam'd white as snow:
As the gilcups did quiver among
  The white deäisies, a-spread in a sheet.
There a quick-trippèn maïd come along, —
  Aye, a girl wi' her light-steppèn veet.

An' she cried 'I do praÿ, is the road
  Out to Lincham on here, by the meäd?'
An' 'oh! ees,' I meäde answer, an' show'd
  Her the way it would turn an' would leäd:
'Goo along by the beech in the nook,
  Where the childern do plaÿ in the cool,
To the steppèn stwones over the brook, —
  Aye, the grey blocks o' rock at the pool.'

'Then you don't seem a-born an' a-bred,'
  I spoke up, 'at a place here about;'
An' she answer'd wi' cheäks up so red
  As a pi'ny but leäte a-come out,
'No, I liv'd wi' my uncle that died
  Back in Eäpril, an' now I 'm a-come
Here to Ham, to my mother, to bide, —
  Aye, to her house to vind a new hwome.'

I 'm asheämed that I wanted to know
  Any mwore of her childhood or life,
But then, why should so feäir a child grow
  Where noo father did bide wi' his wife;
Then wi' blushes of zunrisèn morn,
  She replied 'that it midden be known,

Oh! they zent me awaÿ to be born, —
  Aye, they hid me when zome would be shown.'

Oh! it meäde me a'most teary-ey'd,
  An' I vound I a'most could ha' groan'd —
What! so winnèn, an' still cast a-zide —
  What! so lovely, an' not to be own'd;
Oh! a God-gift a-treated wi' scorn,
  Oh! a child that a squier should own;
An' to zend her awaÿ to be born! —
  Aye, to hide her where others be shown!

EVENÈN IN THE VILLAGE.

Now the light o' the west is a-turn'd to gloom,
  An' the men be at hwome vrom ground;
An' the bells be a-zendèn all down the Coombe
  From tower, their mwoansome sound.
      An' the wind is still,
     An' the house-dogs do bark,
An' the rooks be a-vled to the elems high an' dark,
  An' the water do roar at mill.

An' the flickerèn light drough the window peäne
  Vrom the candle's dull fleäme do shoot,
An' young Jemmy the smith is a-gone down leäne,
  A-plaÿèn his shrill-vaïced flute.
      An' the miller's man
     Do zit down at his ease
On the seat that is under the cluster o' trees,
  Wi' his pipe an' his cider can.

HAŸ-CARRÈN.

'T is merry ov a zummer's day,
When vo'k be out a-haulèn haÿ
Where boughs, a-spread upon the ground,
Do meäke the staddle big an' round;
An' grass do stand in pook, or lie
In long-back'd weäles or parsels, dry.
There I do vind it stir my heart
To hear the frothèn hosses snort,
A-haulèn on, wi' sleek heäir'd hides,
The red-wheel'd waggon's deep-blue zides.
Aye; let me have woone cup o' drink,
An' hear the linky harness clink,
An' then my blood do run so warm,
An' put sich strangth 'ithin my eärm,
That I do long to toss a pick,
A-pitchèn or a-meäkèn rick.

The bwoy is at the hosse's head,
An' up upon the waggon bed
The lwoaders, strong o' eärm do stan',
At head, an' back at taïl, a man,
Wi' skill to build the lwoad upright
An' bind the vwolded corners tight;
An' at each zide ō'm, sprack an' strong,
A pitcher wi' his long-stem'd prong,
Avore the best two women now
A-call'd to reäky after plough.

When I do pitchy, 't is my pride
Vor Jenny Hine to reäke my zide,
An' zee her fling her reäke, an' reach
So vur, an' teäke in sich a streech;
An' I don't shatter haÿ, an' meäke
Mwore work than needs vor Jenny's reäke.

7

I 'd sooner zee the weäles' high rows
Lik' hedges up above my nose,
Than have light work myzelf, an' vind
Poor Jeäne a-beät an' left behind ;
Vor she would sooner drop down dead,
Than let the pitchers get a-head.

'T is merry at the rick to zee
How picks do wag, an' haÿ do vlee.
While woone's unlwoadèn, woone do teäke
The pitches in ; an' zome do meäke
The lofty rick upright an' roun',
An' tread en hard, an' reäke en down,
An' tip en, when the zun do zet,
To shoot a sudden vall o' wet.
An' zoo 't is merry any day
When vo'k be out a-carrèn haÿ.

SIR FRANCIS HASTINGS DOYLE.

THE DONCASTER ST. LEGER.[1]

THE sun is bright, the sky is clear,
  Above the crowded course,
As the mighty moment draweth near
  Whose issue shows *the horse.*

The fairest of the land are here
To watch the struggle of the year,
The dew of beauty and of mirth,
Lies on the living flowers of earth,
And blushing cheek and kindling eye
Lend brightness to the sun on high:
And every corner of the north
Has poured her hardy yeoman forth;
The dweller by the glistening rills
That sound among the Craven hills;
The stalwart husbandman who holds
His plough upon the eastern wolds;
The sallow shrivelled artisan,
Twisted below the height of man,
Whose limbs and life have mouldered down,
Within some foul and cloudy town,
Are gathered thickly on the lea,
Or streaming from far homes to see
If Yorkshire keeps her old renown;
Or if the dreaded Derby horse
Can sweep in triumph o'er her course;

With the same look in every face,
The same keen feeling, they retrace
The legends of each ancient race:
Recalling Reveller in his pride,
Or Blacklock of the mighty stride,
Or listening to some gray-haired sage
Full of the dignity of age;
How Hambletonian beat of yore
Such rivals as are seen no more;
How his old father loved to tell
Of that long struggle — ended well,
When, strong of heart, the Wentworth Bay
From staggering Herod strode away:
How Yorkshire racers, swift as they,
Would leave this southern horse halfway,
But that the creatures of to-day
Are cast in quite a different mould
From what he recollects of old.
Clear peals the bell; at that known sound,
Like bees, the people cluster round;
On either side upstarting then,
One close dark wall of breathless men,
Far down as eye can stretch, is seen
Along yon vivid strip of green,
Where keenly watched by countless eyes,
'Mid hopes, and fears, and prophecies,
Now fast, now slow, now here, now there,
With hearts of fire, and limbs of air,
Snorting and prancing — sidling by
With arching neck, and glancing eye,
In every shape of strength and grace,
The horses gather for the race;
Soothed for a moment all, they stand
Together, like a sculptured band,
Each quivering eyelid flutters thick,
Each face is flushed, each heart beats quick;

And all around dim murmurs pass,
Like low winds moaning on the grass.
Again — the thrilling signal sound —
And off at once, with one long bound,
Into the speed of thought they leap,
Like a proud ship rushing to the deep.
A start! a start! they 're off, by heaven,
Like a single horse, though twenty-seven,
And 'mid the flash of silks we scan
A Yorkshire Jacket in the van;
   Hurrah! for the bold bay mare!

I 'll pawn my soul her place is there
   Unheaded to the last,
For a thousand pounds, she wins unpast —
   Hurrah! for the matchless mare!

A hundred yards have glided by,
   And they settle to the race,
More keen becomes each straining eye,
   More terrible the pace.
Unbroken yet o'er the gravel road
Like maddening waves the troop has flowed,
   But the speed begins to tell;
And Yorkshire sees, with eye of fear,
The Southron stealing from the rear.
   Ay! mark his action well!
Behind he is, but what repose!
How steadily and clean he goes!
What latent speed his limbs disclose!
What power in every stride he shows!
They see, they feel, from man to man
The shivering thrill of terror ran,
And every soul instinctive knew
It lay between the mighty two.
The world without, the sky above,
Have glided from their straining eyes —

Future and past, and hate and love,
The life that wanes, the friend that dies,
E'en grim remorse, who sits behind
Each thought and motion of the mind,
These now are nothing, Time and Space
Lie in the rushing of the race ;
As with keen shouts of hope and fear
They watch it in its wild career.
Still far ahead of the glittering throng,
Dashes the eager mare along,
And round the turn, and past the hill,
Slides up the Derby winner still.
The twenty-five that lay between
Are blotted from the stirring scene,
And the wild cries which rang so loud,
Sink by degrees throughout the crowd,
To one deep humming, like the tremulous roar
Of seas remote along a northern shore.

In distance dwindling to the eye
Right opposite the stand they lie,
  And scarcely seem to stir ;
Though an Arab scheich his wives would give
For a single steed, that with them could live
  Three hundred yards, without the spur.
But though so indistinct and small,
You hardly see them move at all,
There are not wanting signs, which show
Defeat is busy as they go.
Look how the mass, which rushed away
As full of spirit as the day,
So close compacted for a while,
Is lengthening into single file.
Now inch by inch it breaks, and wide
And spreading gaps the line divide.
As forward still, and far away

Undulates on the tired array
Gay colors, momently less bright,
Fade flickering on the gazers' sight,
Till keenest eyes can scarcely trace
The homeward ripple of the race.
Care sits on every lip and brow.
'Who leads? who fails? how goes it now?'
One shooting spark of life intense,
One throb of refluent suspense,
And a far rainbow-colored light
Trèmbles again upon the sight.
Look to yon turn! Already there
Gleams the pink and black of the fiery mare,
And through *that*, which was but now a gap,
Creeps on the terrible white cap.
Half-strangled in each throat, a shout
Wrung from their fevered spirits out,
Booms through the crowd like muffled drums,
'His jockey moves on him. He comes!'
Then momently like gusts, you heard,
'He 's sixth — he 's fifth — he 's fourth — he 's third;'
And on, like some glancing meteor-flame,
The stride of the Derby winner came.

And during all that anxious time,
(Sneer as it suits you at my rhyme)
The earnestness became sublime;
Common and trite as is the scene,
At once so thrilling, and so mean,
To him who strives his heart to scan,
And feels the brotherhood of man,
That needs *must* be a mighty minute,
When a crowd has but one soul within it.
As some bright ship with every sail
Obedient to the urging gale,
Darts by vext hulls, which side by side,

Dismasted on the raging tide,
Are struggling onward, wild and wide,
Thus, through the reeling field he flew,
And near, and yet more near he drew;
Each leap seems longer than the last,
Now — now — the second horse is past,
And the keen rider of the mare,
With haggard looks of feverish care,
Hangs forward on the speechless air,
By steady stillness nursing in
The remnant of her speed to win.
One other bound — one more — 't is done;
Right up to her the horse has run,
And head to head, and stride for stride,
Newmarket's hope, and Yorkshire's pride,
Like horses harnessed side by side,
    Are struggling to the goal.
Ride! gallant son of Ebor, ride !
For the dear honor of the north,
Stretch every bursting sinew forth,
    Put out thy inmost soul, —
And with knee, and thigh, and tightened rein,
Lift in the mare by might and main;
The feelings of the people reach,
What lies beyond the springs of speech,
So that there rises up no sound
From the wide human life around;
One spirit flashes from each eye,
One impulse lifts each heart throat-high,
One short and panting silence broods,
O'er the wildly-working multitudes,
As on the struggling coursers press,
So deep the eager silentness,
That underneath their feet the turf
Seems shaken, like the eddying surf
    When it tastes the rushing gale,

And the singing fall of the heavy whips,
Which tear the flesh away in strips,
 As the tempest tears the sail,
On the throbbing heart and quivering ear,
Strike vividly distinct, and near.
But mark what an arrowy rush is there,
'He's beat! he's beat!'—by heaven, the mare!
Just on the post, her spirit rare,
When Hope herself might well despair;
When Time had not a breath to spare;
With bird-like dash shoots clean away,
And by half a length has gained the day.
Then how to life that silence wakes!
Ten thousand hats thrown up on high
Send darkness to the echoing sky,
And like the crash of hill-pent lakes,
Out-bursting from their deepest fountains,
Among the rent and reeling mountains,
At once, from thirty thousand throats
 Rushes the Yorkshire roar,
And the name of their northern winner floats
A league from the course, and more.

THE PRIVATE OF THE BUFFS.[8]

LAST night, among his fellow roughs,
 He jested, quaffed, and swore;
A drunken private of the Buffs,
 Who never looked before.
To-day, beneath the foeman's frown,
 He stands in Elgin's place,
Ambassador from Britain's crown,
 And type of all her race.

Poor, reckless, rude, low-born, untaught,
 Bewildered, and alone,

A heart, with English instinct fraught,
  He yet can call his own.
Ay, tear his body limb from limb,
  Bring cord, or axe, or flame :
He only knows, that not through *him*
  Shall England come to shame.

Far Kentish hop-fields round him seemed,
  Like dreams, to come and go ;
Bright leagues of cherry-blossom gleamed,
  One sheet of living snow ;
The smoke, above his father's door,
  In gray soft eddyings hung ;
Must he then watch it rise no more,
  Doomed by himself, so young ?

Yes, honor calls ! — with strength like steel
  He put the vision by.
Let dusky Indians whine and kneel;
  An English lad must die.
And thus, with eyes that would not shrink,
  With knee to man unbent,
Unfaltering on its dreadful brink,
  To his red grave he went.

Vain mightiest fleets of iron framed ;
  Vain those all-shattering guns ;
Unless proud England keep, untamed,
  The strong heart of her sons.
So let his name through Europe ring, —
  A man of mean estate,
Who died, as firm as Sparta's king,
  Because his soul was great.

SIR SAMUEL FERGUSON.

THE FORGING OF THE ANCHOR.

COME, see the Dolphin's anchor forged — 't is at a white
    heat now :
The bellows ceased, the flames decreased — though on the
    forge's brow
The little flames still fitfully play through the sable mound,
And fitfully you still may see the grim smiths ranking round,
All clad in leathern panoply, their broad hands only bare :
Some rest upon their sledges here, some work the windlass
    there.

The windlass strains the tackle-chains, the black mound
    heaves below,
And red and deep a hundred veins burst out at every throe :
It rises, roars, rends all outright — O, Vulcan, what a glow !
'T is blinding white, 't is blasting bright — the high sun
    shines not so !
The high sun sees not, on the earth, such fiery fearful show,
The roof-ribs swarth, the candent hearth, the ruddy lurid
    row
Of smiths that stand, an ardent band, like men before the
    foe,
As, quivering through his fleece of flame, the sailing mon-
    ster, slow
Sinks on the anvil : — all about the faces fiery grow : —
' Hurrah !' they shout, ' leap out — leap out ' : bang, bang
    the sledges go :
Hurrah ! the jetted lightnings are hissing high and low —

A hailing fount of fire is struck at every squashing blow ;
The leathern mail rebounds the hail, the rattling cinders
strow
The ground around ; at every bound the sweltering fountains flow,
And thick and loud the swinking crowd at every stroke pant
'ho!'

Leap out, leap out, my masters ; leap out and lay on load !
Let's forge a goodly anchor — a bower, thick and broad ;
For a heart of oak is hanging on every blow, I bode ;
And I see the good ship riding all in a perilous road —
The low reef roaring on her lee — the roll of ocean poured
From stem to stern, sea after sea, the mainmast by the
board ;
The bulwarks down, the rudder gone, the boat stove at the
chains !
But courage still, brave mariners — the bower yet remains,
And not an inch to flinch he deigns, save when ye pitch
sky high ;
Then moves his head, as though he said, 'Fear nothing
— here am I.'
Swing in your strokes in order, let foot and hand keep
time ;
Your blows make music sweeter far than any steeple's
chime :
But, while ye sling your sledges, sing — and let the
burden be,
The anchor is the anvil-king, and royal craftsmen we !
Strike in, strike in — the sparks begin to dull their rust-
ling red ;
Our hammers ring with sharper din, our work will soon
be sped.
Our anchor soon must change his bed of fiery rich array,
For a hammock at the roaring bows, or an oozy couch
of clay ;

Our anchor soon must change the lay of merry crafts-
    men here,
For the yeo-heave-o, and the heave-away, and the sighing
    seaman's cheer ;
When, weighing slow, at eve they go — far, far from love
    and home ;
And sobbing sweethearts, in a row, wail o'er the ocean foam.

In livid and obdurate gloom he darkens down at last :
A shapely one he is, and strong, as e'er from cat was cast :
A trusted and trustworthy guard, if thou hadst life like me,
What pleasures would thy toils reward beneath the deep
    green sea !
O deep Sea-diver, who might then behold such sights
    as thou ?
The hoary monster's palaces ! methinks what joy 't were
    now
To go plumb plunging down amid the assembly of the
    whales,
And feel the churned sea round me boil beneath their
    scourging tails !
Then deep in tangle-woods to fight the fierce sea unicorn,
And send him foiled and bellowing back, for all his ivory
    horn :
To leave the subtle sworder-fish of bony blade forlorn ;
And for the ghastly-grinning shark, to laugh his jaws
    to scorn :
To leap down on the kraken's back, where 'mid Norwegian
    isles
He lies, a lubber anchorage for sudden shallowed miles :
Till snorting, like an under-sea volcano, off he rolls ;
Meanwhile to swing, a-buffeting the far astonished shoals
Of his back-browsing ocean-calves ; or, haply, in a cove,
Shell-strown, and consecrate of old to some Undiné's love,
To find the long-haired mermaidens ; or, hard by icy lands,
To wrestle with the Sea-serpent, upon cerulean sands.

O broad-armed Fisher of the deep, whose sports can equal
      thine ?
The Dolphin weighs a thousand tons, that tugs thy cable line;
And night by night, 't is thy delight, thy glory day by day,
Through sable sea and breaker white the giant game to
      play —
But shamer of our little sports ! forgive the name I gave —
A fisher's joy is to destroy — thine office is to save.
O lodger in the sea-kings' halls, couldst thou but understand
Whose be the white bones by thy side, or who that drip-
      ping band,
Slow swaying in the heaving wave, that round about thee
      bend,
With sounds like breakers in a dream blessing their an-
      cient friend —
Oh, couldst thou know what heroes glide with larger steps
      round thee,
Thine iron side would swell with pride; thou 'dst leap
      within the sea !

Give honor to their memories who left the pleasant strand,
To shed their blood so freely for the love of Father-land —
Who left their chance of quiet age and grassy churchyard
      grave,
So freely, for a restless bed amid the tossing wave —
Oh, though our anchor may not be all I have fondly sung,
Honor him for their memory, whose bones he goes among !

WILLY GILLILAND.

AN ULSTER BALLAD.

UP in the mountain solitudes, and in a rebel ring,
He has worshipped God upon the hill, in spite of church
      and king;
And sealed his treason with his blood on Bothwell bridge
      he hath ;

So he must fly his father's land, or he must die the death;
For comely Claverhouse has come along with grim Dalzell,
And his smoking rooftree testifies they've done their
    errand well.

In vain to fly his enemies he fled his native land;
Hot persecution waited him upon the Carrick strand;
His name was on the Carrick cross, a price was on his
    head,
A fortune to the man that brings him in alive or dead!
And so on moor and mountain, from the Lagan to the Bann,
From house to house, and hill to hill, he lurked an out-
    lawed man.

At last, when in false company he might no longer bide,
He staid his houseless wanderings upon the Collon side,
There in a cave all under ground he laired his heathy den,
Ah, many a gentleman was fain to earth like hill fox then!
With hound and fishing-rod he lived on hill and stream
    by day;
At night, betwixt his fleet greyhound and his bonny mare
    he lay.

It was a summer evening, and, mellowing and still,
Glenwhirry to the setting sun lay bare from hill to hill;
For all that valley pastoral held neither house nor tree,
But spread abroad and open all, a full fair sight to see,
From Slemish foot to Collon top lay one unbroken green,
Save where in many a silver coil the river glanced between.

And on the river's grassy bank, even from the morning gray,
He at the angler's pleasant sport had spent the summer day:
Ah! many a time and oft I've spent the summer day
    from dawn,
And wondered, when the sunset came, where time and care
    had gone,

Along the reaches curling fresh, the wimpling pools and
    streams,
Where he that day his cares forgot in those delightful
    dreams.

His blithe work done, upon a bank the outlaw rested now,
And laid the basket from his back, the bonnet from his
    brow ;
And there, his hand upon the Book, his knee upon the sod,
He filled the lonely valley with the gladsome word of God ;
And for a persecuted kirk, and for her martyrs dear,
And against a godless church and king he spoke up loud
    and clear.

And now, upon his homeward way, he crossed the Collon
    high,
And over bush and bank and brae he sent abroad his eye ;
But all was darkening peacefully in gray and purple haze,
The thrush was silent in the banks, the lark upon the
    braes —
When suddenly shot up a blaze, from the cave's mouth
    it came ;
And troopers' steeds and troopers' caps are glancing in
    the same !

He couched among the heather, and he saw them, as he
    lay,
With three long yells at parting, ride lightly east away :
Then down with heavy heart he came, to sorry cheer
    came he,
For ashes black were crackling where the green whins
    used to be,
And stretched among the prickly coomb his heart's blood
    smoking round,
From slender nose to breast-bone cleft, lay dead his good
    greyhound !

'They 've slain my dog, the Philistines! they 've ta'en my
 bonny mare!' —
He plunged into the smoky hole; no bonny beast was
 there —
He groped beneath his burning bed, (it burned him to
 the bone,)
Where his good weapon used to be, but broadsword there
 was none;
He reeled out of the stifling den, and sat down on a stone,
And in the shadows of the night 't was thus he made
 his moan —

'I am a houseless outcast; I have neither bed nor board,
Nor living thing to look upon, nor comfort save the Lord:
Yet many a time were better men in worse extremity;
Who succored them in their distress, He now will succor
 me, —
He now will succor me, I know; and, by His holy Name,
I 'll make the doers of this deed right dearly rue the same!

'My bonny mare! I 've ridden you when Claver'se rode
 behind,
And from the thumbscrew and the boot you bore me like
 the wind;
And, while I have the life you saved, on your sleek flank,
 I swear,
Episcopalian rowel shall never ruffle hair!
Though sword to wield they 've left me none — yet Wallace
 wight, I wis,
Good battle did on Irvine side wi' waur weapon than this.' —

His fishing-rod with both his hands he griped it as he spoke,
And, where the butt and top were spliced, in pieces twain
 he broke;
The limber top he cast away, with all its gear abroad,
But, grasping the tough hickory butt, with spike of iron shod,

He ground the sharp spear to a point; then pulled his bon-
    net down,
And, meditating black revenge, set forth for Carrick town.

The sun shines bright on Carrick wall and Carrick Castle
    gray,
And up thine aisle, Saint Nicholas, has ta'en his morning
    way;
And to the North-Gate sentinel displayeth far and near
Sea, hill, and tower, and all thereon, in dewy freshness
    clear,
Save where, behind a ruined wall, himself alone to view,
Is peering from the ivy green a bonnet of the blue.

The sun shines red on Carrick wall and Carrick castle old,
And all the western buttresses have changed their gray
    for gold;
And from thy shrine, Saint Nicholas, the pilgrim of the sky
Hath gone in rich farewell, as fits such royal votary;
But, as his last red glance he takes down past black Slieve-
    a-true,
He leaveth where he found it first, the bonnet of the blue.

Again he makes the turrets gray stand out before the hill;
Constant as their foundation rock, there is the bonnet still!
And now the gates are opened, and forth in gallant show
Prick jeering grooms and burghers blithe, and troopers in
    a row;
But one has little care for jest, so hard bested is he,
To ride the outlaw's bonny mare, for this at last is she!

Down comes her master with a roar, her rider with a groan,
The iron and the hickory are through and through him gone!
He lies a corpse; and where he sat, the outlaw sits again,
And once more to his bonny mare he gives the spur and
    rein;

Then some with sword, and some with gun, they ride and
    run amain ;
But sword and gun, and whip and spur, that day they plied
    in vain !

Ah ! little thought Willy Gilliland, when he on Skerry side
Drew bridle first, and wiped his brow after that weary ride,
That where he lay like hunted brute, a caverned outlaw lone,
Broad lands and yeomen tenantry should yet be there his
    own ;
Yet so it was ; and still from him descendants not a few
Draw birth and lands, and, let me trust, draw love of Free-
    dom too.

GEORGE WALTER THORNBURY.

THE DEATH OF TH' OWD SQUIRE.

'T WAS a wild, mad kind of night, as black as the bottom-
    less pit,
The wind was howling away, like a Bedlamite in a fit,
Tearing the ash-boughs off, and mowing the poplars down,
In the meadows beyond the old flour-mill, where you turn
    off to the town.

And the rain (well, it *did* rain) dashing the window glass,
And deluging on the roof, as the Devil were come to pass ;
The gutters were running in floods outside the stable door,
And the spouts splashed from the tiles, as if they would
    never give o'er.

Lor' how the winders rattled !   You 'd almost ha' thought
    that thieves
Were wrenching at the shutters, while a ceaseless pelt of
    leaves
Flew at the door in gusts ; and I could hear the beck
Calling so loud, I knew at once it was up to a tall man's
    neck.

We was huddling in the harness-room, by a little scrap of
    fire,
And Tom, the coachman, he was there, a-practising for the
    choir ;

But it sounded desmal, anthem did, for Squire was dying
    fast,
And the doctor 'd said, do what he would, ' Squire 's break-
    ing up at last.'

The Death-watch, sure enough, ticked loud just over th' owd
    man's head,
Though he had never once been heard up there since mas-
    ter's boy lay dead ;
And the only sound, beside Tom's toon, was the stirring in
    the stalls,
And the gnawing and the scratching of the rats in the owd
    walls.

We could n't hear Death's foot pass by, but we knew that
    he was near ;
And the chill rain, and the wind and cold, made us all
    shake with fear ;
We listened to the clock upstairs, — 't was breathing soft
    and low,
For the nurse said at the turn of night the old Squire's
    soul must go.

Master had been a wildish man and led a roughish life ;
Did 'nt he shoot the Bowton Squire, who dared write to
    his wife ?
He beat the Rads at Hindon town, I heard in Twenty-nine,
When every pail in market-place was brimmed with red
    port wine.

And as for hunting, bless your soul ! why, for forty year
    or more
He'd kept the Marley hounds, man, as his fayther did
    afore ;
And now to die, and in his bed — the season just begun —
It made him fret, the doctors said, as 't might do any one.

And when the young sharp lawyer came to see him sign
    his will,
Squire made me blow my horn outside as we was going to
    kill ;
And we turned the hounds out in the court — that seemed
    to do him good ;
For he swore, and sent us off to seek a fox in Thornhill
    Wood.

But then the fever it rose high, and he would go see the room
Where Missus died ten years ago when Lammastide shall
    come :
I mind the year, because our mare at Salisbury broke down;
Moreover the town hall was burnt at Steeple Dinton town.

It might be two, or half past two, the wind seemed quite
    asleep ;
Tom, he was off, but I awake sat, watch and ward to keep ;
The moon was up, quite glorious like, the rain no longer
    fell,
When all at once out clashed and clanged the rusty turret
    bell,

That had n't been heard for twenty year, not since the
    Luddite days ;
Tom he leapt up, and I leapt up, for all the house ablaze
Had sure not scared us half as much ; and out we ran like
    mad —
I, Tom, and Joe, the whipper-in, and t' little stable lad.

'He's killed hisself,' that 's the idea that came into my head;
I felt as sure as though I saw Squire Barrowby was dead ;
When all at once a door flew back, and he met us face to
    face ;
His scarlet coat was on his back, and he looked like the
    old race.

The nurse was clinging to his knees, and crying like a
    child;
The maids were sobbing on the stairs, for he looked fierce
    and wild:
'Saddle me Lightning Bess, my man,' that's what he said
    to me;
'The moon is up, we're sure to find at Stop or Etterby.

'Get out the hounds; I'm well to-night, and young again
    and sound;
I'll have a run once more before they put me underground:
They brought my father home feet first, and it never shall
    be said
That his son Joe, who rode so straight, died quietly in his
    bed.

'Brandy!' he cried; 'a tumbler-full, you women howling
    there!'
Then clapped the old black velvet cap upon his long gray
    hair,
Thrust on his boots, snatched down his whip; though he
    was old and weak,
There was a devil in his eye, that would not let me speak.

We loosed the hounds to humor him, and sounded on the
    horn;
The moon was up above the woods, just east of Haggard
    Bourne;
I buckled Lightning's throat-lash fast; the Squire was
    watching me;
He let the stirrups down himself, so quick, yet carefully.

Then up he got and spurred the mare, and ere I well could
    mount,
He drove the yard gate open, man, and called to old Dick
    Blount,

Our huntsman, dead five years ago — for the fever rose
    again,
And was spreading, like a flood of flame, fast up into his
    brain.

Then off he flew before the hounds, yelling to call us on,
While we stood there, all pale and dumb, scarce knowing
    he was gone;
We mounted, and below the hill we saw the fox break out,
And down the covert ride we heard the old Squire's part-
    ing shout.

And in the moonlit meadow mist we saw him fly the rail
Beyond the hurdles by the beck, just half-way down the
    vale;
I saw him breast fence after fence — nothing could turn
    him back;
And in the moonlight after him streamed out the brave old
    pack.

'T was like a dream, Tom cried to me, as we rode free and
    fast;
Hoping to turn him at the brook, that could not well be
    past,
For it was swollen with the rain; but, LORD! 't was not
    to be;
Nothing could stop old Lightning Bess but the broad breast
    of the sea.

The hounds swept on, and well in front the mare had got
    her stride;
She broke across the fallow land that runs by the down side;
We pulled up on Chalk Linton Hill, and as we stood us
    there,
Two fields beyond we saw the Squire fall stone dead from
    the mare.

Then she swept on, and, in full cry, the hounds went out
    of sight;
A cloud came over the broad moon, and something dimmed
    our sight,
As Tom and I bore master home, both speaking under
    breath;
And that 's the way I saw th' owd Squire ride boldly to his
    death.

THE CAVALIER'S ESCAPE.

TRAMPLE! trample! went the roan,
    Trap! trap! went the gray;
But pad! *pad!* PAD! like a thing that was mad,
    My chestnut broke away.—
It was just five miles from Salisbury town,
    And but one hour to day.

Thud! THUD! came on the heavy roan,
    Rap! RAP! the mettled gray;
But my chestnut mare was of blood so rare,
    That she showed them all the way.
Spur on! spur on! I doffed my hat,
    And wished them all good day.

They splashed through miry rut and pool, —
    Splintered through fence and rail;
But chestnut Kate switched over the gate —
    I saw them droop and tail.
To Salisbury town — but a mile of down,
    Once over this brook and rail.

Trap! trap! I heard their echoing hoofs
    Past the walls of mossy stone;
The roan flew on at a staggering pace,
    But blood is better than bone.

I patted old Kate, and gave her the spur,
  For I knew it was all my own.

But trample ! trample ! came their steeds,
  And I saw their wolf's eyes burn ;
I felt like a royal hart at bay,
  And made me ready to turn.
I looked where highest grew the May,
  And deepest arched the fern.

I flew at the first knave's sallow throat, —
  One blow, and he was down.
The second rogue fired twice, and missed ;
  I sliced the villain's crown.
Clove through the rest, and flogged brave Kate,
  Fast, fast to Salisbury town !

Pad ! pad ! they came on the level sward,
  Thud ! thud ! upon the sand ;
With a gleam of swords, and a burning match,
  And a shaking of flag and hand :
But one long bound, and I passed the gate,
  Safe from the canting band.

THE JESTER'S SERMON.

THE Jester shook his hood and bells, and leaped upon a
    chair,
The pages laughed, the women screamed, and tossed their
    scented hair ;
The falcon whistled, staghounds bayed, the lapdog barked
    without,
The scullion dropped the pitcher brown, the cook railed at
    the lout !
The steward, counting out his gold, let pouch and money
    fall,
And why ? because the Jester rose to say grace in the hall !

The page played with the heron's plume, the steward with
    his chain,
The butler drummed upon the board, and laughed with
    might and main ;
The grooms beat on their metal cans, and roared till they
    were red,
But still the Jester shut his eyes and rolled his witty head ;
And when they grew a little still, read half a yard of text,
And, waving hand, struck on the desk, then frowned like
    one perplexed.

'Dear sinners all,' the fool began, 'man's life is but a
    jest,
A dream, a shadow, bubble, air, a vapor at the best,
In a thousand pounds of law I find not a single ounce of
    love ;
A blind man killed the parson's cow in shooting at the
    dove ;
The fool that eats till he is sick must fast till he is well ;
The wooer who can flatter most will bear away the belle.

'Let no man halloo he is safe till he is through the wood ;
He who will not when he may, must tarry when he should.
He who laughs at crooked men should need walk very
    straight ;
O, he who once has won a name may lie abed till eight !
Make haste to purchase house and land, be very slow to
    wed ;
True coral needs no painter's brush, nor need be daubed
    with red.

'The friar, preaching, cursed the thief (the pudding in his
    sleeve).
To fish for sprats with golden hooks is foolish, by your
    leave, —
To travel well, — an ass's ears, ape's face, hog's mouth,
    and ostrich legs.

He does not care a pin for thieves who limps about and
     begs.
Be always first man at a feast and last man at a fray;
The short way round, in spite of all, is still the longest
     way.
When the hungry curate licks the knife, there's not much
     for the clerk;
When the pilot, turning pale and sick, looks up — the
     storm grows dark.'

Then loud they laughed, the fat cook's tears ran down
     into the pan:
The steward shook, that he was forced to drop the brim-
     ming can;
And then again the women screamed, and every staghound
     bayed, —
And why? because the motley fool so wise a sermon made.

DENIS FLORENCE MacCARTHY.

FROM 'THE VOYAGE OF ST. BRENDAN.'[9]

PART I.

THE VOCATION.

O ITA! mother of my heart and mind —
  My nourisher — my fosterer — my friend,
Who taught me first, to God's great will resigned,
  Before his shining altar-steps to bend,
Who poured his word upon my soul like balm,
  And on mine eyes what pious fancy paints,
And on mine ear the sweetly swelling psalm,
  And all the sacred knowledge of the saints.

Who but to thee, my mother, should be told,
  Of all the wonders I have seen afar? —
Islands more green, and suns of brighter gold
  Than this dear land, or yonder blazing star;
Of hills that bear the fruit-trees on their tops,
  And seas that dimple with eternal smiles;
Of airs from heaven that fan the golden crops,
  O'er the great ocean, 'mid the blessèd isles!

Thou knowest, O my mother! how to thee,
  The blessed Ercus led me when a boy,
And how within thine arms and at thy knee
  I learned the love that death cannot destroy;

And how I parted hence with bitter tears,
  And felt when turning from thy friendly door,
In the reality of ripening years,
  My paradise of childhood was no more.

I wept — but not with sin such tear-drops flow;
  I sighed — for earthly things with heaven entwine;
Tears make the harvest of the heart to grow,
  And love, though human, is almost divine.
The heart that loves not knows not how to pray;
  That eye can never smile that never weeps;
'T is through our sighs Hope's kindling sunbeams play,
  And through our tears the bow of Promise peeps.

I grew to manhood by the western wave,
  Among the mighty mountains on the shore;
My bed the rock within some natural cave,
  My food, whate'er the seas or seasons bore;
My occupation, morn and noon and night:
  The only dream my hasty slumbers gave,
Was Time's unheeding, unreturning flight,
  And the great world that lies beyond the grave.

And thus, where'er I went, all things to me
  Assumed the one deep color of my mind;
Great Nature's prayer rose from the murmuring sea,
  And sinful man sighed in the wintry wind.
The thick-veiled clouds by shedding many a tear,
  Like penitents, grew purified and bright,
And, bravely struggling through earth's atmosphere,
  Passed to the regions of eternal light.

I loved to watch the clouds, now dark and dun,
  In long procession and funeral line,
Pass with slow pace across the glorious sun,
  Like hooded monks before a dazzling shrine.

And now with gentler beauty as they rolled
   Along the azure vault in gladsome May,
Gleaming pure white, and edged with broidered gold,
   Like snowy vestments on the Virgin's day.

And then I saw the mighty sea expand
   Like Time's unmeasured and unfathomed waves,
One with its tide-marks on the ridgy sand,
   The other with its line of weedy graves;
And as beyond the outstretched wave of Time
   The eye of Faith a brighter land may meet,
So did I dream of some more sunny clime
   Beyond the waste of waters at my feet:

Some clime where man, unknowing and unknown,
   For God's refreshing Word still gasps and faints;
Or happier rather some Elysian zone,
   Made for the habitation of His saints;
Where Nature's love the sweat of labor spares,
   Nor turns to usury the wealth it lends,
Where the rich soil spontaneous harvest bears,
   And the tall tree with milk-filled clusters bends.

The thought grew stronger with my growing days,
   Even like to manhood's strengthening mind and limb,
And often now amid the purple haze
   That evening breathed upon the horizon's rim —
Methought, as there I sought my wished-for home,
   I could descry amid the waters green,
Full many a diamond shrine and golden dome,
   And crystal palaces of dazzling sheen.

And then I longed with impotent desire,
   Even for the bow whereby the Python bled,
That I might send one dart of living fire
   Into that land, before the vision fled;

And thus at length fix thy enchanted shore,
  Hy Brasail — Eden of the western wave !
That thou again wouldst fade away no more,
  Buried and lost within thy azure grave.

But angels came and whispered as I dreamt,
  This is no phantom of a frenzied brain —
God shows this land from time to time to tempt
  Some daring mariner across the main :
By thee the mighty venture must be made,
  By thee shall myriad souls to Christ be won!
Arise, depart, and trust to God for aid !
  . I woke, and kneeling cried, His will be done !

PART VI.

THE PROMISED LAND.

As on this world the young man turns his eyes,
  When forced to try the dark sea of the grave,
Thus did we gaze upon that paradise,
  Fading, as we were borne across the wave.
And as a brighter world dawns by degrees
  Upon Eternity's serenest strand,
Thus having passed through dark and gloomy seas,
  At length we reached the long-sought Promised Land.

The wind had died upon the ocean's breast,
  When, like a silvery vein through the dark ore,
A smooth, bright current, gliding to the west,
  Bore our light bark to that enchanted shore.
It was a lovely plain — spacious and fair,
  And blessed with all delights that earth can hold,
Celestial odors filled the fragrant air
That breathed around that green and pleasant wold.

There may not rage of frost, nor snow, nor rain,
   Injure the smallest and most delicate flower,
Nor fall of hail wound the fair, healthful plain,
   Nor the warm weather, nor the winter's shower.
That noble land is all with blossoms flowered,
   Shed by the summer breezes as they pass ;
Less leaves than blossoms on the trees are showered,
   And flowers grow thicker in the fields than grass.

Nor hills, nor mountains, there stand high and steep,
   Nor stony cliffs tower o'er the frightened waves,
Nor hollow dells, where stagnant waters sleep,
   Nor hilly risings, nor dark mountain caves ;
Nothing deformed upon its bosom lies,
   Nor on its level breast rests aught unsmooth ; —
A green, glad meadow under golden skies,
   Blooming forever in perpetual youth.

That glorious land stands higher o'er the sea,
   By twelve-fold fathom measure, than we deem
The highest hills beneath the heavens to be.
   There the bower glitters, and the green woods gleam.
All o'er that pleasant plain, calm and serene,
   The fruits ne'er fall, but, hung by God's own hand,
Cling to the trees that stand forever green,
   Obedient to their Maker's first command.

Summer and winter are the woods the same,
   Hung with bright fruits and leaves that never fade ;
Such will they be, beyond the reach of flame,
   Till Heaven, and Earth, and Time shall have decayed.
Here might Iduna in her fond pursuit,
   As fabled by the northern sea-born men,
Gather her golden and immortal fruit,
   That brings their youth back to the gods again.

9

Of old, when God, to punish sinful pride,
  Set round the deluged world the ocean flood,
When all the earth lay 'neath the vengeful tide,
  This glorious land above the waters stood.
Such shall it be at last, even as at first,
  Until the coming of the final doom,
When the dark chambers — men's death-homes shall — burst,
  And man shall rise to judgment from the tomb.

There, there is never enmity, nor rage,
  Nor poisoned calumny, nor envy's breath,
Nor shivering poverty, nor decrepit age,
  Nor loss of vigor, nor the narrow death,
Nor idiot laughter, nor the tears men weep,
  Nor painful exile from one's native soil,
Nor sin, nor pain, nor weariness, nor sleep,
  Nor lust of riches, nor the poor man's toil.

There, never falls the rain-cloud as with us,
  Nor gapes the earth with the dry summer's thirst,
But liquid streams, wondrously curious,
  Out of the ground with fresh, fair bubblings burst.
Sea-cold and bright the pleasant waters glide
  Over the soil and through the shady bowers;
Flowers fling their colored radiance o'er the tide,
  And the white streams their crystals o'er the flowers.

Such was the land for man's enjoyment made
  When from this troubled life his soul doth wend:
Such was the land through which entranced we strayed,
  For fifteen days, nor reached its bound nor end.
Onward we wandered in a blissful dream,
  Nor thought of food, nor needed earthly rest;
Until at length we reached a mighty stream,
  Whose broad, bright waves flowed from the east to west.

We were about to cross its placid tide,
　　When lo ! an angel on our vision broke.
Clothèd in white, upon the further side
　　He stood majestic, and thus sweetly spoke :
'Father, return ! thy mission now is o'er ;
　　God, who did call thee here, now bids thee go.
Return in peace unto thy native shore,
　　And tell the mighty secrets thou dost know.

'In after years, in God's own fitting time,
　　This pleasant land again shall reappear ;
And other men shall preach the truth sublime
　　To the benighted people dwelling here.
But ere that hour, this land shall all be made,
　　For mortal man, a fitting, natural home,
Then shall the giant mountain fling its shade,
　　And the strong rock stem the white torrent's foam.

'Seek thy own isle — Christ's newly-bought domain.
　　Which Nature with an emerald pencil paints ;
Such as it is, long, long shall it remain,
　　The school of truth, the college of the saints,
The student's bower, the hermit's calm retreat,
　　The stranger's home, the hospitable hearth,
The shrine to which shall wander pilgrim feet
　　From all the neighboring nations of the earth.

'But in the end upon that land shall fall
　　A bitter scourge, a lasting flood of tears,
When ruthless tyranny shall level all
　　The pious trophies of its earlier years :
Then shall this land prove thy poor country's friend,
　　And shine, a second Eden, in the west ;
Then shall this shore its friendly arms extend,
　　And clasp the outcast exile to its breast.'

He ceased, and vanished from our dazzled sight,
    While harps and sacred hymns rang sweetly o'er:
For us, again we winged our homeward flight
    O'er the great ocean to our native shore;
And as a proof of God's protecting hand,
    And of the wondrous tidings that we bear,
The fragrant perfume of that heavenly land
    Clings to the very garments that we wear.

SUMMER LONGINGS.

AH ! my heart is weary waiting,
        Waiting for the May —
Waiting for the pleasant rambles
Where the fragrant hawthorn brambles,
        With the woodbine alternating,
            Scent the dewy way.
        Ah ! my heart is weary waiting,
            Waiting for the May.

Ah ! my heart is sick with longing,
        Longing for the May —
Longing to escape from study,
To the young face fair and ruddy,
        And the thousand charms belonging
            To the summer's day.
        Ah ! my heart is sick with longing,
            Longing for the May.

Ah ! my heart is sore with sighing,
        Sighing for the May —
Sighing for their sure returning,
When the summer beams are burning,
        Hopes and flowers that, dead or dying,
            All the winter lay.
        Ah ! my heart is sore with sighing,
            Sighing for the May.

Ah! my heart is pained with throbbing,
  Throbbing for the May —
Throbbing for the seaside billows,
Or the water-wooing willows;
  Where, in laughing and in sobbing,
    Glide the streams away.
  Ah! my heart, my heart is throbbing,
    Throbbing for the May.

  Waiting sad, dejected, weary,
    Waiting for the May.
Spring goes by with wasted warnings,
Moonlit evenings, sunbright mornings;
  Summer comes, yet dark and dreary
    Life still ebbs away:
  Man is ever weary, weary,
    Waiting for the May!

THE PILLAR TOWERS OF IRELAND.

THE pillar towers of Ireland, how wondrously they stand
By the lakes and rushing rivers through the valleys of our
    land;
In mystic file, through the isle, they lift their heads sublime,
These gray old pillar temples — these conquerors of time!

Beside these gray old pillars, how perishing and weak
The Roman's arch of triumph, and the temple of the Greek,
And the gold domes of Byzantium, and the pointed Gothic
    spires,
All are gone, one by one, but the temples of our sires!

The column, with its capital, is level with the dust,
And the proud halls of the mighty and the calm homes of
    the just;
For the proudest works of man, as certainly, but slower
Pass like the grass at the sharp scythe of the mower!

But the grass grows again when in majesty and mirth,
On the wing of the Spring comes the Goddess of the
      Earth ;
But for man in this world no spring-tide e'er returns
To the labors of his hands or the ashes of his urns !

Two favorites hath Time — the pyramids of Nile,
And the old mystic temples of our own dear isle ;
As the breeze o'er the seas, where the halcyon has its
      nest,
Thus Time o'er Egypt's tombs and the temples of the
      West !

The names of their founders have vanished in the gloom,
Like the dry branch in the fire or the body in the tomb;
But to-day, in the ray, their shadows still they cast —
These temples of forgotten Gods — these relics of the past!

Around these walls have wandered the Briton and the
      Dane —
The captives of Armorica, the cavaliers of Spain —
Phœnician and Milesian, and the plundering Norman
      Peers —
And the swordsmen of brave Brian, and the chiefs of later
      years !

How many different rites have these gray old temples
      known ?
To the mind what dreams are written in these chronicles
      of stone !
What terror and what error, what gleams of love and truth,
Have flashed from these walls since the world was in its
      youth ?

Here blazed the sacred fire, and, when the sun was gone,
As a star from afar to the traveller it shone ;

And the warm blood of the victim have these gray old
    temples drunk,
And the death-song of the Druid and the matin of the
    Monk.

Here was placed the holy chalice that held the sacred wine,
And the gold cross from the altar, and the relics from the
    shrine,
And the mitre shining brighter with its diamonds than the
    East,
And the crozier of the Pontiff, and the vestments of the
    Priest !

Where blazed the sacred fire, rung out the vesper bell, —
Where the fugitive found shelter, became the hermit's cell ;
And hope hung out its symbol to the innocent and good,
For the Cross o'er the moss of the pointed summit stood !

There may it stand for ever, while this symbol doth impart
To the mind one glorious vision, or one proud throb to the
    heart ;
While the breast needeth rest may these gray old temples
    last,
Bright prophets of the future, as preachers of the past !

CAROLINE ELIZABETH NORTON.

THE KING OF DENMARK'S RIDE.

WORD was brought to the Danish King
 (Hurry!)
That the love of his heart lay suffering,
And pined for the comfort his voice would bring:
 (O, ride as though you were flying!)
Better he loves each golden curl
On the brow of that Scandinavian girl
Than his rich crown jewels of ruby and pearl:
 And his rose of the isles is dying!

Thirty nobles saddled with speed;
 (Hurry!)
Each one mounting a gallant steed
Which he kept for battle and days of need;
 (O, ride as though you were flying!)
Spurs were struck in the foaming flank;
Worn-out chargers staggered and sank;
Bridles were slackened, and girths were burst;
But ride as they would, the king rode first,
 For his rose of the isles lay dying!

His nobles are beaten, one by one;
 (Hurry!)
They have fainted, and faltered, and homeward gone;
His little fair page now follows alone,
 For strength and for courage trying!

The king looked back at that faithful child;
Wan was the face that answering smiled;
They passed the drawbridge with clattering din,
Then he dropped; and only the king rode in
　Where his rose of the isles lay dying!

The king blew a blast on his bugle horn;
　(Silence!)
No answer came; but faint and forlorn
An echo returned on the cold gray morn,
　Like the breath of a spirit sighing.
The castle portal stood grimly wide;
None welcomed the king from that weary ride;
For dead, in the light of the dawning day,
The pale sweet form of the welcomer lay,
　Who had yearned for his voice while dying!

The panting steed, with a drooping crest,
　Stood weary.
The king returned from her chamber of rest,
The thick sobs choking in his breast;
　And, that dumb companion eying,
The tears gushed forth which he strove to check;
He bowed his head on his charger's neck:
'O steed, that every nerve didst strain,
Dear steed, our ride hath been in vain
　To the halls where my love lay dying!'

BINGEN ON THE RHINE.

A SOLDIER of the Legion lay dying in Algiers,
There was lack of woman's nursing, there was dearth of
　woman's tears;
But a comrade stood beside him, while his life-blood ebbed
　away,
And bent, with pitying glances, to hear what he might say.

The dying soldier faltered, and he took that comrade's
    hand,
And he said, 'I nevermore shall see my own, my native
    land;
Take a message, and a token, to some distant friends of
    mine,
For I was born at Bingen, — at Bingen on the Rhine.

'Tell my brothers and companions, when they meet and
    crowd around,
To hear my mournful story, in the pleasant vineyard ground,
That we fought the battle bravely, and when the day was
    done,
Full many a corse lay ghastly pale beneath the setting sun;
And, mid the dead and dying, were some grown old in
    wars, —
The death-wound on their gallant breasts, the last of many
    scars ;
And some were young, and suddenly beheld life's morn
    decline, —
And one had come from Bingen, — fair Bingen on the
    Rhine.

'Tell my mother that her other son shall comfort her old
    age ;
For I was still a truant bird, that thought his home a cage.
For my father was a soldier, and even as a child
My heart leaped forth to hear him tell of struggles fierce
    and wild ;
And when he died, and left us to divide his scanty hoard,
I let them take whate'er they would, — but kept my father's
    sword ;
And with boyish love I hung it where the bright light used
    to shine,
On the cottage wall at Bingen, — calm Bingen on the
    Rhine.

'Tell my sister not to weep for me, and sob with drooping
head,
When the troops come marching home again with glad and
gallant tread,
But to look upon them proudly, with a calm and steadfast
eye,
For her brother was a soldier too, and not afraid to die;
And if a comrade seek her love, I ask her in my name
To listen to him kindly, without regret or shame,
And to hang the old sword in its place (my father's sword
and mine)
For the honor of old Bingen, — dear Bingen on the Rhine.

'There 's another, — not a sister; in the happy days gone by
You 'd have known her by the merriment that sparkled in
her eye;
Too innocent for coquetry, — too fond for idle scorning, —
O friend! I fear the lightest heart makes sometimes heav-
iest mourning!
Tell her the last night of my life (for, ere the moon be
risen,
My body will be out of pain, my soul be out of prison), —
I dreamed I stood with *her*, and saw the yellow sunlight shine
On the vine-clad hills of Bingen, —fair Bingen on the Rhine.

'I saw the blue Rhine sweep along, —I heard, or seemed
to hear,
The German songs we used to sing, in chorus sweet and
clear;
And down the pleasant river, and up the slanting hill,
The echoing chorus sounded, through the evening calm
and still;
And her glad blue eyes were on me, as we passed, with
friendly talk,
Down many a path beloved of yore, and well-remembered
walk!

And her little hand lay lightly, confidingly in mine, —
But we 'll meet no more at Bingen, — loved Bingen on the
    Rhine.'

His trembling voice grew faint and hoarse, — his grasp
    was childish weak, —
His eyes put on a dying look, — he sighed and ceased to
    speak ;
His comrade bent to lift him, but the spark of life had
    fled, —
The soldier of the Legion in a foreign land is dead !
And the soft moon rose up slowly, and calmly she looked
    down
On the red sand of the battle-field, with bloody corses
    strewn ;
Yes, calmly on that dreadful scene her pale light seemed
    to shine,
As it shone on distant Bingen, — fair Bingen on the Rhine.

THE MOTHER'S HEART.

WHEN first thou camest, gentle, shy, and fond,
    My eldest born, first hope, and dearest treasure,
My heart received thee with a joy beyond
    All that it yet had felt of earthly pleasure ;
Nor thought that any love again might be
So deep and strong as that I felt for thee.

Faithful and true, with sense beyond thy years,
    And natural piety that leaned to heaven ;
Wrung by a harsh word suddenly to tears,
    Yet patient to rebuke when justly given ;
Obedient, easy to be reconciled,
And meekly cheerful ; such wert thou, my child !

Not willing to be left — still by my side,
    Haunting my walks, while summer-day was dying ;

Nor leaving in thy turn, but pleased to glide
　　Through the dark room where I was sadly lying;
Or by the couch of pain, a sitter meek,
Watch the dim eye, and kiss the fevered cheek.

O boy! of such as thou are oftenest made
　　Earth's fragile idols; like a tender flower,
No strength in all thy freshness, prone to fade,
　　And bending weakly to the thunder-shower;
Still, round the loved, thy heart found force to bind,
And clung, like woodbine shaken in the wind!

Then THOU, my merry love, — bold in thy glee,
　　Under the bough, or by the firelight dancing,
With thy sweet temper, and thy spirit free, —
　　Didst come, as restless as a bird's wing glancing,
Full of a wild and irrepressible mirth,
Like a young sunbeam to the gladdened earth!

Thine was the shout, the song, the burst of joy,
　　Which sweet from childhood's rosy lip resoundeth;
Thine was the eager spirit naught could cloy,
　　And the glad heart from which all grief reboundeth;
And many a mirthful jest and mock reply
Lurked in the laughter of thy dark-blue eye.

And thine was many an art to win and bless,
　　The cold and stern to joy and fondness warming;
The coaxing smile, the frequent soft caress,
　　The earnest, tearful prayer all wrath disarming!
Again my heart a new affection found,
But thought that love with thee had reached its bound.

At length THOU camest, — thou, the last and least,
　　Nicknamed 'the Emperor' by thy laughing brothers,
Because a haughty spirit swelled thy breast,
　　And thou didst seek to rule and sway the others,

Mingling with every playful infant wile
A mimic majesty that made us smile.

And O, most like a regal child wert thou !
  An eye of resolute and successful scheming !
Fair shoulders, curling lips, and dauntless brow,
  Fit for the world's strife, not for poet's dreaming ;
And proud the lifting of thy stately head,
And the firm bearing of thy conscious tread.

Different from both ! yet each succeeding claim
  I, that all other love had been forswearing,
Forthwith admitted, equal and the same ;
  Nor injured either by this love's comparing,
Nor stole a fraction for the newer call, —
But in the mother's heart found room for all !

WILLIAM COX BENNETT.

BABY MAY.

CHEEKS as soft as July peaches;
Lips whose dewy scarlet teaches
Poppies paleness; round large eyes
Ever great with new surprise;
Minutes filled with shadeless gladness:
Minutes just as brimmed with sadness;
Happy smiles and wailing cries;
Crows and laughs and tearful eyes;
Lights and shadows, swifter born
Than on wind-swept autumn corn;
Ever some new tiny notion,
Making every limb all motion;
Catchings up of legs and arms;
Throwings back and small alarms;
Clutching fingers; straightening jerks;
Twining feet whose each toe works;
Kickings up and straining risings;
Mother's ever new surprisings;
Hands all wants and looks all wonder
At all things the heavens under;
Tiny scorns of smiled reprovings
That have more of love than lovings;
Mischiefs done with such a winning
Archness that we prize such sinning;
Breakings dire of plates and glasses;
Graspings small at all that passes;

Pullings off of all that's able
To be caught from tray or table;
Silences — small meditations
Deep as thoughts of cares for nations
Breaking into wisest speeches
In a tongue that nothing teaches;
All the thoughts of whose possessing
Must be wooed to light by guessing;
Slumbers — such sweet angel-seemings
That we'd ever have such dreamings;
Till from sleep we see thee breaking,
And we'd always have thee waking;
Wealth for which we know no measure;
Pleasure high above all pleasure;
Gladness brimming over gladness;
Joy in care; delight in sadness;
Loveliness beyond completeness;
Sweetness distancing all sweetness;
Beauty all that beauty may be; —
That's May Bennett; that's my baby.

BABY'S SHOES.

O, THOSE little, those little blue shoes!
Those shoes that no little feet use.
    O the price were high
    That those shoes would buy,
Those little blue unused shoes!

For they hold the small shape of feet
That no more their mother's eyes meet,
    That, by God's good will,
    Years since, grew still,
And ceased from their totter so sweet.

And O, since that baby slept,
So hushed, how the mother has kept,

With a tearful pleasure,
That little dear treasure,
And o'er them thought and wept!

For they mind her forevermore
Of a patter along the floor;
And blue eyes she sees
Look up from her knees
With the look that in life they wore.

As they lie before her there,
There babbles from chair to chair
A little sweet face
That's a gleam in the place,
With its little gold curls of hair.

Then O wonder not that her heart
From all else would rather part
Than those tiny blue shoes
That no little feet use,
And whose sight makes such fond tears start!

INVOCATION TO RAIN IN SUMMER.

O GENTLE, gentle summer rain,
Let not the silver lily pine,
The drooping lily pine in vain
To feel that dewy touch of thine, —
To drink thy freshness once again,
O gentle, gentle summer rain!

In heat the landscape quivering lies;
The cattle pant beneath the tree;
Through parching air and purple skies
The earth looks up, in vain, for thee;

For thee — for thee, it looks in vain,
O gentle, gentle summer rain.

Come thou, and brim the meadow streams,
    And soften all the hills with mist,
O falling dew ! from burning dreams
    By thee shall herb and flower be kissed,
And Earth shall bless thee yet again,
O gentle, gentle summer rain.

MARY HOWITT.

THE FAIRIES OF THE CALDON LOW.

A MIDSUMMER LEGEND.

'AND where have you been, my Mary,
  And where have you been from me?'
'I 've been to the top of the Caldon Low,
  The midsummer-night to see!'

'And what did you see, my Mary,
  All up on the Caldon Low?'
'I saw the glad sunshine come down,
  And I saw the merry winds blow.'

'And what did you hear, my Mary,
  All up on the Caldon hill?'
'I heard the drops of the water made,
  And the ears of the green corn fill.'

'Oh! tell me all, my Mary —
  All, all that ever you know;
For you must have seen the fairies,
  Last night on the Caldon Low.'

'Then take me on your knee, mother;
  And listen, mother of mine:
A hundred fairies danced last night,
  And the harpers they were nine;

' And their harp-strings rung so merrily
    To their dancing feet so small ;
But oh ! the words of their talking
    Were merrier far than all.'

' And what were the words, my Mary,
    That then you heard them say ? '
' I 'll tell you all, my mother ;
    But let me have my way.

' Some of them played with the water,
    And rolled it down the hill ;
" And this," they said, " shall speedily turn
    The poor old miller's mill ;

' " For there has been no water
    Ever since the first of May ;
And a busy man will the miller be
    At dawning of the day.

' " Oh ! the miller, how he will laugh
    When he sees the mill-dam rise !
The jolly old miller, how he will laugh
    Till the tears fill both his eyes ! "

' And some they seized the little winds
    That sounded over the hill ;
And each put a horn unto his mouth,
    And blew both loud and shrill ;

' " And there," they said, " the merry winds go
    Away from every horn ;
And they shall clear the mildew dank
    From the blind, old widow's corn.

' " Oh ! the poor, blind widow,
    Though she has been blind so long,
She 'll be blithe enough when the mildew 's gone,
    And the corn stands tall and strong."

' And some they brought the brown lint-seed,
    And flung it down from the Low;
" And this," they said, "by the sunrise,
    In the weaver's croft shall grow.

' " Oh ! the poor, lame weaver,
    How will he laugh outright
When he sees his dwindling flax-field
    All full of flowers by night ! "

' And then outspoke a brownie,
    With a long beard on his chin ;
" I have spun up all the tow," said he,
    " And I want some more to spin.

' " I 've spun a piece of hempen cloth,
    And I want to spin another ;
A little sheet for Mary's bed,
    And an apron for her mother."

' With that I could not help but laugh,
    And I laughed out loud and free ;
And then on the top of the Caldon Low
    There was no one left but me.

' And all on the top of the Caldon Low
    The mists were cold and gray,
And nothing I saw but the mossy stones
    That round about me lay.

' But, coming down from the hill-top,
    I heard afar below
How busy the jolly miller was,
    And how the wheel did go.

' And I peeped into the widow's field,
    And, sure enough, were seen
The yellow ears of the mildewed corn
    All standing stout and green.

'And down by the weaver's croft I stole,
  To see if the flax were sprung ;
But I met the weaver at his gate,
  With the good news on his tongue.

'Now this is all I heard, mother,
  And all that I did see ;
So prithee make my bed, mother,
  For I 'm tired as I can be.'

FRANCIS MAHONY.

THE BELLS OF SHANDON.

> Sabbata pango ;
> Funera plango ;
> Solemnia clango.
>   INSCRIPTION ON AN OLD BELL.

WITH deep affection
And recollection
I often think of
  Those Shandon bells,
Whose sounds so wild would,
In the days of childhood,
Fling round my cradle
  Their magic spells.

On this I ponder
Where'er I wander,
And thus grow fonder,
  Sweet Cork, of thee, —
With thy bells of Shandon,
That sound so grand on
The pleasant waters
  Of the river Lee.

I 've heard bells chiming
Full many a clime in,
Tolling sublime in
  Cathedral shrine,
While at a glibe rate
Brass tongues would vibrate ;

But all their music
  Spoke naught like thine.

For memory, dwelling
On each proud swelling
Of thy belfry, knelling
  Its bold notes free,
Made the bells of Shandon
Sound far more grand on
The pleasant waters
  Of the river Lee.

I 've heard bells tolling
Old Adrian's Mole in,
Their thunder rolling
  From the Vatican, —
And cymbals glorious
Swinging uproarious
In the gorgeous turrets
  Of Notre Dame;

But thy sounds were sweeter
Than the dome of Peter
Flings o'er the Tiber,
  Pealing solemnly.
Oh! the bells of Shandon
Sound far more grand on
The pleasant waters
  Of the river Lee.

There 's a bell in Moscow;
While on tower and kiosk O
In St. Sophia
  The Turkman gets,
And loud in air
Calls men to prayer,

From the tapering summit
   Of tall minarets.

Such empty phantom
I freely grant them;
But there 's an anthem
   More dear to me, —
'T is the bells of Shandon,
That sound so grand on
The pleasant waters
   Of the river Lee.

THE LADYE OF LEE.

THERE 's a being bright whose beams
Light my days and gild my dreams
Till my life all sunshine seems — 't is the ladye of Lee.

Oh! the joy that Beauty brings,
While her merry laughter rings
And her voice of silver sings — how she loves but me!

There 's a grace in every limb,
There 's a charm in every whim,
And the diamond cannot dim — the dazzling of her e'e.

But there 's a light amid
All the lustre of her lid
That from the crowd is hid — and only I can see.

'T is the glance by which is shown
That she loves but me alone;
That she is all mine own — this ladye of Lee.

Then say, can it be wrong
If the burden of my song
Be, how fondly I 'll belong to this ladye of Lee?

GERALD MASSEY.

THE BALLAD OF BABE CHRISTABEL.

WHEN Danaë-Earth bares all her charms,
   And gives the God her perfect flower,
   Who in the sunshine's golden shower,
Leaps warm into her amorous arms!

When buds are bursting on the brier,
   And all the kindled greenery glows,
   And life hath richest overflows,
And morning fields are fringed with fire:

When young Maids feel Love stir i' the blood,
   And wanton with the kissing leaves
   And branches, and the quick sap heaves,
And dances to a ripened flood;

Till, blown to its hidden heart with sighs,
   Love's red rose burns i' the cheek so dear,
   And, as sea-jewels upward peer,
Love-thoughts melt through their swimming eyes:

When Beauty walks in bravest dress,
   And, fed with April's mellow showers,
   The earth laughs out with sweet May-flowers,
That flush for very happiness:

And Spider-Puck such wonder weaves
   O' nights, and nooks of greening gloom
   Are rich with violets that bloom
In the cool dark of dewy leaves:

When Rose-buds drink the fiery wine
  Of Dawn, with crimson stains i' the mouth,
  All thirstily as yearning youth
From Love's hand drinks the draught divine;

And honeyed plots are drowsed with Bees:
  And Larks rain music by the shower,
  While singing, singing hour by hour,
Song like a Spirit sits i' the Trees!

When fainting hearts forget their fears,
  And in the poorest Life's salt cup
  Some rare wine runs, and Hope builds up
Her rainbow over Memory's tears!

It fell upon a merry May morn,
  I' the perfect prime of that sweet time
  When daisies whiten, woodbines climb, —
The dear Babe Christabel was born.

. . . .

Babe Christabel was royally born!
  For when the earth was flushed with flowers,
  And drenched with beauty in rainbow showers,
She came through golden gates of Morn.

No chamber arras-pictured round,
  Where sunbeams golden gorgeous gloom,
  And touch its glories into bloom,
And footsteps fall withouten sound,

Was her Birth-place that merry May-morn;
  No gifts were heaped, no bells were rung,
  No healths were crowned, no songs were sung,
When dear Babe Christabel was born:

But Nature on the darling smiled,
  And with her beauty's blessing crowned:
  Love brooded o'er the hallowed ground,
And there were Angels with the child!

And May her kisses of love did blow
  On amorous airs, that came to her
  With gifts of Frankincense and Myrrh,
As came the Magi long ago

To worship Bethlehem's baby-King,
  Spring-Birds make welcoming merriment,
  And all the Flowers for welcome sent
The secret sweetness of the Spring.

With glancing lights and shimmering shade,
  And cheeks that touched and ripelier burned,
  May-Roses in at the lattice yearned
A-tiptoe, and Good Morrow bade.

No purple and fine linen might
  Be hoarded up for her sweet sake:
  But Mother's love shall clothe and make
The little wearer richly dight!

Wide worlds of worship are their eyes,
  Their loyal hearts are worlds of love,
  Who fondly clasp the stranger Dove,
And read its news from Paradise.

Their looks praise God—souls sing for glee:
  They think if this old world had toiled
  Through ages to bring forth their child,
It hath a glorious destiny.

She grew, a sweet and sinless child,
  In sun and shadow, — calm and strife ;
  A Rainbow on the dark of Life,
From Love's own radiant heaven down-smiled !

In lonely loneliness she grew, —
  A shape all music, light, and love,
  With startling looks, so eloquent of
The spirit burning into view.

At childhood she could seldom play
  With merry heart, whose flashings rise
  Like splendor-wingèd butterflies
From honeyed hearts of flowers in May :

The fields with flowers flamed out and flushed,
  The Roses into crimson yearned,
  With cloudy fire the wall-flowers burned,
And blood-red Sunsets bloomed and blushed. —

And still her cheek was pale as pearl, —
  It took no tint of Summer's wealth
  Of color, warmth, and wine of Health : —
Ah ! Death's hand whitely pressed the Girl !

No blushes swarmed to the sun's kiss
  Where violet-veins ran purple light,
  So tenderly thro' Parian white
Touching you into tenderness.

A spirit-look was in her face,
  That shadowed a miraculous range
  Of meanings, ever rich and strange,
Or lightened glory in the place.

Such mystic lore was in her eyes,
  And light of other worlds than ours,
  She looked as she had fed on flowers,
And drunk the dews of Paradise.

Her brow — fit home for daintiest dreams —
   With such a dawn of light was crowned,
   And reeling ringlets showerèd round,
Like sunny sheaves of golden beams :

And she would talk so weirdly-wild,
   And grow upon your wonderings,
   As tho' her stature rose on wings !
And you forgot she was a Child.

Ah ! she was one of those who come
   With pledgèd promise not to stay
   Long, ere the angels let them stray
To nestle down in earthly home :

And, thro' the windows of her eyes,
   We often saw her saintly soul,
   Serene, and sad, and beautiful,   /
Go sorrowing for lost Paradise.

In Earth she took no lusty root,
   Her beauty of promise to disclose,
   And round into the Woman-Rose,
And climb into Life's crowning fruit.

She came — like music in the night
   Floating as heaven in the brain,
   A moment oped, and shut again,
And all is dark where all was light.

She came — as comes the light of smiles
   O'er earth, and every budding thing
   Makes quick with beauty — alive with Spring ;
Then goeth to Hesperian Isles.

Midnight was trancèd solemnly
   Thinking of Dawn : Her Star-thoughts burned !
   The Trees like burdened Prophets yearned,
Rapt in a wind of prophecy.

When, like the Night, the shadow of Woe
 On all things laid its hand death-dark,
 Our last hope went out like a spark,
And a cry smote heaven like a blow !

We sat and watched by Life's dark stream,
 Our love-lamp blown about the night,
 With hearts that lived as lived its light,
And died as died its precious gleam.

In Death's face hers flashed up and smiled,
 As smile the young flowers in their prime,
 I' the face of their gray murderer Time,
And Death for true love kissed our child.

She thought our good-night kiss was given,
 And like a lily her life did close ;
 Angels uncurtained that repose,
And the next waking dawned in heaven.

  . . . .

ADELAIDE ANNE PROCTER.

A WOMAN'S QUESTION.

BEFORE I trust my Fate to thee,
　Or place my hand in thine,
Before I let thy Future give
　Color and form to mine,
Before I peril all for thee, question thy soul to-night for me.

I break all slighter bonds, nor feel
　A shadow of regret :
Is there one link within the Past,
　That holds thy spirit yet ?
Or is thy Faith as clear and free as that which I can pledge
　　to thee ?

Does there within thy dimmest dreams
　A possible future shine,
Wherein thy life could henceforth breathe,
　Untouched, unshared by mine ?
If so, at any pain or cost, O, tell me before all is lost.

Look deeper still.　If thou canst feel
　Within thy inmost soul,
That thou hast kept a portion back,
　While I have staked the whole ;
Let no false pity spare the blow, but in true mercy tell me
　　so.

Is there within thy heart a need
　That mine cannot fulfil,

One chord that any other hand
  Could better wake or still?
Speak now — lest at some future day my whole life wither
    and decay.

Lives there within thy nature hid
  The demon-spirit Change,
Shedding a passing glory still
  On all things new and strange? —
It may not be thy fault alone — but shield my heart against
    thy own.

Couldst thou withdraw thy hand one day
  And answer to my claim,
That Fate, and that to-day's mistake,
  Not thou — had been to blame?
Some soothe their conscience thus: but thou wilt surely
    warn and save me now.

Nay, answer *not* — I dare not hear,
  The words would come too late;
Yet I would spare thee all remorse,
  So, comfort thee, my Fate —
Whatever on my heart may fall — remember, I *would* risk
    it all!

GOD'S GIFTS.

God gave a gift to Earth: — a child,
Weak, innocent, and undefiled,
Opened its ignorant eyes and smiled.

It lay so helpless, so forlorn,
Earth took it coldly and in scorn,
Cursing the day when it was born.

She gave it first a tarnished name,
For heritage, a tainted fame,
Then cradled it in want and shame.

11

All influence of Good or Right,
All ray of God's most holy light,
She curtained closely from its sight.

Then turned her heart, her eyes away,
Ready to look again, the day
Its little feet began to stray.

In dens of guilt the baby played,
Where sin, and sin alone, was made
The law that all around obeyed.

With ready and obedient care,
He learnt the tasks they taught him there ;
Black sin for lesson — oaths for prayer.

Then Earth arose, and, in her might,
To vindicate her injured right,
Thrust him in deeper depths of night.

Branding him with a deeper brand
Of shame, he could not understand,
The felon outcast of the land.

———————

God gave a gift to Earth : — a child,
Weak, innocent, and undefiled,
Opened its ignorant eyes and smiled.

And Earth received the gift, and cried
Her joy and triumph far and wide,
Till echo answered to her pride.

She blessed the hour when first he came
To take the crown of pride and fame,
Wreathed through long ages for his name.

Then bent her utmost art and skill
To train the supple mind and will,
And guard it from a breath of ill.

She strewed his morning path with flowers,
And Love, in tender dropping showers,
Nourished the blue and dawning hours.

She shed, in rainbow hues of light,
A halo round the Good and Right,
To tempt and charm the baby's sight.

And every step, of work or play,
Was lit by some such dazzling ray,
Till morning brightened into day.

And then the World arose, and said —
Let added honors now be shed
On such a noble heart and head !

O World, both gifts were pure and bright,
Holy and sacred in God's sight : —
God will judge them and thee aright !

THE ANGEL OF DEATH.

WHY shouldst thou fear the beautiful angel, Death,
  Who waits thee at the portals of the skies,
Ready to kiss away thy struggling breath,
  Ready with gentle hand to close thine eyes?

How many a tranquil soul has passed away,
  Fled gladly from fierce pain and pleasures dim,
To the eternal splendor of the day ;
  And many a troubled heart still calls for him.

Spirits too tender for the battle here
  Have turned from life, its hopes, its fears, its charms ;
And children, shuddering at a world so drear,
  Have smiling passed away into his arms.

He whom thou fearest will, to ease its pain,
　Lay his cold hand upon thy aching heart:
Will soothe the terrors of thy troubled brain,
　And bid the shadow of earth's grief depart.

He will give back what neither time, nor might,
　Nor passionate prayer, nor longing hope restore
(Dear as to long-blind eyes recovered sight),
　He will give back those who are gone before.

O, what were life, if life were all?　Thine eyes
　Are blinded by their tears, or thou wouldst see
Thy treasures wait thee in the far-off skies,
　And Death, thy friend, will give them all to thee

HUSH.

'I CAN scarcely hear,' she murmured,
　'For my heart beats loud and fast,
But surely, in the far, far distance,
　I can hear a sound at last.'
　　'It is only the reapers singing,
　　　As they carry home their sheaves,
　　And the evening breeze has risen,
　　　And rustles the dying leaves.'

'Listen! there are voices talking.'
　Calmly still she strove to speak,
Yet her voice grew faint and trembling,
　And the red flushed in her cheek.
　　'It is only the children playing
　　　Below, now their work is done,
　　And they laugh that their eyes are dazzled
　　　By the rays of the setting sun.'

Fainter grew her voice, and weaker,
　As with anxious eye she cried,

'Down the avenue of chestnuts,
   I can hear a horseman ride.'
     'It was only the deer that were feeding
      In a herd on the clover grass,
      They were startled, and fled to the thicket,
       As they saw the reapers pass.'

Now the night arose in silence,
   Birds lay in their leafy nest,
And the deer couched in the forest,
   And the children were at rest:
     There was only a sound of weeping
      From watchers around a bed,
     But Rest to the weary spirit,
      Peace to the quiet Dead!

A CHANT.

'Benedictus qui venit in nomine Domini.'

WHO is the Angel that cometh?
      Life!
Let us not question what he brings,
      Peace or Strife,
Under the shade of his mighty wings,
     One by one,
     Are his secrets told;
     One by one,
Lit by the rays of each morning sun,
   Shall a new flower its petals unfold,
   With the mystery hid in its heart of gold.
We will arise and go forth to greet him,
   Singing, gladly, with one accord; —
'Blessèd is he that cometh
   In the name of the Lord!'

Who is the Angel that cometh?
            Joy!
Look at his glittering rainbow wings —
            No alloy
Lies in the radiant gifts he brings;
        Tender and sweet,
    He is come to-day,
        Tender and sweet:
While chains of love on his silver feet
    Will hold him in lingering fond delay.
    But greet him quickly, he will not stay,
Soon he will leave us; but though for others
    All his brightest treasures are stored; —
'Blessèd is he that cometh
        In the name of the Lord!'

Who is the Angel that cometh?
            Pain!
Let us arise and go forth to greet him;
            Not in vain
Is the summons come for us to meet him;
        He will stay,
    And darken our sun;
        He will stay
A desolate night, a weary day.
    Since in that shadow our work is done,
    And in that shadow our crowns are won,
Let us say still, while his bitter chalice
    Slowly into our hearts is poured, —
'Blessèd is he that cometh
        In the name of the Lord!'

Who is the Angel that cometh?
            Death!
But do not shudder and do not fear;
        Hold your breath,

For a kingly presence is drawing near,
 Cold and bright
  Is his flashing steel,
 Cold and bright
The smile that comes like a starry light
 To calm the terror and grief we feel;
 He comes to help and to save and heal :
Then let us, baring our hearts and kneeling,
 Sing, while we wait this Angel's sword, —
'Blessèd is he that cometh
  In the name of the Lord ! '

WILLIAM ALLINGHAM.

LOVELY MARY DONNELLY.

To an Irish tune.

OH, lovely Mary Donnelly, it's you I love the best!
If fifty girls were round you I'd hardly see the rest.
Be what it may the time of day, the place be where it will,
Sweet looks of Mary Donnelly, they bloom before me still.

Her eyes like mountain water that's flowing on a rock,
How clear they are, how dark they are! and they give me
    many a shock.
Red rowans warm in sunshine and wetted with a show'r,
Could ne'er express the charming lip that has me in its
    pow'r.

Her nose is straight and handsome, her eyebrows lifted up,
Her chin is very neat and pert, and smooth like a china cup;
Her hair's the brag of Ireland, so weighty and so fine;
It's rolling down upon her neck, and gathered in a twine.

The dance o' last Whit-Monday night exceeded all before,
No pretty girl for miles about was missing from the floor;
But Mary kept the belt of love, and O but she was gay!
She danced a jig, she sung a song, that took my heart away.

When she stood up for dancing, her steps were so com-
    plete,
The music nearly killed itself to listen to her feet;

The fiddler moaned his blindness, he heard her so much
    praised,
But blessed his luck to not be deaf when once her voice
    she raised.

And evermore I 'm whistling or lilting what you sung;
Your smile is always in my heart, your name beside my
    tongue;
But you 've as many sweethearts as you 'd count on both
    your hands,
And for myself there 's not a thumb or little finger stands.

'T is you 're the flower o' womankind in country or in town;
The higher I exalt you, the lower I 'm cast down.
If some great lord should come this way, and see your
    beauty bright,
And you to be his lady, I 'd own it was but right.

O might we live together in a lofty palace hall,
Where joyful music rises, and where scarlet curtains fall !
O might we live together in a cottage mean and small,
With sods of grass the only roof, and mud the only wall !

O lovely Mary Donnelly, your beauty 's my distress.
It 's far too beauteous to be mine, but I 'll never wish it
    less.
The proudest place would fit your face, and I am poor and
    low;
But blessings be about you, dear, wherever you may go !

THE FAIRIES.

A CHILD'S SONG.

Up the airy mountain,
   Down the rushy glen,
We dare n't go a hunting
   For fear of little men;

Wee folk, good folk,
  Trooping all together;
Green jacket, red cap,
  And white owl's feather!

Down along the rocky shore
  Some make their home,
They live on crispy pancakes
  Of yellow-tide foam;
Some in the reeds
  Of the black mountain-lake,
With frogs for their watch-dogs,
  All night awake.

High on the hill-top
  The old King sits;
He is now so old and gray
  He 's nigh lost his wits.
With a bridge of white mist
  Columbkill he crosses,
On his stately journeys
  From Slieveleague to Rosses;
Or going up with music
  On cold starry nights,
To sup with the Queen
  Of the gay Northern Lights.

They stole little Bridget
  For seven years long;
When she came down again
  Her friends were all gone.
They took her lightly back,
  Between the night and morrow;
They thought that she was fast asleep,
  But she was dead with sorrow.
They have kept her ever since
  Deep within the lakes,

On a bed of flag-leaves,
  Watching till she wakes.

By the craggy hillside,
  Through the mosses bare,
They have planted thorn-trees
  For pleasure here and there.
Is any man so daring
  As dig them up in spite,
He shall find their sharpest thorns
  In his bed at night.

Up the airy mountain,
  Down the rushy glen,
We dare n't go a hunting
  For fear of little men;
Wee folk, good folk,
  Trooping all together;
Green jacket, red cap,
  And white owl's feather!

THE MILKMAID.

To the tune of ' It was an old Beggarman.'

O WHERE are you going so early? he said;
Good luck go with you, my pretty maid;
To tell you my mind I 'm half afraid,
  But I wish I were your sweetheart.
    When the morning sun is shining low,
    And the cocks in every farmyard crow
      I 'll carry your pail,
      O'er hill and dale,
    And I 'll go with you a-milking.

I 'm going a-milking, sir, says she,
Through the dew, and across the lea;

You ne'er would even yourself to me,
Or take me for your sweetheart.
    When the morning sun, etc.

Now give me your milking-stool awhile,
To carry it down to yonder stile;
I 'm wishing every step a mile,
    And myself your only sweetheart.
        When the morning sun, etc.

O, here 's the stile in-under the tree,
And there 's the path in the grass for me,
And I thank you kindly, sir, says she,
    And wish you a better sweetheart.
        When the morning sun, etc.

Now give me your milking-pail, says he,
And while we 're going across the lea,
Pray reckon your master's cows to me,
    Although I 'm not your sweetheart.
        When the morning sun, etc.

Two of them red, and two of them white,
Two of them yellow and silky bright,
She told him her master's cows aright,
    Though he was not her sweetheart.
        When the morning sun, etc.

She sat and milked in the morning sun,
And when her milking was over and done,
She found him waiting, all as one
    As if he were her sweetheart.
        When the morning sun, etc.

He freely offered his heart and hand;
Now she has a farm at her command,

And cows of her own to graze the land;
Success to all true sweethearts!
    When the morning sun is shining low,
    And the cocks in every farmyard crow,
        I 'll carry your pail
        O'er hill and dale,
    And I 'll go with you a-milking.

TO EÄRINÈ.

> ' Eärinè,
> Who had her very being, and her name,
> With the first knots or buddings of the Spring.'
> BEN JONSON.

SAINT Valentine kindles the crocus,
    Saint Valentine wakens the birds;
I would that his power could evoke us
    In tender and musical words!

I mean, us unconfident lovers,
    Whose doubtful or stammering tongue
No help save in rhyming discovers;
    Since what can't be said may be sung.

So, Fairest and Sweetest, your pardon
    (If no better welcome) I pray!
There 's spring-time in grove and in garden;
    Perchance it may breathe in my lay.

I think and I dream (did you know it?)
    Of somebody's eyes, her soft hair,
The neck bending whitely below it,
    The dress that she chances to wear.

Each tone of her voice I remember,
    Each turn of her head, of her arm:
Methinks, had she faults out of number,
    Being hers, they were certain to charm.

From her every distance I measure;
　　Each mile of a journey, I say —
‘ I ’m so much the nearer my treasure,’
　　Or ‘so much the further away.’

And love writes my almanac also;
　　The good days and bad days occur,
The fasts and the festivals fall so,
　　By seeing or not seeing her.

Who know her, they ’re happy, they only;
　　Whatever she looks on turns bright;
Wherever she is not, is lonely,
　　Wherever she is, is delight.

So friendly her face that I tremble,
　　On friendship so sweet having ruth:
But why should I longer dissemble?
　　Or will you not guess at the truth?

And that is — dear Maiden, I love you!
　　You sweetest, and brightest and best! —
Good luck to the roof-tree above you,
　　The floor where your footstep is pressed!

May some new deliciousness meet you
　　On every new day of the Spring;
Each flower in its turn bloom to greet you,
　　Lark, mavis, and nightingale sing!

May kind vernal powers in your bosom
　　Their tenderest influence shed!
May I, when the rose is in blossom,
　　Enweave you a crown, white and red!

THE TOUCHSTONE.

A MAN there came, whence none can tell,
  Bearing a Touchstone in his hand;
  And tested all things in the land
By its unerring spell.

Quick birth of transmutation smote
  The fair to foul, the foul to fair;
  Purple nor ermine did he spare,
Nor scorn the dusty coat.

Of heirloom jewels, prized so much,
  Were many changed to chips and clods,
  And even statues of the Gods
Crumbled beneath its touch.

Then angrily the people cried,
  'The loss outweighs the profit far;
  Our goods suffice us as they are;
We will not have them tried.'

And since they could not so prevail
  To check his unrelenting quest,
  They seized him, saying — 'Let him test
How real it is, our jail!'

But, though they slew him with a sword,
  And in a fire his Touchstone burned,
  Its doings could not be o'erturned,
Its undoings restored.

And when, to stop all future harm,
  They strewed its ashes on the breeze;
  They little guessed each grain of these
Conveyed the perfect charm.

North, south, in rings and amulets,
  Throughout the crowded world 't is borne;
  Which, as a fashion long outworn,
Its ancient mind forgets.

SONG.

O Spirit of the Summertime!
  Bring back the roses to the dells;
The swallow from her distant clime,
  The honey-bee from drowsy cells.

Bring back the friendship of the sun;
  The gilded evenings, calm and late,
When merry children homeward run,
  And peeping stars bid lovers wait.

Bring back the singing; and the scent
  Of meadowlands at dewy prime; —
Oh, bring again my heart's content,
  Thou Spirit of the Summertime!

MEADOWSWEET.

Through grass, through ambered cornfields, our slow
    Stream —
  Fringed with its flags and reeds and rushes tall
  And Meadowsweet, the chosen from them all
By wandering children, yellow as the cream
Of those great cows — winds on as in a dream
  By mill and footbridge, hamlet old and small
(Red roofs, gray tower), and sees the sunset gleam
  On mullioned windows of an ivied Hall.

There, once upon a time, the heavy King
  Trod out its perfume from the Meadowsweet,
  Strewn like a woman's love beneath his feet,

In stately dance or jovial banqueting,
When all was new ; and in its wayfaring
  Our Streamlet curved, as now, through grass and wheat.

HEATHER.

VAST barren hills and moors, cliffs over lakes,
  Great headlands by the sea — a lonely land !
  With Fishers' huts beside a yellow strand
Where wave on wave in foam and thunder breaks,
Or else a tranquil blue horizon takes
  Sunlight and shadow. Few can understand
  The poor folk's ancient tongue, sweet, simple, grand,
Wherein a dreamy old-world half awakes.

And on these hills a thousand years ago
  Their fathers wandered, sun and stars for clock,
With minds to wing above and creep below ;
  Heard what we hear, the ocean's solemn shock,
Saw what we see, this Heather-flow'r aglow,
  Empurpling league-long slope and crested rock.

12

SABINE BARING-GOULD.

THE UNIVERSAL MOTHER.

PIRKE RABBI ELIESER, II.

WHEN by the hand of God man was created,
He took the dust of earth from every quarter —
From east to west, and from the north and south —
That wheresoever man might wander forth,
He should be still at home; and, when a-dying,
On some far distant western shore, and seeking
A shelter in the bosom of the Mother,
The earth might not refuse to clasp him, saying,

' My offspring art thou not, O roving Eastern.'
Wherever now the foot of Man shall bear him,
Wherever by the final call o'ertaken,
He is no stranger reckoned, nor an outcast,
But hears exclaim the Universal Mother,
' Come, child of mine, and slumber in my bosom.'

THE SWALLOWS OF CITEAUX.

UNDER eaves, against the towers,
All the spring, their muddy bowers
    Swallows build about Citeaux.
Round the chapter house and hall,
From the dawn to evenfall,
    They are fluttering to and fro

On their never-flagging wing.
With the psalms the brethren sing
    Blends their loud incessant cry ;

In and out the plastered nest,
Never taking thought of rest,
　　Chattering these swallows fly.

They distract the monk who reads,
Him as well who tells his beads,
　　Him who writes his chronicle :
In the cloister old and gray
They are jubilant and gay,
　　In the very church as well.

On the dormitory beds,
In refectory o'er the heads —
　　At the windows rich with paint,
Ever dashing, — in and out
With the maddest, noisiest rout,
　　As would surely vex a saint.

To the abbot then complain
Pious monks : — ' Shall these remain
　　To disturb us at our prayers ?
Bid us nests and eggs destroy,
Then the birds will not annoy
　　Any more our deafened ears.'

Quoth the abbot, smiling — ' Say,
Have not we, too, homes of clay,
　　Quite as fragile, not more fair ?
Brothers, and shall we resolve
Their tabernacles to dissolve,
　　Asking God our own to spare ? '

Not another word of blame,
But they turned away in shame.
　　So the little birds had peace,
And the parapets among
Built and laid, and hatched their young,
　　Making wonderful increase.

When declined the autumn sun,
When, the yellow harvest done,
     Sat the swallows in a row
On the ridging of the roof,
Patiently, as in behoof
     Of a licence ere they 'd go.

Forth from out the western door
Came the abbot; him before
     Went a brother with his crook,
And a boy a bell who rung
And a silver censer swung,
     While another bore the book.

Then the abbot raised his hand,
Looking to the swallow band,
     Saying, ' Ite, missa est !
Christian birds, depart in peace,
As your cares of summer cease,
     Swallows, enter on your rest.

' Now the winter snow must fall,
Wrapping earth as with a pall,
     And the stormy winds arise ;
Go to distant lands where glow
Deathless suns, where falls not snow
     From the ever azure skies.

' Go ! dear heralds of the road,
To the dim unknown abode
     In the verdant Blessed Isles,
Whither we shall speed some day,
Leaving crumbling homes of clay
     For the land where summer smiles :

'Go in peace ! your hours have run ;
Go, the day of work is done ;
    Go in peace, my sons ! ' he said,
Then the swallows spread the wing,
Making all the welkin ring
    With their cry, and southward sped.

THE RELIGIOUS POETS.

THE RELIGIOUS POETS.

JOHN HENRY NEWMAN.

THE GREEK FATHERS.

LET heathen sing thy heathen praise,
Fall'n Greece! the thought of holier days
  In my sad heart abides;
For sons of thine in Truth's first hour
Were tongues and weapons of His power,
Born of the Spirit's fiery shower,
  Our fathers and our guides.

All thine is Clement's varied page;
And Dionysius, ruler sage,
  In days of doubt and pain;
And Origen with eagle eye;
And saintly Basil's purpose high
To smite imperial heresy,
  And cleanse the Altar's stain.

From thee the glorious preacher came,
With soul of zeal and lips of flame,
  A court's stern martyr-guest;
And thine, O inexhaustive race!
Was Nazianzen's heaven-taught grace;
And royal-hearted Athanase,
  With Paul's own mantle blest.

DAY-LABORERS.

'And He said, It is finished.'

ONE only, of God's messengers to man,
Finished the work of grace, which He began;
   E'en Moses wearied upon Nebo's height,
   Though loth to leave the fight
With the doomed foe, and yield the sun-bright land
    To Joshua's armèd band.

And David wrought in turn a strenuous part,
Zeal for God's house consuming him in heart;
   And yet he might not build, but only bring
   Gifts for the Heavenly King;
And these another reared, his peaceful son,
    Till the full work was done.

List, Christian warrior! thou whose soul is fain
To rid thy Mother of her present chain; —
   Christ will avenge His Bride; yea, even now
   Begins the work, and thou
Shalt spend in it thy strength, but, ere He save,
    Thy lot shall be the grave.

LIBERALISM.

'Jehu destroyed Baal out of Israel. Howbeit from the sins of Jeroboam Jehu departed not from after them, to wit, the golden calves that were in Bethel, and that were in Dan.'

YE cannot halve the Gospel of God's grace;
   Men of presumptuous heart! I know you well.
   Ye are of those who plan that we should dwell,
Each in his tranquil home and holy place;
Seeing the Word refines all natures rude,
And tames the stirrings of the multitude.

And ye have caught some echoes of its lore,
  As heralded amid the joyous choirs ;
  Ye marked it spoke of peace, chastised desires,
Good-will and mercy, — and ye heard no more ;
But, as for zeal and quick-eyed sanctity,
And the dread depths of grace, ye passed them by.

And so ye halve the Truth ; for ye in heart,
  At best, are doubters whether it be true,
  The theme discarding, as unmeet for you,
Statesmen or Sages. O new-compassed art
Of the ancient Foe ! — but what, if it extends
O'er our own camp, and rules amid our friends ?

OUR FUTURE.

'What I do, thou knowest not now ; but thou shalt know hereafter.'

      Did we but see,
When life first opened, how our journey lay
Between its earliest and its closing day,
  Or view ourselves, as we one time shall be,
Who strive for the high prize, such sight would break
The youthful spirit, though bold for Jesu's sake.

      But Thou, dear Lord !
Whilst I traced out bright scenes which were to come,
Isaac's pure blessings, and a verdant home,
  Didst spare me, and withhold Thy fearful word ;
Wiling me year by year, till I am found
A pilgrim pale, with Paul's sad girdle bound.

THE PILLAR OF THE CLOUD.

Lead, Kindly Light, amid the encircling gloom,
    Lead Thou me on !
The night is dark, and I am far from home —
    Lead Thou me on !

Keep Thou my feet; I do not ask to see
The distant scene, — one step enough for me.

I was not ever thus, nor prayed that Thou
      Shouldst lead me on.
I loved to choose and see my path, but now
      Lead Thou me on!
I loved the garish day, and, spite of fears,
Pride ruled my will: remember not past years.

So long Thy power hath blest me, sure it still
      Will lead me on,
O'er moor and fen, o'er crag and torrent, till
      The night is gone;
And with the morn those angel faces smile
Which I have loved long since, and lost awhile.

FROM 'THE MARRIED AND THE SINGLE.' [10]

Ah, who has hither drawn my backward feet,
Changing for worldly strife my lone retreat? —
Where, in the silent chant of holy deeds,
I praise my God, and tend the sick soul's needs;
By toils of day, and vigils of the night,
By gushing tears, and blessèd lustral rite.
I have no sway amid the crowd, no art
In speech, no place in council or in mart.
Nor human law, nor judges throned on high,
Smile on my face, and to my words reply.
Let others seek earth's honors; be it mine
One law to cherish, and to track one line,
Straight on towards heaven to press with single bent,
To know and love my God, and then to die content.

FROM 'THE DREAM OF GERONTIUS.'[11]

§ 1.

GERONTIUS.

JESU, MARIA — I am near to death,
  And Thou art calling me; I know it now.
Not by the token of this faltering breath,
  This chill at heart, this dampness on my brow, —
(Jesu, have mercy! Mary, pray for me!)
  'T is this new feeling, never felt before,
(Be with me, Lord, in my extremity!)
  That I am going, that I am no more.
'T is this strange innermost abandonment,
  (Lover of souls! great God! I look to Thee,)
This emptying out of each constituent
  And natural force, by which I come to be.
Pray for me, O my friends; a visitant
  Is knocking his dire summons at my door,
The like of whom, to scare me and to daunt,
  Has never, never come to me before;
'T is death, — O loving friends, your prayers! — 't is he! —
As though my very being had given way,
  As though I was no more a substance now,
And could fall back on nought to be my stay,
  (Help, loving Lord! Thou my sole Refuge, Thou,)
And turn no whither, but must needs decay
  And drop from out the universal frame
Into that shapeless, scopeless, blank abyss,
  That utter nothingness, of which I came:
This is it that has come to pass in me;
Oh, horror! this it is, my dearest, this;
So pray for me, my friends, who have not strength to pray.

ASSISTANTS.

KYRIE eleïson, Christe eleïson, Kyrie eleïson.
Holy Mary, pray for him.
All holy Angels, pray for him.
Choirs of the righteous, pray for him.
Holy Abraham, pray for him.
St. John Baptist, St. Joseph, pray for him.
St. Peter, St. Paul, St. Andrew, St. John,
All Apostles, all Evangelists, pray for him.
All holy disciples of the Lord, pray for him.
All holy Innocents, pray for him.
All holy Martyrs, all holy Confessors,
All holy Hermits, all holy Virgins,
All ye Saints of God, pray for him.

GERONTIUS.

Rouse thee, my fainting soul, and play the man;
  And through such waning span
Of life and thought as still has to be trod,
  Prepare to meet thy God.
And while the storm of that bewilderment
  Is for a season spent,
And, ere afresh the ruin on me fall,
  Use well the interval.

ASSISTANTS.

Be merciful, be gracious; spare him, Lord !
Be merciful, be gracious; Lord, deliver him !
From the sins that are past;
  From Thy frown and Thine ire;
    From the perils of dying;
    From any complying
    With sin, or denying
    His God, or relying
      On self, at the last;

From the nethermost fire;
  From all that is evil;
  From power of the devil;
  Thy servant deliver,
  For once and for ever.

By Thy birth, and by Thy Cross,
Rescue him from endless loss;
By Thy death and burial,
Save him from a final fall;
By Thy rising from the tomb,
  By Thy mounting up above,
  By the Spirit's gracious love,
Save him in the day of doom.

GERONTIUS.

Sanctus fortis, Sanctus Deus,
  De profundis oro te,
Miserere, Judex meus,
  Parce mihi, Domine.
Firmly I believe and truly
  God is Three, and God is One;
And I next acknowledge duly
  Manhood taken by the Son.
And I trust and hope most fully
  In that manhood crucified;
And each thought and deed unruly
  Do to death, as He has died.
Simply to His grace and wholly
  Light and life and strength belong,
And I love, supremely, solely,
  Him the holy, Him the strong.
Sanctus fortis, Sanctus Deus,
  De profundis oro te,
Miserere, Judex meus,
  Parce mihi, Domine.

And I hold in veneration,
  For the love of Him alone,
Holy Church, as His creation,
  And her teachings, as His own.
And I take with joy whatever
  Now besets me, pain or fear,
And with a strong will I sever
  All the ties which bind me here.
Adoration aye be given,
  With and through the angelic host,
To the God of earth and heaven,
  Father, Son, and Holy Ghost.
Sanctus fortis, Sanctus Deus,
  De profundis oro te,
Miserere, Judex meus,
  Mortis in discrimine.

I can no more ; for now it comes again,
That sense of ruin, which is worse than pain,
That masterful negation and collapse
Of all that makes me man; as though I bent
  Over the dizzy brink
Of some sheer infinite descent ;
Or worse, as though
Down, down for ever I was falling through
The solid framework of created things,
And needs must sink and sink
 · Into the vast abyss.   And, crueller still,
  A fierce and restless fright begins to fill
The mansion of my soul.   And, worse and worse,
  Some bodily form of ill
Floats on the wind, with many a loathsome curse,
Tainting the hallowed air, and laughs, and flaps
Its hideous wings,
And makes me wild with horror and dismay.
O Jesu help ! pray for me, Mary, pray !

Some Angel, Jesu ! such as came to Thee
In Thine own agony —
Mary, pray for me. Joseph, pray for me. Mary, pray for me.

ASSISTANTS.

Rescue him, O Lord, in this his evil hour,
As of old so many by Thy gracious power : — (Amen.)
Enoch and Elias from the common doom ; (Amen.)
Noe from the waters in a saving home ; (Amen.)
Abraham from th' abounding guilt of Heathenesse ; (Amen.)
Job from all his multiform and fell distress ; (Amen.)
Isaac, when his father's knife was raised to slay ; (Amen.)
Lot from burning Sodom on its judgment-day ; (Amen.)
Moses from the land of bondage and despair ; (Amen.)
Daniel from the hungry lions in their lair ; (Amen.)
And the Children Three amid the furnace-flame ; (Amen.)
Chaste Susanna from the slander and the shame; (Amen.)
David from Golia and the wrath of Saul ; (Amen.)
And the two Apostles from their prison-thrall; (Amen.)
Thecla from her torments ; (Amen :)
　　　　　　　　　　— so to show Thy power,
Rescue this Thy servant in his evil hour.

GERONTIUS.

Novissima hora est; and I fain would sleep.
The pain has wearied me — Into Thy hands,
O Lord, into Thy hands —
O Lord, into Thy hands —

THE PRIEST.

Proficiscere, anima Christiana, de hoc mundo !
Go forth upon thy journey, Christian soul !
Go from this world ! Go, in the Name of God
The Omnipotent Father, who created thee !
Go, in the Name of Jesus Christ, our Lord,
Son of the living God, who bled for thee !

13

Go, in the Name of the Holy Spirit, who
Hath been poured out on thee ! Go, in the name
Of Angels and Archangels ; in the name
Of Thrones and Dominations ; in the name
Of Princedoms and of Powers ; and in the name
Of Cherubim and Seraphim, go forth !
Go, in the name of Patriarchs and Prophets ;
And of Apostles and Evangelists,
Of Martyrs and Confessors ; in the name
Of holy Monks and Hermits ; in the name
Of holy Virgins ; and all Saints of God,
Both men and women, go !   Go on thy course;
And may thy place to-day be found in peace,
And may thy dwelling be the Holy Mount
Of Sion : — through the Name of Christ, our Lord.

§ 5.

ANGEL.

— Hark to those sounds !
They come of tender beings angelical,
Least and most childlike of the sons of God.

FIRST CHOIR OF ANGELICALS.

Praise to the Holiest in the height,
  And in the depth be praise :
In all His words most wonderful ;
  Most sure in all His ways !

To us His elder race He gave
  To battle and to win,
Without the chastisement of pain,
  Without the soil of sin.

The younger son He willed to be
  A marvel in His birth :
Spirit and flesh his parents were ;
  His home was heaven and earth.

The Eternal blessed His child, and armed,
  And sent him hence afar,
To serve as champion in the field
  Of elemental war.

To be His Viceroy in the world
  Of matter, and of sense;
Upon the frontier, towards the foe,
  A resolute defence.

ANGEL.

We now have passed the gate, and are within
The House of Judgment; and whereas on earth
Temples and palaces are formed of parts
Costly and rare, but all material,
So in the world of spirits nought is found,
I mould withal, and form into a whole,
But what is immaterial   and thus
The smallest portions of this edifice,
Cornice, or frieze, or balustrade, or stair
The very pavement is made up of life —
Of holy, blessèd, and immortal beings,
Who hymn their Maker's praise continually.

SECOND CHOIR OF ANGELICALS.

Praise to the Holiest in the height,
  And in the depth be praise:
In all His words most wonderful;
  Most sure in all His ways!

Woe to thee, man! for he was found
  A recreant in the fight;
And lost his heritage of heaven,
  And fellowship with light.

Above him now the angry sky,
  Around the tempest's din;

Who once had Angels for his friends,
    Had but the brutes for kin.

O man! a savage kindred they;
    To flee that monster brood
He scaled the seaside cave, and clomb
    The giants of the wood.

With now a fear, and now a hope,
    With aids which chance supplied,
From youth to eld, from sire to son,
    He lived, and toiled, and died.

He dreed his penance age by age;
    And step by step began
Slowly to doff his savage garb,
    And be again a man.

And quickened by the Almighty's breath
    And chastened by His rod,
And taught by angel-visitings,
    At length he sought his God;

And learned to call upon His Name,
    And in His faith create
A household and a father-land,
    A city and a state.

Glory to Him who from the mire
    In patient length of days,
Elaborated into life
    A people to His praise!

.   .   .   .

ANGEL.

We have gained the stairs
Which rise towards the Presence-chamber; there

A band of mighty Angels keep the way
On either side, and hymn the Incarnate God.

ANGELS OF THE SACRED STAIR.

Father, whose goodness none can know, but they
  Who see Thee face to face,
By man hath come the infinite display
  Of Thy victorious grace ;
But fallen man — the creature of a day —
  Skills not that love to trace.
It needs, to tell the triumph Thou hast wrought,
An Angel's deathless fire, an Angel's reach of thought.

It needs that very Angel, who with awe,
  Amid the garden shade,
The great Creator in His sickness saw,
  Soothed by a creature's aid,
And agonized, as victim of the Law
  Which He Himself had made ;
For who can praise Him in His depth and height,
But he who saw Him reel amid that solitary fight ?

.   .   .   .

§ 6.

ANGEL.

Thy judgment now is near, for we are come
Into the veilèd presence of our God.

SOUL.

I hear the voices that I left on earth.

ANGEL.

It is the voice of friends around thy bed,
Who say the 'Subvenite' with the priest.
Hither the echoes come; before the Throne
Stands the great Angel of the Agony,
The same who strengthened Him, what time he knelt

Lone in that garden shade, bedewed with blood.
That Angel best can plead with Him for all
Tormented souls, the dying and the dead.

ANGEL OF THE AGONY.

Jesu ! by that shuddering dread which fell on Thee ;
Jesu ! by that cold dismay which sickened Thee ;
Jesu ! by that pang of heart which thrilled in Thee ;
Jesu ! by that mount of sins which crippled Thee ;
Jesu ! by that sense of guilt which stifled Thee ;
Jesu ! by that innocence which girdled Thee ;
Jesu ! by that sanctity which reigned in Thee ;
Jesu ! by that Godhead which was one with Thee ;
Jesu ! spare these souls which are so dear to Thee ;
Who in prison, calm and patient, wait for Thee ;
Hasten, Lord, their hour, and bid them come to Thee,
To that glorious Home, where they shall ever gaze on Thee.

SOUL.

I go before my Judge.   Ah ! —

ANGEL.

              — Praise to His Name !
The eager spirit has darted from my hold,
And, with intemperate energy of love,
Flies to the dear feet of Emmanuel ;
But, ere it reach them, the keen sanctity,
Which with its effluence, like a glory, clothes
And circles round the Crucified, has seized,
And scorched, and shrivelled it ; and now it lies
Passive and still before the awful Throne.
O happy, suffering soul ! for it is safe,
Consumed, yet quickened, by the glance of God.

SOUL.

Take me away, and in the lowest deep
There let me be,

And there in hope the lone night-watches keep,
       Told out for me.
There, motionless and happy in my pain,
       Lone, not forlorn, —
There will I sing my sad perpetual strain,
       Until the morn.
There will I sing, and soothe my stricken breast,
       Which ne'er can cease
To throb, and pine, and languish, till possest
       Of its Sole Peace.
There will I sing my absent Lord and Love : —
       Take me away,
That sooner I may rise, and go above,
And see Him in the truth of everlasting day.

RICHARD CHENEVIX TRENCH.

THE MONK AND BIRD.

As he who finds one flower sharp thorns among,
  Plucks it, and highly prizes, though before
Careless regard on thousands he has flung,
  As fair as this or more ;

Not otherwise perhaps this argument
  Won from me, where I found it, such regard,
That I esteemed no labor thereon spent
  As wearisome or hard.

In huge and antique volume did it lie,
  That by two solemn clasps was duly bound,
As neither to be opened nor laid by
  But with due thought profound.

There fixèd thought to questions did I lend,
  Which hover on the bounds of mortal ken,
And have perplexed, and will unto the end
  Perplex the brains of men ;

Of what is time, and what eternity,
  Of all that seems and is not — forms of things —
Till my tired spirit followed painfully
  On flagging weary wings ;

So that I welcomed this one resting-place,
  Pleased as a bird, which, when its forces fail,
Lights panting in the ocean's middle space
  Upon a sunny sail.

And now the grace of fiction, which has power
　To render things impossible believed,
And win them with the credence of an hour
　To be for truths received —

That grace must help me, as it only can,
　Winning such transient credence, while I tell
What to a cloistered solitary man
　In distant times befell.

Him little might our earthly grandeur feed,
　Who to the uttermost was vowed to be
A follower of his Master's barest need
　In holy poverty.

Nor might he know the gentle mutual strife
　Of home-affections, which can more or less
Temper with sweet the bitter of our life,
　And lighten its distress.

Yet we should err to deem that he was left
　To bear alone our being's lonely weight,
Or that his soul was vacant and bereft
　Of pomp and inward state:

Morn, when before the sun his orb unshrouds,
　Swift as a beacon torch the light has sped,
Kindling the dusky summits of the clouds
　Each to a fiery red —

The slanted columns of the noon-day light,
　Let down into the bosom of the hills,
Or sunset, that with golden vapor bright
　The purple mountains fills —

These made him say, — If God has so arrayed
　A fading world that quickly passes by,
Such rich provision of delight has made
　For every human eye,

What shall the eyes that wait for him survey,
　Where his own presence gloriously appears
In worlds that were not founded for a day,
　But for eternal years ?

And if at seasons this world's undelight
　Oppressed him, or the hollow at its heart,
One glance at those enduring mansions bright
　Made gloomier thoughts depart ;

Till many times the sweetness of the thought
　Of an eternal country — where it lies
Removed from care and mortal anguish, brought
　Sweet tears into his eyes.

Thus, not unsolaced, he longwhile abode,
　Filling all dreary melancholy time
And empty spaces of the heart with God,
　And with this hope sublime :

Even thus he lived, with little joy or pain
　Drawn through the channels by which men receive —
Most men receive the things which for the main
　Make them rejoice or grieve.

But for delight, on spiritual gladness fed,
　And obvious to temptations of like kind ;
One such, from out his very gladness bred,
　It was his lot to find.

When first it came, he lightly put it by,
　But it returned again to him ere long,
And ever having got some new ally,
　And every time more strong —

A little worm that gnawed the life away
　Of a tall plant, the canker of its root,
Or like as when from some small speck decay
　Spreads o'er a beauteous fruit.

For still the doubt came back, — Can God provide
  For the large heart of man what shall not pall,
Nor through eternal ages' endless tide
  On tired spirits fall?

Here but one look tow'rd heaven will oft repress
  The crushing weight of undelightful care;
But what were there beyond, if weariness
  Should ever enter there?

Yet do not sweetest things here soonest cloy?
  Satiety the life of joy would kill,
If sweet with bitter, pleasure with annoy
  Were not attempered still.

This mood endured, till every act of love,
  Vigils of praise and prayer, and midnight choir,
All shadows of the service done above,
  And which, while his desire,

And while his hope was heavenward, he had loved,
  As helps to disengage him from the chain
That fastens unto earth — all these now proved
  Most burdensome and vain.

What must have been the issue of that mood
  It were a thing to fear — but that one day,
Upon the limits of an ancient wood,
  His thoughts him led astray.

Darkling he went, nor once applied his ear,
  (On a loud sea of agitations thrown,)
Nature's low tones and harmonies to hear,
  Heard by the calm alone.

The merry chirrup of the grasshopper,
  Sporting among the roots of withered grass,
The dry leaf rustling to the wind's light stir,
  Did each unnoted pass:

He, walking in a trance of selfish care,
  Not once observed the beauty shed around,
The blue above, the music in the air,
  The flowers upon the ground:

Till from the centre of that forest dim
  Came to him such sweet singing of a bird,
As, sweet in very truth, then seemed to him
  The sweetest ever heard.

That lodestar drew him onward inward still,
  Deeper than where the village children stray,
Deeper than where the woodman's glittering bill
  Lops the large boughs away —

Into a central space of glimmering shade,
  Where hardly might the straggling sunbeams pass,
Which a faint lattice-work of light had made
  Upon the long lank grass.

He did not sit, but stood and listened there,
  And to him listening the time seemed not long,
While that sweet bird above him filled the air
  With its melodious song.

He heard not, saw not, felt not aught beside,
  Through the wide worlds of pleasure and of pain,
Save the full flowing and the ample tide
  Of that celestial strain.

As though a bird of Paradise should light
  A moment on a twig of this bleak earth,
And singing songs of Paradise invite
  All hearts to holy mirth,

And then take wing to Paradise again,
  Leaving all listening spirits raised above
The toil of earth, the trouble, and the pain,
  And melted all in love:

Such hidden might, such power was in the sound;
　But when it ceased sweet music to unlock,
The spell that held him sense and spirit-bound
　Dissolved with a slight shock.

All things around were as they were before —
　The trees, and the blue sky, and sunshine bright,
Painting the pale and leafstrewn forest-floor
　With patches of faint light.

But as when music doth no longer thrill,
　Light shudderings yet along the chords will run,
Or the heart vibrates tremulously still,
　Although its prayer be done,

So his heart fluttered all the way he went,
　Listening each moment for the vesper bell;
For a long hour he deemed he must have spent
　In that untrodden dell.

And once it seemed that something new or strange
　Had past upon the flowers, the trees, the ground;
Some slight but unintelligible change
　On everything around:

Such change, where all things undisturbed remain,
　As only to the eye of him appears,
Who absent long, at length returns again —
　The silent work of years.

And ever grew upon him more and more
　Fresh marvel — for, unrecognized of all,
He stood a stranger at the convent door:
　New faces filled the hall.

Yet was it long ere he received the whole
　Of that strange wonder — how, while he had stood
Lost in deep gladness of his inmost soul,
　Far hidden in that wood,

Three generations had gone down unseen
    Under the thin partition that is spread —
The thin partition of thin earth — between
    The living and the dead.

Nor did he many days to earth belong,
    For like a pent-up stream, released again,
The years arrested by the strength of song
    Came down on him amain;

Sudden as a dissolving thaw in spring;
    Gentle as when upon the first warm day,
Which sunny April in its train may bring,
    The snow melts all away.

They placed him in his former cell, and there
    Watched him departing; what few words he said
Were of calm peace and gladness, with one care
    Mingled — one only dread —

Lest an eternity should not suffice
    To take the measure and the breadth and height
Of what there is reserved in Paradise —
    Its ever-new delight.

'*DUST TO DUST.*'

OH blessing wearing semblance of a curse,
We fear thee, thou stern sentence — yet to be
Linked to immortal bodies were far worse
    Than thus to be set free.

For mingling with the life-blood through each vein
The venom of the serpent's bite has run,
And only thus might be expelled again —
    Thus only health be won.

Shall we not then a gracious sentence own,
Now since the leprosy has fretted through
The entire house, that Thou wilt take it down,
    And build it all anew?

Build it this time (since Thou wilt build again),
A holy house where righteousness may dwell;
And we, though in the unbuilding there be pain,
    Will still affirm, — 't is well.

PRAYER.

WHEN prayer delights the least, then learn to say,
Soul, now is greatest need that thou shouldst pray.

Crookèd and warped I am, and I would fain
Straighten myself by thy right line again.

Oh come, warm sun, and ripen my late fruits;
Pierce, genial showers, down to my parchèd roots.

My well is bitter; cast therein the tree,
That sweet henceforth its brackish waves may be.

Say what is prayer, when it is prayer indeed?
The mighty utterance of a mighty need.

The man is praying, who doth press with might
Out of his darkness into God's own light.

White heat the iron in the furnace won;
Withdrawn from thence, 't is cold and hard anon.

Flowers from their stalks divided, presently
Droop, fail, and wither in the gazer's eye.

The greenest leaf divided from its stem
To speedy withering doth itself condemn.

The largest river from its fountain head
Cut off, leaves soon a parched and dusty bed.

All things that live from God their sustenance wait,
And sun and moon are beggars at his gate.

All skirts extended of thy mantle hold,
When angel-hands from heaven are scattering gold.

THE LENT JEWELS.

A JEWISH APOLOGUE.

In schools of wisdom all the day was spent:
His steps at eve the Rabbi homeward bent,
With homeward thoughts, which dwelt upon the wife
And two fair children who consoled his life.
She, meeting at the threshold, led him in,
And with these words preventing, did begin:
' I, greeting ever your desired return,
Yet greet it most to-day; for since this morn
I have been much perplexed and sorely tried
Upon one point, which you shall now decide.
Some years ago, a friend into my care
Some jewels gave, rich precious gems they were;
But having given them in my charge, this friend
Did afterward nor come for them, nor send,
But in my keeping suffered them so long,
That now it almost seems to me a wrong
That he should suddenly arrive to-day,
To take those jewels, which he left, away.
What think you?   Shall I freely yield them back,
And with no murmuring? — so henceforth to lack
Those gems myself, which I had learned to see
Almost as mine for ever, mine in fee.'

' What question can be here? your own true heart
Must needs advise you of the only part;
That may be claimed again which was but lent,
And should be yielded with no discontent;
Nor surely can we find in this a wrong,
That it was left us to enjoy it long.'

'Good is the word,' she answered; 'may we now
And evermore that it is good allow!'
And, rising, to an inner chamber led,
And there she showed him, stretched upon one bed,
Two children pale, and he the jewels knew,
Which God had lent him, and resumed anew.

'*BY GRECIAN ANNALS IT REMAINS UNTOLD.*'

By Grecian annals it remained untold,
But may be read in Eastern legend old,
How when great Alexander died, he bade
That his two hands uncovered should be laid
Outside the bier — for men therewith to see,
(Men who had seen him in his majesty,)
That he had gone the common way of all,
And nothing now his own in death might call;
Nor of the treasures of two empires aught
Within those empty hands unto the grave had brought.

'*SOME MURMUR WHEN THEIR SKY IS CLEAR.*'

SOME murmur, when their sky is clear
    And wholly bright to view,
If one small speck of dark appear
    In their great heaven of blue:
And some with thankful love are filled,
    If but one streak of light,

One ray of God's good mercy gild
　　The darkness of their night.

In palaces are hearts that ask,
　　In discontent and pride,
Why life is such a dreary task,
　　And all good things denied :
And hearts in poorest huts admire
　　How Love has in their aid,
Love that not ever seems to tire,
　　Such rich provision made.

'*LORD, WHAT A CHANGE WITHIN US ONE SHORT HOUR!*'

LORD, what a change within us one short hour
　　Spent in thy presence will prevail to make !
　　What heavy burdens from our bosoms take,
What parchèd ground refresh, as with a shower !
We kneel, and all around us seems to lower ;
　　We rise, and all, the distant and the near,
　　Stands forth in sunny outline, brave and clear ;
We kneel how weak, we rise how full of power.
　　Why therefore should we do ourselves this wrong
　　Or others — that we are not always strong,
That we are ever overborne with care,
　　That we should ever weak or heartless be,
Anxious or troubled, when with us is prayer,
　　And joy and strength and courage are with Thee.

'*LORD, MANY TIMES I AM AWEARY QUITE.*'

LORD, many times I am aweary quite
　　Of mine own self, my sin, my vanity —
Yet be not Thou, or I am lost outright,
　　Weary of me.

And hate against myself I often bear,
    And enter with myself in fierce debate :
Take Thou my part against myself, nor share
        In that just hate.

Best friends might loathe us, if what things perverse
    We know of our own selves, they also knew :
Lord, Holy One ! if Thou who knowest worse
        Shouldst loathe us too !

FREDERICK WILLIAM FABER.

THE SHADOW OF THE ROCK.

THE Shadow of the Rock!
Stay, Pilgrim! stay!
Night treads upon the heels of day;
There is no other resting-place this way.
The Rock is near,
The well is clear,
Rest in the Shadow of the Rock.

The Shadow of the Rock!
The desert wide
Lies round thee like a trackless tide,
In waves of sand forlornly multiplied.
The sun is gone,
Thou art alone,
Rest in the Shadow of the Rock.

The Shadow of the Rock!
All come alone,
All, ever since the sun hath shone,
Who travelled by this road have come alone.
Be of good cheer,
A home is here,
Rest in the Shadow of the Rock.

The Shadow of the Rock!
Night veils the land;
How the palms whisper as they stand!

How the well tinkles faintly through the sand !
  Cool water take
  Thy thirst to slake,
 Rest in the Shadow of the Rock.

  The Shadow of the Rock !
   Abide ! Abide !
This Rock moves ever at thy side,
Pausing to welcome thee at eventide.
   Ages are laid
   Beneath its shade,
 Rest in the Shadow of the Rock !

  The Shadow of the Rock !
   Always at hand,
Unseen it cools the noon-tide land,
And quells the fire that flickers in the sand.
   It comes in sight
   Only at night,
 Rest in the Shadow of the Rock.

  The Shadow of the Rock !
   Mid skies storm-riven
It gathers shadows out of heaven,
And holds them o'er us all night cool and even.
   Through the charmed air
   Dew falls not there,
 Rest in the Shadow of the Rock.

  The Shadow of the Rock !
   To angel's eyes
This Rock its shadow multiplies,
And at this hour in countless places lies.
   One Rock, one Shade,
   O'er thousands laid,
 Rest in the Shadow of the Rock.

The Shadow of the Rock !
To weary feet,
That have been diligent and fleet,
The sleep is deeper and the shade more sweet.
O weary ! rest,
Thou art sore pressed,
Rest in the Shadow of the Rock.

The Shadow of the Rock !
Thy bed is made ;
Crowds of tired souls like thine are laid
This night beneath the self-same placid shade.
They who rest here
Wake with heaven near,
Rest in the Shadow of the Rock.

The Shadow of the Rock !
Pilgrim ! sleep sound ;
In night's swift hours with silent bound
The Rock will put thee over leagues of ground,
Gaining more way
By night than day ;
Rest in the Shadow of the Rock.

The Shadow of the Rock !
One day of pain
Thou scarce wilt hope the Rock to gain,
Yet there wilt sleep thy last sleep on the plain ;
And only wake
In heaven's day-break,
Rest in the Shadow of the Rock.

THE WILL OF GOD.

I worship Thee, sweet Will of God!
   And all Thy ways adore,
And every day I live I seem
   To love Thee more and more.

Thou wert the end, the blessed rule
   Of our Saviour's toils and tears;
Thou wert the passion of His Heart
   Those Three-and-thirty years.

And He hath breathed into my soul
   A special love of Thee,
A love to lose my will in His,
   And by that loss be free.

I love to see Thee bring to nought
   The plans of wily men;
When simple hearts outwit the wise,
   Oh Thou art loveliest then!

The headstrong world, it presses hard
   Upon the Church full oft,
And then how easily Thou turn'st
   The hard ways into soft.

I love to kiss each print where Thou
   Hast set Thine unseen feet:
I cannot fear Thee, blessed Will!
   Thine empire is so sweet.

When obstacles and trials seem
   Like prison-walls to be,
I do the little I can do,
   And leave the rest to Thee.

I know not what it is to doubt ;
  My heart is ever gay ;
I run no risk, for come what will
  Thou always hast Thy way.

I have no cares, O blessed Will !
  For all my cares are Thine ;
I live in triumph, Lord ! for Thou
  Hast made Thy triumphs mine.

And when it seems no chance or change
  From grief can set me free,
Hope finds its strength in helplessness,
  And gaily waits on Thee.

Man's weakness waiting upon God
  Its end can never miss,
For men on earth no work can do
  More angel-like than this.

Ride on, ride on triumphantly,
  Thou glorious Will ! ride on ;
Faith's pilgrim sons behind Thee take
  The road that Thou hast gone.

He always wins who sides with God,
  To him no chânce is lost ;
God's will is sweetest to him when
  It triumphs at his cost.

Ill that He blesses is our good,
  And unblest good is ill ;
And all is right that seems most wrong,
  If it be His sweet will !

EVENING HYMN AT THE ORATORY.

SWEET Saviour! bless us ere we go;
   Thy word into our minds instil;
And make our lukewarm hearts to glow
   With lowly love and fervent will.
Through life's long day and death's dark night,
O gentle Jesus! be our light.

The day is done; its hours have run;
   And Thou hast taken count of all,
The scanty triumphs grace hath won,
   The broken vow, the frequent fall.
Through life's long day and death's dark night,
O gentle Jesus! be our light.

Grant us, dear Lord! from evil ways
   True absolution and release;
And bless us more than in past days
   With purity and inward peace.
Through life's long day and death's dark night,
O gentle Jesus! be our light.

Do more than pardon; give us joy,
   Sweet fear and sober liberty,
And loving hearts without alloy,
   That only long to be like Thee.
Through life's long day and death's dark night,
O gentle Jesus! be our light.

Labor is sweet, for Thou hast toiled,
   And care is light, for Thou hast cared;
Let not our works with self be soiled,
   Nor in unsimple ways ensnared,
Through life's long day and death's dark night,
O gentle Jesus! be our light.

For all we love, the poor, the sad,
  The sinful, — unto Thee we call;
Oh let Thy mercy make us glad;
  Thou art our Jesus and our All.
Through life's long day and death's dark night,
O gentle Jesus ! be our light.

Sweet Saviour ! bless us; night is come;
  Mary and Philip near us be !
Good angels watch about our home,
  And we are one day nearer Thee.
Through life's long day and death's dark night,
O gentle Jesus ! be our light.

THE RIGHT MUST WIN.

OH it is hard to work for God,
  To rise and take His part
Upon this battlefield of earth,
  And not sometimes lose heart?

He hides Himself so wondrously,
  As though there were no God;
He is least seen when all the powers
  Of ill are most abroad.

Or He deserts us at the hour
  The fight is all but lost;
And seems to leave us to ourselves
  Just when we need Him most.

Yes, there is less to try our faith,
  In our mysterious creed,
Than in the godless look of earth,
  In these our hours of need.

Ill masters good; good seems to change
   To ill with greatest ease ;
And, worst of all, the good with good
   Is at cross purposes.

The Church, the Sacraments, the Faith,
   Their uphill journey take,
Lose here what there they gain, and, if
   We lean upon them, break.

It is not so, but so it looks ;
   And we lose courage then ;
And doubts will come if God hath kept
   His promises to men.

Ah ! God is other than we think ;
   His ways are far above,
Far beyond reason's height, and reached
   Only by childlike love.

The look, the fashion of God's ways
   Love's lifelong study are ;
She can be bold, and guess, and act,
   When reason would not dare.

She has a prudence of her own ;
   Her step is firm and free ;
Yet there is cautious science too
   In her simplicity.

Workmen of God ! Oh lose not heart,
   But learn what God is like ;
And in the darkest battlefield
   Thou shalt know where to strike.

Thrice blest is he to whom is given
   The instinct that can tell
That God is on the field when he
   Is most invisible.

Blest too is he who can divine
  Where real right doth lie,
And dares to take the side that seems
  Wrong to man's blindfold eye.

Then learn to scorn the praise of men,
  And learn to lose with God;
For Jesus won the world through shame,
  And beckons thee His road.

God's glory is a wondrous thing,
  Most strange in all its ways,
And, of all things on earth, least like
  What men agree to praise.

As He can endless glory weave
  From what men reckon shame,
In His own world He is content
  To play a losing game.

Muse on His justice, downcast soul!
  Muse and take better heart;
Back with thine angel to the field,
  And bravely do thy part.

God's justice is a bed, where we
  Our anxious hearts may lay,
And, weary with ourselves, may sleep
  Our discontent away.

For right is right, since God is God;
  And right the day must win;
To doubt would be disloyalty,
  To falter would be sin.

PERFECTION.

Oh how the thought of God attracts
  And draws the heart from earth,
And sickens it of passing shows
  And dissipating mirth!

'T is not enough to save our souls,
  To shun the eternal fires;
The thought of God will rouse the heart
  To more sublime desires.

God only is the creature's home,
  Though rough and strait the road;
Yet nothing less can satisfy
  The love that longs for God.

Oh utter but the Name of God
  Down in your heart of hearts,
And see how from the world at once
  All tempting light departs.

A trusting heart, a yearning eye,
  Can win their way above;
If mountains can be moved by faith,
  Is there less power in love?

How little of that road, my soul!
  How little hast thou gone!
Take heart, and let the thought of God
  Allure thee further on.

The freedom from all wilful sin,
  The Christian's daily task, —
Oh these are graces far below
  What longing love would ask!

Dole not thy duties out to God,
  But let thy hand be free:

Look long at Jesus; His sweet Blood,
  How was it dealt to thee?

The perfect way is hard to flesh;
  It is not hard to love;
If thou wert sick for want of God,
  How swiftly wouldst thou move!

Good is the cloister's silent shade,
  Cold watch and pining fast;
Better the mission's wearing strife,
  If there thy lot be cast.

Yet none of these perfection needs : —
  Keep thy heart calm all day,
And catch the words the Spirit there
  From hour to hour may say.

Then keep thy conscience sensitive;
  No inward token miss:
And go where grace entices thee; —
  Perfection lies in this.

Be docile to thine unseen Guide,
  Love Him as He loves thee;
Time and obedience are enough,
  And thou a saint shalt be.

THE PILGRIMS OF THE NIGHT.

HARK! hark! my soul! angelic songs are swelling
  O'er earth's green fields and ocean's wave-beat shore;
How sweet the truth those blessèd strains are telling
  Of that new life when sin shall be no more!
        Angels of Jesus,
          Angels of light,
        Singing to welcome
          The pilgrims of the night!

Darker than night life's shadows fall around us,
  And, like benighted men, we miss our mark;
God hides Himself, and grace hath scarcely found us.
  Ere death finds out his victims in the dark.
        Angels of Jesus,
          Angels of light,
        Singing to welcome
          The pilgrims of the night!

Onward we go, for still we hear them singing,
  Come, weary souls! for Jesus bids you come!
And through the dark, its echoes sweetly ringing,
  The music of the Gospel leads us home.
        Angels of Jesus,
          Angels of light,
        Singing to welcome
          The pilgrims of the night!

Far, far away, like bells at evening pealing,
  The voice of Jesus sounds o'er land and sea,
And laden souls, by thousands meekly stealing,
  Kind Shepherd! turn their weary steps to Thee.
        Angels of Jesus,
          Angels of light,
        Singing to welcome
          The pilgrims of the night!

Rest comes at length; though life be long and dreary,
  The day must dawn, and darksome night be past;
All journeys end in welcomes to the weary,
  And heaven, the heart's true home, will come at last.
        Angels of Jesus,
          Angels of light,
        Singing to welcome
          The pilgrims of the night!

Cheer up, my soul! faith's moonbeams softly glisten
  Upon the breast of life's most troubled sea;
And it will cheer thy drooping heart to listen
    To those brave songs which angels mean for thee.
          Angels of Jesus,
            Angels of light,
          Singing to welcome
            The pilgrims of the night!

Angels! sing on, your faithful watches keeping,
  Sing us sweet fragments of the songs above;
While we toil on, and soothe ourselves with weeping,
    Till life's long night shall break in endless love.
          Angels of Jesus,
            Angels of light,
          Singing to welcome
            The pilgrims of the night!

JOHN KEBLE.

FROM 'THE CHRISTIAN YEAR.'[12]

EVENING.

Abide with us : for it is toward evening, and the day is far spent. — St. Luke xxiv. 29.

'T is gone, that bright and orbèd blaze,
Fast fading from our wistful gaze ;
Yon mantling cloud has hid from sight
The last faint pulse of quivering light.

In darkness and in weariness
The traveller on his way must press,
No gleam to watch on tree or tower,
Whiling away the lonesome hour.

Sun of my soul ! Thou Saviour dear,
It is not night if Thou be near :
Oh may no earth-born cloud arise
To hide Thee from thy servant's eyes.

When round thy wondrous works below
My searching rapturous glance I throw,
Tracing out Wisdom, Power, and Love,
In earth or sky, in stream or grove ; —

Or by the light thy words disclose
Watch Time's full river as it flows,
Scanning thy gracious Providence,
Where not too deep for mortal sense : —

15

When with dear friends sweet talk I hold,
And all the flowers of life unfold; —
Let not my heart within me burn,
Except in all I Thee discern.

When the soft dews of kindly sleep
My wearied eyelids gently steep,
Be my last thought, how sweet to rest
For ever on my Saviour's breast.

Abide with me from morn till eve,
For without Thee I cannot live:
Abide with me when night is nigh,
For without Thee I dare not die.

Thou Framer of the light and dark,
Steer through the tempest thine own ark:
Amid the howling wintry sea
We are in port if we have Thee.

The Rulers of this Christian land,
'Twixt Thee and us ordained to stand, —
Guide Thou their course, O Lord, aright,
Let all do all as in thy sight.

Oh by thine own sad burthen, borne
So meekly up the hill of scorn,
Teach Thou thy Priests their daily cross
To bear as thine, nor count it loss!

If some poor wandering child of thine
Have spurned, to-day, the voice divine,
Now, Lord, the gracious work begin;
Let him no more lie down in sin.

Watch by the sick: enrich the poor
With blessings from thy boundless store:
Be every mourner's sleep to-night
Like infants' slumbers, pure and light.

Come near and bless us when we wake,
Ere through the world our way we take :
· Till in the ocean of thy love
We lose ourselves in heaven above.

FIRST SUNDAY IN LENT.

THE CITY OF REFUGE.

Haste thee, escape thither ; for I cannot do anything till thou be
come thither.   Therefore the name of the city was called Zoar. — GEN-
ESIS xix. 22.

'ANGEL of wrath ! why linger in mid air,
    While the devoted city's cry
Louder and louder swells ? and canst thou spare,
    Thy full-charged vial standing by ? '
Thus, with stern voice, unsparing Justice pleads :
    He hears her not — with softened gaze
His eye is following where sweet Mercy leads,
And till she give the sign, his fury stays.

Guided by her, along the mountain road,
    Far through the twilight of the morn,
With hurrying footsteps from th' accursed abode
    He sees the holy household borne :
Angels, or more, on either hand are nigh,
    To speed them o'er the tempting plain,
Lingering in heart, and with frail sidelong eye
Seeking how near they may unharmed remain.

' Ah wherefore gleam those upland slopes so fair ?
    And why, through every woodland arch,
Swells yon bright vale, as Eden rich and rare,
    Where Jordan winds his stately march ;
If all must be forsaken, ruined all,
    If God have planted but to burn ? —

Surely not yet th' avenging shower will fall,
Though to my home for one last look I turn.'

Thus while they waver, surely long ago
    They had provoked the withering blast,
But that the merciful Avengers know
    Their frailty well, and hold them fast.
'Haste, for thy life escape, nor look behind ' —
    Ever in thrilling sounds like these
They check the wandering eye, severely kind,
Nor let the sinner lose his soul at ease.

And when, o'erwearied with the steep ascent,
    We for a nearer refuge crave,
One little spot of ground in mercy lent,
    One hour of home before the grave,
Oft in his pity o'er his children weak,
    His hand withdraws the penal fire,
And where we fondly cling, forbears to wreak
Full vengeance, till our hearts are weaned entire.

Thus, by the merits of one righteous man,
    The Church, our Zoar, shall abide,
Till she abuse, so sore, her lengthened span,
    Even Mercy's self her face must hide.
Then, onward yet a step, thou hard-won soul ;
    Though in the Church thou know thy place,
The mountain farther lies — there seek thy goal,
There breathe at large, o'erpast thy dangerous race.

Sweet is the smile of home ; the mutual look
    When hearts are of each other sure ;
Sweet all the joys that crowd the household nook,
    The haunt of all affections pure ;
Yet in the world even these abide, and we
    Above the world our calling boast:
Once gain the mountain top, and thou art free :
Till then, who rest, presume ; who turn to look, are lost.

MONDAY BEFORE EASTER.

CHRIST WAITING FOR THE CROSS.

Doubtless thou art our father, though Abraham be ignorant of us, and Israel acknowledge us not. — ISAIAH lxiii. 16.

'FATHER to me Thou art and Mother dear,
    And Brother too, kind husband of my heart'—
So speaks Andromache in boding fear,
    Ere from her last embrace her hero part—
So evermore, by Faith's undying glow,
We own the Crucified in weal or woe.

Strange to our ears the church-bells of our home,
    The fragrance of our old paternal fields
May be forgotten; and the time may come
    When the babe's kiss no sense of pleasure yields
Even to the doting mother: but thine own
Thou never canst forget, nor leave alone.

There are who sigh that no fond heart is theirs,
    None loves them best — O vain and selfish sigh!
Out of the bosom of His love He spares —
    The Father spares the Son, for thee to die:
For thee He died — for thee He lives again:
O'er thee He watches in His boundless reign.

Thou art as much His care, as if beside
    Nor man nor angel lived in heaven or earth:
Thus sunbeams pour alike their glorious tide
    To light up worlds, or wake an insect's mirth:
They shine and shine with unexhausted store —
Thou art thy Saviour's darling — seek no more.

On thee and thine, thy warfare and thine end,
    Even in His hour of agony He thought,
When, ere the final pang His soul should rend,
    The ransomed spirits one by one were brought

To his mind's eye — two silent nights and days
In calmness for His far-seen hour He stays.

Ye vaulted cells where martyred seers of old
    Far in the rocky walls of Sion sleep,
Green terraces and archèd fountains cold,
    Where lies the cypress shade so still and deep,
Dear sacred haunts of glory and of woe,
Help us, one hour, to trace His musings high and low:

One heart-ennobling hour! It may not be:
    Th' unearthly thoughts have passed from earth away,
And fast as evening sunbeams from the sea
    Thy footsteps all in Sion's deep decay
Were blotted from the holy ground: yet dear
Is every stone of hers; for Thou wast surely here.

There is a spot within this sacred dale
    That felt Thee kneeling — touched thy prostrate brow:
One angel knows it. O might prayer avail
    To win that knowledge! sure each holy vow
Less quickly from th' unstable soul would fade,
Offered where Christ in agony was laid.

Might tear of ours once mingle with the blood
    That from His aching brow by moonlight fell,
Over the mournful joy our thoughts would brood,
    Till they had framed within a guardian spell
To chase repining fancies, as they rise,
Like birds of evil wing, to mar our sacrifice.

So dreams the heart self-flattering, fondly dreams; —
    Else wherefore, when the bitter waves o'erflow,
Miss we the light, Gethsemane, that streams
    From thy dear name, where in His page of woe
It shines, a pale kind star in winter's sky?
Who vainly reads it there, in vain had seen Him die.

SECOND SUNDAY AFTER EASTER.

BALAAM.

He hath said, which heard the words of God, and knew the knowledge of the most High, which saw the vision of the Almighty, falling into a trance, but having his eyes open: I shall see him, but not now: I shall behold him, but not nigh: there shall come a Star out of Jacob, and a Sceptre shall rise out of Israel, and shall smite the corners of Moab, and destroy all the children of Sheth. — NUMBERS xxiv. 16, 17.

O FOR a sculptor's hand,
That thou mightst take thy stand,
Thy wild hair floating on the eastern breeze,
Thy tranced yet open gaze
Fixed on the desert haze,
As one who deep in heaven some airy pageant sees.

In outline dim and vast
Their fearful shadows cast
The giant forms of empires on their way
To ruin: one by one
They tower and they are gone,
Yet in the Prophet's soul the dreams of avarice stay.

No sun or star so bright
In all the world of light
That they should draw to heaven his downward eye:
He hears th' Almighty's word,
He sees the angel's sword,
Yet low upon the earth his heart and treasure lie.

Lo from yon argent field,
To him and us revealed,
One gentle star glides down, on earth to dwell.
Chained as they are below
Our eyes may see it glow,
And as it mounts again, may track its brightness well.

To him it glared afar,
A token of wild war,
The banner of his Lord's victorious wrath:
    But close to us it gleams,
    Its soothing lustre streams
Around our home's green walls, and on our churchway path.

We in the tents abide
Which he at distance eyed
Like goodly cedars by the waters spread,
    While seven red altar-fires
    Rose up in wavy spires,
Where on the mount he watched his sorceries dark and
    dread.

He watched till morning's ray
On lake and meadow lay,
And willow-shaded streams, that silent sweep
    Around the bannered lines,
    Where by their several signs
The desert-wearied tribes in sight of Canaan sleep.

He watched till knowledge came
Upon his soul like flame,
Not of those magic fires at random caught:
    But true prophetic light
    Flashed o'er him, high and bright,
Flashed once, and died away, and left his darkened thought.

And can he choose but fear,
Who feels his God so near,
That when he fain would curse, his powerless tongue
    In blessing only moves? —
    Alas! the world he loves
Too close around his heart her tangling veil hath flung.

Sceptre and Star divine,
Who in Thine inmost shrine
Hast made us worshippers, O claim Thine own;
More than thy seers we know —
O teach our love to grow
Up to thy heavenly light, and reap what Thou hast sown.

SUNDAY AFTER ASCENSION.

SEED TIME.

As every man hath received the gift, even so minister the same one to another, as good stewards of the manifold grace of God. — 1 St. Peter iv. 10.

THE Earth that in her genial breast
Makes for the down a kindly nest,
Where wafted by the warm south-west
It floats at pleasure,
Yields, thankful, of her very best,
To nurse her treasure:

True to her trust, tree, herb, or reed,
She renders for each scattered seed,
And to her Lord with duteous heed
Gives large increase:
Thus year by year she works unfeed,
And will not cease.

Woe worth these barren hearts of ours,
Where Thou hast set celestial flowers,
And watered with more balmy showers,
Than e'er distilled
In Eden, on th' ambrosial bowers —
Yet nought we yield.

Largely Thou givest, gracious Lord,
Largely thy gifts should be restored;
Freely Thou givest, and thy word
  Is, ' freely give.'
He only, who forgets to hoard,
  Has learned to live.

Wisely Thou givest — all around
Thine equal rays are resting found,
Yet varying so on various ground
  They pierce and strike,
That not two roseate cups are crowned
  With dew alike:

Even so, in silence, likest Thee,
Steals on soft-handed Charity,
Tempering her gifts, that seem so free,
  By time and place,
Till not a woe the bleak world see,
  But finds her grace:

Eyes to the blind, and to the lame
Feet, and to sinners wholesome blame,·
To starving bodies food and flame
  By turn she brings,
To humbled souls, that sink for shame,
  Lends heaven ward wings:

Leads them the way our Saviour went,
And shows Love's treasure yet unspent;
As when th' unclouded heavens were rent
  Opening his road,
Nor yet his Holy Spirit sent
  To our abode.

Ten days th' eternal doors displayed
Were wondering, so th' Almighty bade,
Whom Love enthroned would send, in aid

Of souls that mourn,
Left orphans in Earth's dreary shade
As soon as born.

Open they stand, that prayers in throngs
May rise on high, and holy songs,
Such incense as of right belongs
        To the true shrine,
Where stands the Healer of all wrongs
        In light divine;

The golden censer in his hand,
He offers hearts from every land,
Tied to his own by gentlest band
        Of silent Love:
About Him wingèd blessings stand
        In act to move.

A little while, and they shall fleet
From Heaven to Earth, attendants meet
On the life-giving Paraclete
        Speeding his flight,
With all that sacred is and sweet,
        On saints to light.

Apostles, Prophets, Pastors, all
Shall feel the shower of Mercy fall,
And starting at th' Almighty's call,
        Give what He gave,
Till their high deeds the world appal,
        And sinners save.

TWENTIETH SUNDAY AFTER TRINITY.

MOUNTAIN SCENERY.

Hear ye, O mountains, the Lord's controversy, and ye strong foundations of the earth. — MICAH vi. 2.

WHERE is thy favored haunt, eternal Voice,
    The region of thy choice,
Where, undisturbed by sin and earth, the soul
    Owns thine entire control ? —
'T is on the mountain's summit dark and high,
    When storms are hurrying by :
'T is 'mid the strong foundations of the earth,
    Where torrents have their birth.

No sounds of worldly toil ascending there,
    Mar the full burst of prayer ;
Lone Nature feels that she may freely breathe,
    And round us and beneath
Are heard her sacred tones : the fitful sweep
    Of winds across the steep,
Through withered bents — romantic note and clear,
    Meet for a hermit's ear, —

The wheeling kite's wild solitary cry,
    And, scarcely heard so high,
The dashing waters when the air is still
    From many a torrent rill
That winds unseen beneath the shaggy fell,
    Tracked by the blue mist well :
Such sounds as make deep silence in the heart
    For Thought to do her part.

'T is then we hear the voice of God within,
    Pleading with care and sin :

'Child of my love ! how have I wearied thee ?
    Why wilt thou err from me ?
Have I not brought thee from the house of slaves,
    Parted the drowning waves,
And set my saints before thee in the way,
    Lest thou shouldst faint or stray ?

'What ? was the promise made to thee alone ?
    Art thou th' excepted one ?
An heir of glory without grief or pain ?
    O vision false and vain !
There lies thy cross ; beneath it meekly bow ;
    It fits thy stature now :
Who scornful pass it with averted eye,
    'T will crush them by and by.

' Raise thy repining eyes, and take true measure
    Of thine eternal treasure ;
The Father of thy Lord can grudge thee nought,
    The world for thee was bought,
And as this landscape broad — earth, sea, and sky —
    All centres in thine eye,
So all God does, if rightly understood,
    Shall work thy final good.'

TWENTY-FOURTH SUNDAY AFTER TRINITY.

IMPERFECTION OF HUMAN SYMPATHY.

The heart knoweth his own bitterness ; and a stranger doth not in-
termeddle with his joy. — PROVERBS xiv. 10.

WHY should we faint and fear to live alone,
    Since all alone, so Heaven has willed, we die ;
Nor even the tenderest heart, and next our own,
    Knows half the reasons why we smile and sigh ?

Each in his hidden sphere of joy or woe
   Our hermit spirits dwell, and range apart,
Our eyes see all around in gloom or glow —
   Hues of their own, fresh borrowed from the heart.

And well it is for us our God should feel
   Alone our secret throbbings : so our prayer
May readier spring to Heaven, nor spend its zeal
   On cloud-born idols of this lower air.

For if one heart in perfect sympathy
   Beat with another, answering love for love,
Weak mortals, all entranced, on earth would lie,
   Nor listen for those purer strains above.

Or what if Heaven for once its searching light
   Lent to some partial eye, disclosing all
The rude bad thoughts, that in our bosom's night
   Wander at large, nor heed Love's gentle thrall ?

Who would not shun the dreary uncouth place ?
   As if, fond leaning where her infant slept,
A mother's arm a serpent should embrace :
   So might we friendless live, and die unwept.

Then keep the softening veil in mercy drawn,
   Thou who canst love us, tho' Thou read us true ;
As on the bosom of th' aerial lawn
   Melts in dim haze each coarse ungentle hue.

So too may soothing Hope thy leave enjoy
   Sweet visions of long severed hearts to frame :
Though absence may impair, or cares annoy,
   Some constant mind may draw us still the same.

We in dark dreams are tossing to and fro,
   Pine with regret, or sicken with despair,
The while she bathes us in her own chaste glow,
   And with our memory wings her own fond prayer.

O bliss of child-like innocence, and love
　　Tried to old age! creative power to win,
And raise new worlds, where happy fancies rove,
　　Forgetting quite this grosser world of sin.

Bright are their dreams, because their thoughts are clear,
　　Their memory cheering: but th' earth-stained spright,
Whose wakeful musings are of guilt and fear,
　　Must hover nearer earth, and less in light.

Farewell, for her, th' ideal scenes so fair —
　　Yet not farewell her hope, since Thou hast deigned,
Creator of all hearts! to own and share
　　The woe of what Thou mad'st, and we have stained.

Thou know'st our bitterness — our joys are thine —
　　No stranger Thou to all our wanderings wild:
Nor could we bear to think how every line
　　Of us, thy darkened likeness and defiled,

Stands in full sunshine of thy piercing eye,
　　But that Thou call'st us Brethren: sweet repose
Is in that word — the Lord who dwells on high
　　Knows all, yet loves us better than He knows.

ALL SAINTS' DAY.

Hurt not the earth, neither the sea, nor the trees, till we have sealed
the servants of our God in their foreheads. — REVELATION vii. 3.

WHY blow'st thou not, thou wintry wind,
　　Now every leaf is brown and sere,
And idly droops, to thee resigned,
　　The fading chaplet of the year?
Yet wears the pure aerial sky
Her summer veil, half drawn on high,
Of silvery haze, and dark and still
The shadows sleep on every slanting hill.

How quiet shows the woodland scene !
  Each flower and tree, its duty done,
Reposing in decay serene,
  Like weary men when age is won,
Such calm old age as conscience pure
And self-commanding hearts ensure,
Waiting their summons to the sky,
Content to live, but not afraid to die.

Sure if our eyes were purged to trace
  God's unseen armies hovering round,
We should behold by angels' grace
  The four strong winds of Heaven fast bound,
Their downward sweep a moment staid
On ocean cove and forest glade,
Till the last flower of autumn shed
Her funeral odors on her dying bed.

So in thine awful armory, Lord,
  The lightnings of the judgment day
Pause yet awhile, in mercy stored,
  Till willing hearts wear quite away
Their earthly stains; and spotless shine
On every brow in light divine
The Cross by angel hands impressed,
The seal of glory won and pledge of promised rest.

Little they dream, those haughty souls
  Whom empires own with bended knee,
What lowly fate their own controls,
  Together linked by Heaven's decree ; —
As bloodhounds hush their baying wild
To wanton with some fearless child,
So Famine waits, and War with greedy eyes,
Till some repenting heart be ready for the skies.

Think ye the spires that glow so bright
  In front of yonder setting sun,
Stand by their own unshaken might?
  No — where th' upholding grace is won,
We dare not ask, nor Heaven would tell,
But sure from many a hidden dell,
From many a rural nook unthought of there,
Rises for that proud world the saints' prevailing prayer.

On, champions blest, in Jesus' name,
  Short be your strife, your triumph full,
Till every heart have caught your flame,
  And lightened of the world's misrule,
Ye soar those elder saints to meet,
Gathered long since at Jesus' feet,
No world of passions to destroy,
Your prayers and struggles o'er, your task all praise and joy.

16

HORATIUS BONAR.

THE SHEPHERDS' PLAIN.

'Dum servant *oves* invenerunt *Agnum* Dei.' — JEROME.

BLESSÈD night, when first that plain
Echoed with the joyful strain, —
'Peace has come to earth again.'

Blessèd hills, that heard the song
Of the glorious angel-throng,
Swelling all your slopes along.

Happy shepherds, on whose ear
Fell the tidings glad and dear, —
'God to man is drawing near.'

Happy shepherds, on whose eye
Shone the glory from on high,
Of the heavenly Majesty.

Happy, happy Bethlehem,
Judah's least but brightest gem,
Where the rod from Jesse's stem,

Scion of a princely race,
Sprung in heaven's own perfect grace,
Yet in feeble lowliness.

This the woman's promised seed,
Abram's mighty son indeed;
Succorer of earth's great need.

This the victor in our war,
This the glory seen afar,
This the light of Jacob's star!

Happy Judah, rise and own
Him, the heir of David's throne,
David's Lord, and David's Son.

Babe of promise, born at last,
After weary ages past,
When our hopes were overcast.

Babe of weakness, can it be,
That earth's last great victory
Is to be achieved by thee?

Child of meekness, can it be
That the proud rebellious knee
Of this world shall bend to thee?

Child of poverty, art thou
He to whom all heaven shall bow,
And all earth shall pay the vow?

Can that feeble head alone
Bear the weight of such a crown,
As belongs to David's Son?

Can these helpless hands of thine,
Wield a sceptre so divine,
As belongs to Jesse's line?

Heir of pain and toil, whom none
In this evil day will own,
Art thou the Eternal One?

Thou, o'er whom the sword and rod
Wave, in haste, to drink thy blood,
Art thou very Son of God?

Thus revealed to shepherds' eyes,
Hidden from the great and wise,
Entering earth in lowly guise, —

Entering by this narrow door,
Laid upon this rocky floor,
Placed in yonder manger poor.

We adore thee as our King,
And to thee our song we sing;
Our best offering to thee bring.

Guarded by the shepherds' rod,
'Mid their flock, thy poor abode,
Thus we own thee, Lamb of God.

Lamb of God, thy lowly name,
King of kings, we thee proclaim;
Heaven and earth shall hear its fame.

Bearer of our sins' sad load,
Wielder of the iron rod,
Judah's Lion, Lamb of God !

Mighty King of righteousness,
King of glory, king of peace,
Never shall thy kingdom cease !

Thee, earth's heir and Lord, we own
Raise again its fallen throne,
Take its everlasting crown.

Blessèd Babe of Bethlehem,
Owner of earth's diadem,
Claim, and wear the radiant gem.

Scatter darkness with thy light,
End the sorrows of our night,
Speak the word, and all is bright.

Spoil the spoiler of the earth,
Bring creation's second birth,
Promised day of song and mirth.

'T is thine Israel's voice that calls,
Build again thy Salem's walls,
Dwell within her holy halls.

'T is thy Church's voice that cries,
Rend these long unrended skies,
Bridegroom of the Church, arise.

Take to thee thy power and reign,
Purify this earth again ;
Cleanse it from each curse and stain.

Sun of peace, no longer stay,
Let the shadows flee away,
And the long night end in day.

Let the dayspring from on high,
That arose in Judah's sky,
Cover earth eternally.

Babe of Bethlehem, to thee,
Infant of eternity,
Everlasting glory be !

A LITTLE WHILE.

BEYOND the smiling and the weeping
    I shall be soon ;
Beyond the waking and the sleeping,
Beyond the sowing and the reaping,
    I shall be soon.
  Love, rest, and home !
  Sweet hope !
  Lord, tarry not, but come.

Beyond the blooming and the fading,
    I shall be soon ;
Beyond the shining and the shading,
Beyond the hoping and the dreading,
    I shall be soon.
  Love, rest, and home !
  Sweet hope !
  Lord, tarry not, but come.

Beyond the rising and the setting
    I shall be soon ;
Beyond the calming and the fretting,
Beyond remembering and forgetting,
    I shall be soon.
  Love, rest, and home !
  Sweet hope !
  Lord, tarry not, but come.

Beyond the gathering and the strowing
    I shall be soon ;
Beyond the ebbing and the flowing,
Beyond the coming and the going,
    I shall be soon.
  Love, rest, and home !
  Sweet hope !
  Lord, tarry not, but come.

Beyond the parting and the meeting
    I shall be soon ;
Beyond the farewell and the greeting,
Beyond this pulse's fever-beating,
    I shall be soon. '
  Love, rest, and home !
  Sweet hope !
  Lord, tarry not, but come.

Beyond the frost-chain and the fever
    I shall be soon;
Beyond the rock-waste and the river,
Beyond the ever and the never,
    I shall be soon.
   Love, rest, and home!
   Sweet hope!
   Lord, tarry not, but come.

THE NIGHT AND THE MORNING.

To dream a troubled dream, and then awaken
   To the soft gladness of a summer sky;
To dream ourselves alone, unloved, forsaken,
   And then to wake 'mid smiles, and love, and joy;

To look at evening on the storm's rude motion,
   The cloudy tumult of the fretted deep;
And then at day-burst upon that same ocean,
   Soothed to the stillness of its stillest sleep —

So runs our course — so tells the church her story,
   So to the end shall it be ever told;
Brief shame on earth, but after shame the glory,
   That wanes not, dims not, never waxes old.

Lord Jesus, come, and end this troubled dreaming!
   Dark shadows vanish, rosy twilight break!
Morn of the true and real, burst forth, calm-beaming
   Day of the beautiful, arise, awake!

HENRY ALFORD.

'COME UNTO THE FEAST.'

RISE, said the Master, come unto the feast : —
She heard the call and rose with willing feet ;
But thinking it not otherwise than meet
For such a bidding to put on her best,
She is gone from us for a few short hours
Into her bridal closet, there to wait
For the unfolding of the palace gate,
That gives her entrance to the blissful bowers.
We have not seen her yet, though we have been
Full often to her chamber door, and oft
Have listened underneath the postern green,
And laid fresh flowers, and whispered short and soft ;
But she hath made no answer ; and the day
From the clear west is fading fast away.

THE DEAD.

THE dead alone are great !
While heavenly plants abide on earth,
The soil is one of dewless death ;
But when they die, a mourning shower
Comes down and makes their memories flower
With odors sweet though late.

The dead alone are fair !
While they are with us, strange lines play
Before our eyes, and chase away
God's light ; but let them pale and die,

And swell the stores of memory —
    There is no envy there.

    The dead alone are dear!
While they are here, long shadows fall
From our own forms, and darken all;
But when they leave us, all the shade
Is round our own sad footsteps made,
    And they are bright and clear.

    The dead alone are blest!
While they are here, clouds mar the day
And bitter snow-falls nip their May;
But when the tempest-time is done,
The light and heat of Heaven's own sun
    Broods on their land of rest.

THE PILOT.

My bark is wafted on the strand
    By breath divine;
And on the helm there rests a hand
    Other than mine.

One who was known in storms to sail,
    I have on board;
Above the roaring of the gale,
    I have my Lord.

He holds me when the billows smite;
    I shall not fall.
If sharp, 't is short; if long, 't is light —
    He tempers all.

Safe to the land! safe to the land
    The end is this,
And then with Him go hand in hand
    Far into bliss.

CHAUNCEY HARE TOWNSHEND.

FROM 'SERMONS IN SONNETS.' [18]

XIII.

O, speak good of the Lord, all ye works of his, in all places of his
dominions. — PSALM ciii. 22.

ANSWER, with all thy pulses, throb and speak,
Thou tender, palpitating heart of God!
Through earth, through air, and caves of ocean broad
All thronged with myriad beings, strong or weak
In terror, or deep love! Flush on the cheek
Of morn, breathe sweet from evening's dewy sod!
Tremble in music, 'mid the choral ode
That from the soft vale to the mountain peak
Whispers or thunders! — Art Thou cold, or dead,
Or vengeful? — Hush! A holy silence reigns:
That our own heart, stilling our throbbing veins,
And only with its own assurance fed,
May be itself Thy answer and abode,
O tender, palpitating heart of God!

XVI.

Who is he that condemneth? It is Christ that died. — ROMANS
viii. 24.

PERCHANCE I whisper to my happy soul,
'Thought of past sin should burthens on thee lay,
And send thee weeping on a dreary way,
And self-abased.' — But then, beyond control

Of such mistrust, new pleasures still unroll
Their calm sweet glories to the visual ray
Of inward faith; and heavenly voices say
Unto my spirit, 'Joy is the great pole
Of thy existence. Not as mortals do
The Saviour doth: He raiseth from the ground
The crushed one, and restores from every wound
The self-respect of man. No friend untrue
Is He, with past offence to make thee sad.
Smiles He? Thou canst not choose but to be glad.'

XXXI.

Marvel not that I said, Ye must be born again. — St. John iii.

Born out of God, with pain and bitter tears,
Back unto God we must be born again,
Also with struggle and reluctant pain!
Our mortal days are types of greater years;
And all that to our body's eye appears
In this great universe of loss and gain
Shadows our inner life, and is a chain
That ever linketh us by hopes and fears —
By Terror and by Trust — by Life and Death —
With grandeur. All this world is but a womb
Unto another. As we draw our breath,
We weep as infants do when first they come
Into this orb. So strive we in our thirst
To drink Heaven's air, which pains us at the first.

XXXIII.

Perfect love casteth out fear. — i John iv. 18.

Seest thou with dread creation's mystery?
Dost thou life's drear enigma beat in vain?
Hast thou a cloud upon thy heart and brain?
Love — only love — and all resolved shall be!

Art thou a fool in this world's subtlety?
Must thou thy fond belief still rue with pain
In all thy fancy deemed was joy and gain?
Love — only love — and wisdom comes to thee!
But, mind, thy love must be a heavenly fire:
For flames, from any earthly shrine ascending,
Kindled in vanity, in woe expire,
And leave experience o'er but ashes bending.
Then, too, the fear of God's avenging rod
Can only be escaped by loving God!

XLVII.

Nevertheless, though I am sometime afraid, yet put I my trust in thee. — PSALM lvi.

FORSAKE me not! Oh, if Thou couldst indeed,
For me were blotted out earth, sea, and sky!
Give me Thyself, what canst Thou then deny?
Thyself, if Thou deny me, all is need!
Without Thee, I am but a worthless weed
Fit to be thrown away. But Thou be nigh,
And flowers, and fruit, and festal luxury,
Unto my drooping and my dearth succeed.
My God, forgive these seeming doubts of Thee!
I play with language, but I feel no fears!
To me Thy faithfulness so true appears,
My very sins have no alarm for me.
Not like the world, disheriting its child,
Dost Thou prove fickle, where Thou once hast smiled.

.

ARTHUR PENRHYN STANLEY.

LIFE AND DEATH.

THE DIVINE LIFE.

'Who lived amongst men.' — (In the Original Draft of the Nicene
Creed — from the Creed of the Church of Palestine.)

WHERE shall we find the Lord?
Where seek his face adored?
Is it apart from men,
In deep sequestered den,
By Jordan's desert flood,
Or mountain solitude,
Or lonely mystic shrine,
That heaven reveals the Life Divine?

Where shall we trace the Lord?
'T was at the festal board,
Amid the innocent mirth
And hallowed joys of earth,
Close neighbor, side by side,
With bridegroom and with bride,
While flowed the cheering wine,
That first appeared the Life Divine.

What was the blest abode
Where dwelt the Son of God?
Beside the busy shore,
Where thousands pressed the door,

Where town with hamlet vied,
Where eager traffic plied, —
There with his calm design
Was wrought and taught the Life Divine.

What were the souls he sought?
What moved his inmost thought?
The friendless and the poor,
The woes none else could cure,
The grateful sinner's cry,
The heathen's heavenward sigh, —
Each in their lot and line
Drew forth the Love and Life Divine.

Where did he rest the while
His most benignant smile?
The little children's charms
That nestled in his arms,
The flowers that round him grew,
The birds that o'er him flew,
Were Nature's sacred sign
To breathe the spell of Love Divine.

Where shall the Lord repose,
When pressed by fears and foes?
Amid the friends he loves,
In Bethany's dear groves,
Or at the parting feast,
Where yearning host and guest
In converse sweet recline,
Is closed in peace the Life Divine.

O Thou who once did come
In holy, happy home,
Teaching and doing good,
To bless our daily food :.

Compassionating mind,
That grasped all human kind,
Even now among us shine,
True glory of the Life Divine.

THE PERFECT DEATH.

Disce mori.

WHERE shall we learn to die?
Go, gaze with steadfast eye
On dark Gethsemane,
Or darker Calvary,
Where, thro' each lingering hour,
The Lord of grace and power,
Most lowly and most High,
Has taught the Christian how to die.

When in the olive shade
His long last prayer he prayed,
When on the cross to heaven
His parting spirit was given,
He showed that to fulfil
The Father's gracious will,
Not asking how or why,
Alone prepares the soul to die.

No word of angry strife,
No anxious cry for life;
By scoff and torture torn
He speaks not scorn for scorn;
Calmly forgiving those
Who deem themselves his foes,
In silent majesty
He points the way at peace to die.

Delighting to the last
In memories of the past;

Glad at the parting meal
In lowly tasks to kneel;
Still yearning to the end
For mother and for friend;
His great humility
Loves in such acts of love to die.

Beyond his depths of woes
A wider thought arose, —
Along his path of gloom,
Thought for his country's doom,
Athwart all pain and grief,
Thought for the contrite thief, —
The far-stretched sympathy
Lives on when all beside shall die.

Bereft, but not alone,
The world is still his own;
The realm of deathless truth
Still breathes immortal youth;
Sure, though in shudd'ring dread,
That all is finishèd.
With purpose fixed and high
The Friend of all mankind must die.

O! by those weary hours
Of slowly ebbing powers,
By those deep lessons heard
In each expiring word;
By that unfailing love
Lifting the soul above,
When our last end is nigh,
So teach us, Lord, with thee to die!

HENRY FRANCIS LYTE.

'MY BELOVĒD IS MINE, AND I AM HIS.'

IMITATED FROM QUARLES.

LONG did I toil, and knew no earthly rest;
   Far did I rove, and found no certain home:
At last I sought them in His sheltering breast,
   Who opes His arms, and bids the weary come.
With Him I found a home, a rest divine;
And I since then am His, and He is mine.

Yes, He is mine! and nought of earthly things,
   Not all the charms of pleasure, wealth, or power,
The fame of heroes, or the pomp of kings,
   Could tempt me to forego His love an hour.
Go, worthless world, I cry, with all that's thine!
Go! I my Saviour's am, and He is mine.

The good I have is from His stores supplied:
   The ill is only what He deems the best.
He for my friend, I'm rich with nought beside;
   And poor without Him, though of all possessed.
Changes may come — I take, or I resign,
Content, while I am His, while He is mine.

Whate'er may change, in Him no change is seen,
   A glorious sun, that wanes not, nor declines:
Above the clouds and storms He walks serene,
   And on His people's inward darkness shines.

All may depart — I fret not nor repine,
While I my Saviour's am, while He is mine.

He stays me falling; lifts me up when down;
  Reclaims me wandering; guards from every foe;
Plants on my worthless brow the victor's crown,
  Which in return before His feet I throw,
Grieved that I cannot better grace His shrine
Who deigns to own me His, as He is mine.

While here, alas! I know but half His love,
  But half discern Him, and but half adore;
But when I meet Him in the realms above,
  I hope to love Him better, praise Him more,
And feel, and tell, amid the choir divine,
How fully I am His, and He is mine.

ABIDE WITH ME.

Abide with us: for it is toward evening, and the day is far spent. —
St. Luke xxiv. 29.

  Abide with me! Fast falls the eventide;
  The darkness deepens: Lord, with me abide!
  When other helpers fail, and comforts flee,
  Help of the helpless, O abide with me!

  Swift to its close ebbs out life's little day;
  Earth's joys grow dim; its glories pass away:
  Change and decay in all around I see;
  O Thou, who changest not, abide with me!

  Not a brief glance I beg, a passing word,
  But as Thou dwell'st with Thy disciples, Lord,
  Familiar, condescending, patient, free,
  Come, not to sojourn, but abide, with me!

Come not in terrors, as the King of kings;
But kind and good, with healing in Thy wings:
Tears for all woes, a heart for every plea.
Come, Friend of sinners, and thus bide with me!

Thou on my head in early youth didst smile,
And, though rebellious and perverse meanwhile,
Thou hast not left me, oft as I left Thee.
On to the close, O Lord, abide with me!

I need Thy presence every passing hour.
What but Thy grace can foil the Tempter's power?
Who like Thyself my guide and stay can be?
Through cloud and sunshine, O abide with me!

I fear no foe with Thee at hand to bless:
Ills have no weight, and tears no bitterness.
Where is death's sting? where, grave, thy victory?
I triumph still, if Thou abide with me.

Hold Thou Thy cross before my closing eyes;
Shine through the gloom, and point me to the skies:
Heaven's morning breaks, and earth's vain shadows flee.
In life and death, O Lord, abide with me!

EDWARD HENRY BICKERSTETH.

'*UNTIL HE COME.*'

' TILL He come ! ' — oh, let the words
Linger on the trembling chords ;
Let the little while between,
In their golden light be seen ;
Let us think how heaven and home
Lie beyond that ' Till He come.'

When the weary ones we love
Enter on their rest above,
Seems the earth so poor and vast,
All our life-joy overcast ?
Hush ! be every murmur dumb ;
It is only ' Till He come.'

Clouds and conflicts round us press ;
Would we have one sorrow less ?
All the sharpness of the cross,
All that tells the world is loss,
Death and darkness and the tomb
Only whisper, ' Till He come.'

See, the feast of love is spread !
Drink the wine and break the bread ;
Sweet memorials ! — till the Lord
Call us round His heavenly board ;
Some from earth, from glory some,
Severed only — till He come.

FROM 'YESTERDAY, TO-DAY, AND FOREVER.'[14]

THE FIRST SABBATH.

FROM BOOK IV., THE CREATION OF ANGELS AND OF MEN.

'BUT now the evening sang her vesper song,
And lit her silver lamps; and vanishing
From view of thy first parents, not from ours,
Messiah rose into the heavens serene,
And, gazing on His fair and finished work
Outstretched before Him, saw that it was good,
And blessed it, and in blessing sanctified;
Nor sooner ceased, than all the marshalled host
Of angels poured their rapture forth in songs
Of Hallelujah and melodious praise.
No jar was heard.   Then sang the morning stars
Together, and the first-born sons of God
Shouted for joy, a shout whose echoes yet
Ring in my ear for jubilant delight.
And He with gracious smile received our praise,
Lingering enamoured o'er His new-made world,
The latest counsel of His love, the while
Your earth her earliest holiest Sabbath kept,
Gladdened with new seraphic symphonies,
And the first echoes of the human voice.

'Too quickly it passed.   And then, ere we retraced
Our several paths of service and of rest,
Messiah called us round His feet once more,
And said to all, " Angels, behold your charge,
Your pledge of fealty, your test of faith.
Thine, Lucifer, of heavenly princes first,
Earth is thy province, of all provinces

Henceforth the one that shares My first regards.
This is thy birthright, which, except thyself,
None can revoke : this firmamental heaven
Thy throne ordained ; and yonder orb thy realm.
Thee, My vicegerent, thee I constitute
God of the world and guardian of mankind.
Only let this thy lofty service link
Thee closer to thy Lord ; apart from Whom
This post will prove thy pinnacle of pride,
Whence falling thou wilt fall to the lowest hell ;
But under Me thy seat of endless joy :
If faithless found, thy everlasting shame ;
If faithful, this thy infinite renown.
For, lowly as seems the earth compared with heaven,
We, the Triune, have sworn that through mankind
The angels and celestial potentates
Shall all receive their full beatitude ;
Yea, that Myself, the Uncreated Word,
Joined to mankind, shall of mankind elect
My Church, My chosen Bride, to share with Me
My glory and My throne and endless love.
I am the Bridegroom, and the Bride is Mine :
But yours, ye angel choirs, may be the joy
Pure and unselfish of the Bridegroom's friend.
Only be humble : ministry is might,
And loving servitude is sceptral rule.
Ye are My servants, and in serving men
Ye honor Me, and I will honor you."

'So spake the Son, and forthwith rose sublime,
His pathway heralded with choral hymns,
Till on the heavenly Zion He regained
His Father's bosom and His Father's throne.'

FREDERICK W. H. MYERS.

LOVE AND FAITH.

Lo if a man magnanimous and tender,
Lo if a woman desperately true,
Make the irrevocable sweet surrender,
Show to each other what the Lord can do, —

Each, as I know, a helping and a healing,
Each to the other strangely a surprise,
Heart to the heart its mystery revealing,
Soul to the soul in melancholy eyes, —

Where wilt thou find a roving or a rending
Able to sever them in twain again?
God hath begun, and God's shall be the ending,
Safe in his bosom and aloof from men.

Her thou mayest separate but shalt not sunder,
Tho' thou distress her for a little while; —
Rapt in a worship, ravished in a wonder,
Stayed on the stedfast promise of a smile,

Scarcely she knoweth if his arms have found her —
Waves of his breath make tremulous the air —
Or if the thrill within her and around her
Be but the distant echo of his prayer.

Nay, and much more; for love in his demanding
Will not be bound in limits of our breath,
Calls her to follow where she sees him standing
Fairer and stronger for the plunge of death; —

Waketh a vision and a voice within her
Sweeter than dreams and clearer than complaint,
' Is it a man thou lovest, and a sinner ?
No ! but a soul, a woman, and a saint ! '

Well, — if to her such prophecy be given,
Strong to illuminate when sight is dim,
Then tho' my Lord be holy in the heaven
How should the heavens sunder me from Him ?

She and her love, — how dimly has she seen him
Dark in a dream and windy in a wraith !
I and my Lord, — between me and between Him
Rises the lucent ladder of my faith.

Ay, and thereon, descending and ascending,
Suns at my side and starry in the air,
Angels, His ministers, their tasks are blending,
Bear me the blessing, render Him the prayer.

A PRAYER.

O FOR one minute hark what we are saying !
   This is not pleasure that we ask of Thee !
Nay, let all life be weary with our praying,
   Streaming of tears and bending of the knee : —

Only we ask thro' shadows of the valley
   Stay of thy staff and guiding of thy rod,
Only, when rulers of the darkness rally,
   Be thou beside us, very near, O God !

A LAST APPEAL.

O SOMEWHERE, somewhere, God unknown,
    Exist and be !
I am dying; I am all alone;
    I must have Thee.

God ! God ! my sense, my soul, my all,
    Dies in the cry : —
Saw'st thou the faint star flame and fall?
    Ah! it was I.

FROM 'SAINT PAUL.'[15]

LET no man think that sudden in a minute
    All is accomplished and the work is done ; —
Though with thine earliest dawn thou shouldst begin it
    Scarce were it ended in thy setting sun.

Oh the regret, the struggle and the failing !
    Oh the days desolate and useless years !
Vows in the night, so fierce and unavailing !
    Stings of my shame and passion of my tears !

How have I seen in Araby Orion,
    Seen without seeing, till he set again,
Known the night-noise and thunder of the lion,
    Silence and sounds of the prodigious plain !

How have I knelt with arms of my aspiring
    Lifted all night in irresponsive air,
Dazed and amazed with overmuch desiring,
    Blank with the utter agony of prayer !

'What,' ye will say, 'and thou who at Damascus
    Sawest the splendor, answeredst the voice,
So hast thou suffered and canst dare to ask us,
    Paul of the Romans, bidding us rejoice?'

Shame on the flame so dying to an ember!
    Shame on the reed so lightly overset!
Yes, I have seen him, can I not remember?
    Yes, I have known him, and shall Paul forget?

I, even I who from the fleshly prison
    Caught, (I believe it but I dare not say,)
Rose to the mid light of the Lord arisen,
    Woke to the waking rapture of the day, —

Ah they are shut, the ears of my divining,
    Sealed are the eyes that should have seen Him then.
Look what a beam from the Belovèd shining!
    Look what a night of treasonable men!

What was their tale of some one on a summit,
    Looking, I think, upon the endless sea, —
One with a fate, and sworn to overcome it,
    One who was fettered and who should be free?

Round him a robe, for shaming and for searing,
    Ate with empoisonment and stung with fire,
He thro' it all was to his lord uprearing
    Desperate patience of a brave desire.

Ay and for me there shot from the beginning
    Pulses of passion broken with my breath;
Oh thou poor soul, enwrapped in such a sinning,
    Bound in the shameful body of thy death!

Well, let me sin, but not with my consenting,
    Well, let me die, but willing to be whole:
Never, O Christ, — so stay me from relenting, —
    Shall there be truce betwixt my flesh and soul.

Oft shall that flesh imperil and outweary
   Soul that would stay it in the straiter scope,
Oft shall the chill day and the even dreary
   Force on my heart the frenzy of a hope: —

Lo as some ship, outworn and overladen,
   Strains for the harbor where her sails are furled; —
Lo as some innocent and eager maiden
   Leans o'er the wistful limit of the world,

Dreams of the glow and glory of the distance,
   Wonderful wooing and the grace of tears,
Dreams with what eyes and what a sweet insistence
   Lovers are waiting in the hidden years: —

Lo as some venturer, from his stars receiving
   Promise and presage of sublime emprise,
Wears evermore the seal of his believing
   Deep in the dark of solitary eyes,

Yea to the end, in palace or in prison,
   Fashions his fancies of the realm to be,
Fallen from the height or from the deeps arisen,
   Ringed with the rocks and sundered of the sea: —

So even I, and with a heart more burning,
   So even I, and with a hope more sweet,
Groan for the hour, O Christ! of thy returning,
   Faint for the flaming of thine advent feet.

    .   .   .   .

Also I ask, but ever from the praying
   Shrinks my soul backward, eager and afraid,
Point me the sum and shame of my betraying,
   Show me, O Love, thy wounds that I have made!

Yes, thou forgivest, but with all forgiving
   Canst not renew mine innocence again:

Make thou, O Christ, a dying of my living,
   Purge from the sin but never from the pain !

So shall all speech of now and of to-morrow,
   All He hath shown me or shall show me yet,
Spring from an infinite and tender sorrow,
   Burst from a burning passion of regret :

Standing afar I summon you anigh him,
   Yes, to the multitudes I shout and say,
'This is my King ! I preach and I deny him,
   Christ ! whom I crucify anew to-day.'

See, when a fireship in mid ocean blazes
   Lone on the battlements a swimmer stands,
Looks for a help, and findeth not, and raises
   High for a moment melancholy hands ;

Then the sad ship, to her own funeral flaring,
   Holds him no longer in her arms, for he
Simple and strong and desolate and daring
   Leaps to the great embraces of the sea.

So when around me for my soul's affrighting,
   Madly red-litten of the woe within,
Faces of men and deeds of their delighting
   Stare in a lurid cruelty of sin,

Thus as I weary me and long and languish,
   Nowise availing from that pain to part, —
Desperate tides of the whole great world's anguish
   Forced thro' the channels of a single heart, —

Then let me feel how infinite around me
   Floats the eternal peace that is to be,
Rush from the demons, for my King has found me,
   Leap from the universe and plunge in Thee !

  .   .   .   .

Lo as some bard on isles of the Aegean
  Lovely and eager when the earth was young,
Burning to hurl his heart into a paean,
  Praise of the hero from whose loins he sprung ; —

He, I suppose, with such a care to carry,
  Wandered disconsolate and waited long,
Smiting his breast, wherein the notes would tarry,
  Chiding the slumber of the seed of song :

Then in the sudden glory of a minute
  Airy and excellent the proëm came,
Rending his bosom, for a god was in it,
  Waking the seed, for it had burst in flame.

So even I athirst for His inspiring,
  I who have talked with Him forget again,
Yes, many days with sobs and with desiring,
  Offer to God a patience and a pain ;   .

Then thro' the mid complaint of my confession,
  Then thro' the pang and passion of my prayer,
Leaps with a start the shock of his possession,
  Thrills me and touches, and the Lord is there.

Lo if some pen should write upon your rafter
  Mene and mene in the folds of flame,
Think you could any memories thereafter
  Wholly retrace the couplet as it came ?

Lo if some strange intelligible thunder
  Sang to the earth the secret of a star,
Scarce could ye catch, for terror and for wonder,
  Shreds of the story that was pealed so far : —

Scarcely I catch the words of His revealing,
　　Hardly I hear Him, dimly understand,
Only the Power that is within me pealing
　　Lives on my lips and beckons to my hand.

Whoso has felt the Spirit of the Highest
　　Cannot confound nor doubt Him nor deny:
Yea with one voice, O world, tho' thou deniest,
　　Stand thou on that side, for on this am I.

Rather the earth shall doubt when her retrieving
　　Pours in the rain and rushes from the sod,
Rather than he for whom the great conceiving
　　Stirs in his soul to quicken into God.

Ay, tho' thou then shouldst strike him from his glory
　　Blind and tormented, maddened and alone,
Even on the cross would he maintain his story,
　　Yes, and in hell would whisper, I have known.

EXPLANATORY NOTES.

EXPLANATORY NOTES.

NOTE 1, PAGE 3. — *The King's Tragedy.* 'Tradition says that Catherine Douglas, in honor of her heroic act when she barred the door with her arm against the murderers of James the First of Scots, received popularly the name of " Barlass." This name remains to her descendants, the Barlas family, in Scotland, who bear for their crest a broken arm. She married Alexander Lovell of Bolunnie. A few stanzas from King James's lovely poem, known as *The King's Quhair,* are quoted in the course of this ballad. The writer must express regret for the necessity which has compelled him to shorten the ten-syllabled lines to eight syllables, in order that they might harmonize with the ballad metre.' *Author's Note.*

NOTE 2, PAGE 27. — *The House of Life* consists of two parts, Pt. I. *Youth and Change,* Pt. II. *Change and Fate,* and contains one hundred and one sonnets.

NOTE 3, PAGE 43. — *The Earthly Paradise,* if regarded as one poem, consists of twelve books and contains some forty thousand lines. The poem, however, is properly a collection of twenty-four separate tales in verse on legendary and mythological subjects. The book receives its name from the story told in the prologue of how certain gentlemen and mariners of Norway, having heard of the Earthly Paradise, set sail to find it, and after many vicissitudes and the lapse of many years reached a western land, where they dwelt for a long time. The different tales are represented as being told by the elders of the city, who had hospitably received the wanderers, and by the wanderers themselves. Two tales are represented as being told in each of the twelve months of the year, which are introduced by a short lyric on the month itself. In *The Man Born to be King,* the author has the following argument prefixed : ' It was foretold to a great king that he who should reign after him should be low-born and poor ; which thing came to pass in the end, for all that the king could do.'

18

NOTE 4, PAGE 59. — The full title is *Love is Enough, or the Freeing of Pharamond, a Morality.* The following is the argument prefixed to the play by the author : 'This story, which is told by way of a morality set before an Emperor and Empress newly wedded, showeth of a King whom nothing but Love might satisfy, who left all to seek Love, and, having found it, found this also, that he had enough, though he lacked all else.'

NOTE 5, PAGE 63. — The full title is *Mano, a Poetical History: of the Time of the Close of the Tenth Century: concerning the adventures of a Norman Knight, which fell part in Normandy, part in Italy.* The poem is divided into four Books, Bk. I. containing seventeen cantos, Bk. II. twelve, Bk. III. eight, Bk. IV. seventeen, and the entire poem contains about five thousand lines. The following is a synopsis of the story told in the poem : Mano, the adopted son of Count Thurold, comes to Rouen with Diantha, the daughter of his adopted father, to raise fresh levies for the Holy Wars in the East. While at Rouen he meets the sisters, Blanche and Joanna, the former of whom he loves and the latter of whom loves him. Being refused by Blanche, Mano sets out with Joanna to visit Gerbert, subsequently Pope. Both Mano and Joanna make Gerbert their confidant, who urges the former to overcome his passion, and sends him on a mission to Italy with the monk Fergant as a companion. Gerbert, after elevation to the Pontificate, inflicts the punishment of banishment from Rome on Mano, who forthwith sets out for Normandy. On his way thither, he encounters Diantha, who has joined a band of peasants in revolt against Duke Richard of Rouen, and in seeking to rescue her is captured by the knights whom the Duke had sent to quell the insurrection of the peasants. He and Diantha are both sentenced to be burnt alive, but Joanna, having learned from Gerbert that Mano is the half-brother of the Duke, hastens to tell him the secret of his prisoner's parentage, and thereby avert Mano's fate. Instead of the Duke, she finds Robert, his brother, the Archbishop of Rouen, who refuses to interfere. Joanna then manages to compass the escape of Diantha, by taking her place in the cell, and both she and Mano are publicly burnt alive.

NOTE 6, PAGE 72. — *Pygmalion* consists of twelve books, and contains some four thousand lines. The subject is the legend of the king and sculptor of Cyprus of that name.

NOTE 7, PAGE 99.—*The Doncaster St. Leger.* 'This poem is intended to illustrate the spirit of Yorkshire racing, now unhappily, or happily, as the case may be, on the decline. The perfect acquaintance of every peasant on the ground with the pedigrees, performances, and characters of the horses engaged — his genuine interest in the result — and the mixture of hatred and contempt which he used to feel for the New-market favorites, who came down to carry off his great national prize, must be well-known to any one who forty years ago crossed the Trent in August or September, — altogether it constituted a peculiar modifica-tion of English feeling, which I thought deserved to be recorded; and in default of a more accomplished Pindar, I have here endeavored to do so *Author's Note.* To line 12, page 100, *When, strong of heart, the Went-worth Bay*, the author has this explanatory note, ' Bay Malton. King Herod, the champion of Newmarket in the famous race alluded to above, broke a blood vessel in the crisis of the contest.'

NOTE 8, PAGE 105.— *The Private of the Buffs.* ' " Some Seiks, and a private of the Buffs " — an East Kent Regiment — " having remained behind with the grog-carts, fell into the hands of the Chinese. On the next morning they were brought before the authorities, and commanded to perform the *kotou*. The Seiks obeyed; but Moyse, the English sol-dier, declaring that he would not prostrate himself before any Chinaman alive, was immediately knocked upon the head, and his body thrown on a dunghill." — *See China Correspondent of The Times.'* *Author's Note.*

NOTE 9, PAGE 125.— *The Voyage of St. Brendan* consists of six parts, and contains altogether eighty-two eight-line stanzas. The subject of the poem is the legend of the Voyage of St. Brendan to Hy-Braisail;. or the Enchanted Island, which was supposed to be visible from the western coast of Ireland every seven years, and which figures extensively in Irish minstrelsy.

NOTE 10, PAGE 188.— The full title is *The Married and the Sin-gle. A Fragment from St. Gregory Nazianzen.* A short poem of some one hundred lines on the respective claims of married and celibate life.

NOTE 11, PAGE 189.— *The Dream of Gerontius* consists of seven parts, and contains about one thousand lines. The purpose of the poem is to represent the vision of a dying Christian, and the Roman Catholic view of the doctrine of Purgatory.

NOTE 12, PAGE 225.— The full title is *The Christian Year. Thoughts in Verse for the Sundays and Holydays throughout the Year,* and it contains one hundred and nine short poems. The following are the author's notes appended to various lines in the selection given : To line 4, verse 4, page 26, — ' Then they willingly received him into the ship : and immediately the ship was at the land whither they went (St. John vi. 21).' To line 3, verse 1, page 229, *Andromache,* — ' Iliad VI. 429.' To line 1, page 230, *two silent nights and days,* — ' In Passion Week from Tuesday evening to Thursday evening : during which time Scripture seems to be nearly silent concerning our Saviour's proceedings.' To line 4, verse 1, page 234, *freely give,* — ' Matthew x. 8.' To line 2, verse 1, Twenty-Fourth Sunday after Trinity, page 237, *Since all alone, so Heaven has willed, we die,* — ' Je mourrai seul. *Pascal.*' To line 1, verse 13, page 29, — ' Thou hast known my soul in adversities (Psalm xxxi. 7).'

NOTE 13, PAGE 250. — *The Sermons in Sonnets* contain sixty-three sonnets.

NOTE 14, PAGE 261. — *Yesterday, To-day, and For Ever* consists of twelve books, and contains some ten thousand lines. The theme is the death of a Christian, his translation to the other world, and a description of the future life. The author has the following notes : *To God of the world, and guardian of mankind,* page 62, line 6, — ' The titles ascribed to Satan and his angels appear to me too explicit to be understood of merely usurped dominion : " The prince of this world " (John xii. 31, etc.), " The god of this world " (2 Cor. iv. 4), " The prince of the power of the air " (Eph. ii. 2), " The rulers of the darkness of this world " (Eph. vi. 12), etc. The devil probably veiled a falsehood under a garb of truth, when he said to our Lord, " All this power will I give Thee, and the glory of them : for that is delivered unto me ; and to whomsoever I will, I give it " (Luke iv. 6).' To *The Bridegroom's Friend,* page 262, line 24, — ' See John iii. 29.'

NOTE 15, PAGE 265. — *Saint Paul* contains one hundred and forty-six verses, and is in form a monologue, wherein the speaker is Saint Paul.

INDEXES.

INDEX OF AUTHORS.

PSEUDONYMS AND LITERARY SOBRIQUETS.

THE authority, in most cases, is *Initials and Pseudonyms* by William Cushing, B. A., 1885. The pseudonyms include such as were used by the author in his prose as well as his poetical works, but not the author's own initials, when those have been adopted as a literary disguise in either instance.

A. . . . . JOHN KEBLE. Pseudonym used in contributions to *Tracts for the Times*, 1840–1848.

ANGLICANUS, L. T.. . . . ARTHUR PENRHYN STANLEY.

B. . . . . BRYAN WALLER PROCTER. Pseudonym used in articles in London *Literary Gazette*.

BENENGELI, CID HAMET . LORD MACAULAY. *Fragments of an Ancient Romance*, 1826.

BERWICK, MISS MARY . . ADELAIDE ANNE PROCTER. Pseudonym used in contributions to *Household Words*; *Legends and Lyrics*, 1858.

BYRON OF HER SEX . . CAROLINE ELIZABETH NORTON. Name given her in a review of *The Dream and other Poems*, in *Quarterly Review*.

CATHOLICUS . . . . . JOHN HENRY NEWMAN. Pseudonym used in article to London *Times*.

CORNWALL, BARRY . . . BRYAN WALLER PROCTER. Pseudonym used in various poetical publications; *Memoir of Charles Lamb*, 1866.

δ . . . . JOHN HENRY NEWMAN. Pseudonym used in verses originally contributed to *The British Magazine*, and subsequently included in *Lyra Apostolica*, 1836.

D. . . . . JOHN HENRY NEWMAN. Pseudonym used in contributions to *Tracts for the Times*, 1840–1848.

γ . . . . JOHN KEBLE. Pseudonym used in verses originally contributed to *The British Magazine*, and subsequently included in *Lyra Apostolica*, 1836.

GENTLEMAN OF THE MID-
    DLE TEMPLE . . . . LORD MACAULAY. *Conversation between Mr. Abraham Cowley and Mr. John Milton touching the Great Civil War*, in *Knight's Quarterly Magazine*, 1824.

HEFFERMAN, MR. MICHAEL SIR SAMUEL FERGUSON. The name of the narrator in the short story of *Father Tom and the Pope, or a Night at the Vatican.*

JESSAMINE, JAMES . . . BRYAN WALLER PROCTER. Pseudonym used in articles in London *Literary Gazette.*

J. H. . . . . DENIS FLORENCE MACCARTHY. *Justina*, 1848.

LIBERTAS . . . . . . CAROLINE ELIZABETH NORTON. *Letters to the Mob*, 1848.

MERTON, TRISTRAM . . LORD MACAULAY. Pseudonym used in *Sketches and Ballads*, contributed to *Knight's Quarterly Magazine.*

PARISH PRIEST, A . . . FREDERICK WILLIAM FABER. *The Blessed Sacrament*, 1845.

PROUT, FATHER . - . . FRANCIS MAHONY. Pseudonym used in contributions to *Fraser's Magazine* under the title of *The Prout Papers. Reliques of Father Prout*, 1860.

QUONGTI, RICHARD . . . LORD MACAULAY. *A Prophetic Account of a Grand National Poem, to be entitled 'The Wellingtoniad,' and to be published A.D. 2824*, in *Knight's Quarterly Magazine*, 1824.

SAVONAROLA, DON JEREMY,
    BENEDICTINE MONK . FRANCIS MAHONY. Pseudonym used
                   in *Facts and Figures from Italy*, 1847;
                   in the form of a series of letters ad-
                   dressed to Charles Dickens.

WALKER, PATRICIUS . . WILLIAM ALLINGHAM. Pseudonym
                   used in contributions to *Fraser's Mag-
                   azine.*

X X X, and also X Y Z . . BRYAN WALLER PROCTER. Pseudo-
                   nyms used in contributions to London
                   Literary Gazette.

YORKE, OLIVER . . . . FRANCIS MAHONY. Pseudonym used
                   as editor of the fictitious *Reliques of
                   Father Prout*, 1860.

INDEX OF FIRST LINES.

University Press : John Wilson and Son, Cambridge.